Fling

CARMICHAEL FAMILY SERIES

ADRIANA LOCKE

Books by Adriana Locke

Amazon Store

Signed copies available on the author's website

Brewer Family Series

The Proposal | The Arrangement | The Invitation

Carmichael Family Series

Flirt | Fling | Fluke | Flaunt | Flame

Landry Family Series

Sway | Swing | Switch | Swear | Swink | Sweet

Landry Family Security Series

Pulse

Gibson Boys Series

Crank | Craft | Cross | Crave | Crazy

The Mason Family Series

Restraint | The Relationship Pact | Reputation | Reckless | Relentless | Resolution

The Marshall Family Series

More Than I Could | This Much Is True

The Exception Series

The Exception | The Perception

Dogwood Lane Series

Tumble | Tangle | Trouble

Standalone Novels

Sacrifice | Wherever It Leads | Written in the Scars | Lucky Number Eleven | Like You Love Me | The Sweet Spot | Nothing But It All | Between Now and Forever

For a complete reading order and more information, visit www.adrianalocke.com.

Cast of Characters

parents
Kixx Carmichael
Damaris Carmichael

siblings
Moss Carmichael [Flirt]
Maddox Carmichael [Fling]
Jess Carmichael [Fluke]
Banks Carmichael [Flaunt]
Foxx Carmichael [Flame]
Paige Carmichael [Sweet]

CHAPTER 1

Ashley

"I'VE MADE A DECISION."

My best friend, Rebecca, looks at me with a *heavy* dose of skepticism. Although I'd like to think that her dubious reaction to my announcement is overblown … it's probably not. That's especially true when my recent rash of spontaneous decisions—*although justified*—is taken into consideration.

Oh, well.

"Not sure I even want to hear this," she says before taking a sip of her drink.

"Becca, I'm going on my honeymoon."

She sputters into a napkin, sending a million particles of tequila into the fabric. The blues of her eyes mist in a watery fog.

I sip my coconut lime margarita and enjoy the evening breeze while Rebecca tries not to die. Even though it's balmy, the air rippling across the rooftop patio is a pleasant reprieve … and a nice distraction from Rebecca's complete overreaction.

"Okay, now that I can breathe again, can you repeat that?" she asks before clearing her throat. "I misheard you."

"I'm going on my honeymoon."

I say the words as though each is its own sentence. Not that the emphasis or the clarity is needed. She heard me. She heard me just fine.

Rebecca holds my gaze. Disbelief mixed with confusion and maybe a sprinkle of amusement is written on her pretty, freckled face.

"Come on," I say, pressing my lips together. "I have to go. How can I let five days in the Caribbean go to waste? What kind of person would I be if I let that happen? I'm a travel agent, for goodness' sake."

She shakes her head, her chestnut tresses dusting her shoulders. She makes a show of holding up her glass and inspecting it. "I haven't drunk enough to be so intoxicated that I'm imagining this conversation, have I?"

"Stop it." I laugh. "Be serious."

"*Be serious*? Okay." She folds her hands together on the table and leans forward, looking me straight in the eye. "I'm worried about you. Are you well?"

A smile stretches across my face. Even though she fights it, she grins too.

I knew it was the right decision to call off my wedding a month before the ceremony was set to take place. What I didn't know—what I didn't envision—was just how relieved I would be when it was all said and done.

When I got out of my lease, put my things in storage, and showed up on Rebecca's doorstep until I figured out what I was going to do— my relief came in waves. And I've basked in it ever since.

I got my power back. I hadn't realized I'd lost so much of it somewhere over the past two years.

"Don't worry about me," I say, licking the salt off my bottom lip. "I'm good."

"I haven't been worrying about you. I've been too busy celebrating the fact that I got my best friend back from Lord Farquaad."

I giggle. "Stop calling him that."

"It's not my fault that he's power-hungry, obsessed with perfection, and has an affinity for red and black. He was one pageboy haircut from me buying him a freaking horse to fulfill his destiny."

I shake with laughter.

"To this day, I'm still confused about why you fell for that guy," Rebecca says.

Yeah, well, me too. "Honestly? At that moment in my life? Dad had just died. I was grieving him and the relationship we never had and was sort of processing the trauma of that situation, I think. And Eton embodied a … power, a sense of control and almost *detachment* that I wished that I had." I swirl the liquid around my glass. "I'm not sure I ever *fell for him*, but that drew me in."

Rebecca starts to say something but reconsiders.

"I'm just thankful I'm home in Kismet Beach right now and not in Orlando," I say. "The rest is water under the bridge at this point."

"I don't know how you stayed away from here for so long. You were gone almost a year. Do you realize that?"

Of course, I realize that. I felt it every day.

Rebecca grins. "Let's steer this conversation away from Duloc."

I snort.

"Are you sure you want to go on your honeymoon?" Rebecca asks carefully. "You were pretty against it last night, and now you've made a one-eighty—which you're allowed to do. I just want to make sure you're not going to get to the Bahamas and start overthinking how you planned the whole thing for you and Eton …"

"*Becca.*" I lower my chin as I watch her over the table. "While I'll admit I've been one to overthink a little—"

"A little?"

"Or a moderate amount. Either way, I sat back and let Eton dictate the past two years of my life. I thought the year of dating long-distance was just rough because of the miles and that the engagement would change things. But the past eight months of living in Orlando …" I scoff. "I walked around on eggshells more and more until I was a shell of myself. And I'm not letting the man who called my travel agency *a gold-digger's hobby to pass time* hover over any of my decisions."

She tilts her head, side-eyeing me. "So this doesn't have anything to do with that book you were reading last night?"

"Ha. No."

"It is titled *Intimacy with Strangers*," she teases me.

"You know," I say, setting my glass down. "You should think about reading my book when I'm done. It might help you relax a little."

"I don't need a book written by some smarmy dude on the back cover with a smile that reminds me of a serial killer just before he turns to the dark side to tell me how to have intimacy with strangers." She laughs, her eyes going wide. "Oh, my gosh! *I get it*. That's how they do it."

I furrow my brow. "Who are *they*, and what do they do?"

"*Serial killers*. They write books angled toward people feeling emotionally fragile and convince them that being intimate with a stranger is somehow healing—"

"The book is not even about sex."

She lifts her glass, her lips pressed together to hide her smile. "At least make the strangers wear condoms and keep your tracking turned on so we can find your body."

I wad my napkin and throw it at her. She ducks, missing it easily, and then plucks it off the ledge behind her.

"All joking aside," I say, our laughter fading. "I have an idea."

"What's that?"

"You should come to the Bahamas with me."

I nibble my bottom lip and wait for her response. It's a shot in the dark, I know, but I'm willing to try.

Rebecca doesn't travel much. She'll go on trips here and there with me and our friend Sara, but she's much more of a homebody than we are. I used to think it was because of finances. But Sara and I always offer to pay, thanks to my inheritance from my father and Sara's kick-ass job. Now I'm not sure.

"Ash, I can't. I wish I could. I just paid my rent, and I need to stay home and get my money's worth."

"Well, I've stayed with you for ten days, and I might be there a while longer. So let me pay the rent this month and—"

"No. That's not an option."

The look she gives me tells me that she's digging her heels in, as expected.

I march on.

"It's an all-expenses-paid trip," I say. "I'll cover the plane ticket because you'd be doing me a favor by going so I don't have to go alone."

She sighs. "Honestly, I'm trying to hoard money. My lease is up in a couple of months, and I'm not sure what I'm going to do. I've been thinking about going home to Texas."

I raise a brow but don't say anything.

"It's the adult decision to stay here and put away some cash. No one is going to come adult my life for me," she says.

Rebecca has mentioned returning to Texas a time or two over the past few months. She seems to have a love/hate relationship with it, and I'm not sure why. I know she left and lived in Indiana for a while before making her way down here a few years ago. I don't pressure her; she closes like a clam. I show my support and give her space as she does me when I need it.

"Okay. I get it. But the option is on the table if you change your mind," I say.

"I appreciate it."

"What do you appreciate?" Sara slides into the booth beside Rebecca, her bracelets jingling against the table. "Sorry, I'm late. The traffic on Beachfront Boulevard is wild tonight."

On cue, a horn blasts below us on the street.

The rooftop patio of La Pachanga, the best Mexican restaurant on this coast of Florida, is my favorite spot in Kismet Beach. It's in the middle of the action—looking down on the main thoroughfare. It's the best perch to watch tourists pose for selfies in front of the huge plastic shark dangling from the surf shop on the corner. From here, you can watch the action and not have to take part.

"*Hel-lo*?" Sara asks, waving her hand at me. "You can't just stop talking when I sit down. I'm nosy. Fill me in."

Ignoring Rebecca's quirked brow, my gaze settles on Sara. Her glossy hair shines in the light.

"Becca is second-guessing my life choices," I say.

Sara looks at Rebecca and drops her jaw. "Don't tell me that you talked her out of coloring her hair again. I swear to all that's holy if you did, I will ..." She pauses. "Well, I don't know what I'll do, but I'll do something hateful. *Mean*. Really petty."

"Nope," Rebecca says, amused. "You're going to love this. You're going to love it more than the time you convinced Ashley to spend a month's wages—"

"*It wasn't a month*," I interject.

"*On a purse*," Rebecca says, ignoring me. "This is bigger than that. You'll be *much more* entertained."

Sara's eyes sparkle. "Enough foreplay. What's going on?"

Rebecca sighs, holding a palm up in front of her. "You can have the honors."

"Well, thanks, considering it's my news."

"*You have news*? What kind of news?" Sara asks. "Don't take this the wrong way, but you've had the best news lately."

I shoot her a look that makes her laugh.

My two best friends are complete opposites. One is mature and logical. She makes soup when I'm sick and talks me out of bad decisions. She always answers the phone—even at four in the morning. She'd be the person I'd call if I needed bail money.

And then there's Sara.

She'll support my honeymoon decision without question. I only need to make sure that she doesn't talk me into some reverse harem situation while I'm in the Bahamas.

Although ...

"So," I say before nibbling the end of a chip. "After much thoughtful deliberation—"

"And a book called *Intimacy with Strangers*," Rebecca interjects.

I stop and turn to her. "I told you—that's a different thing."

"Is it, though?"

"*Yes*," I say, exasperated. "That was about making time for—"

"Cool," Sara says, as impatient as ever. "Talk about that later. What is your big news?"

"You'll be happy to hear that I'm going on my honeymoon," I say, bracing myself for her enthusiasm.

As predicted, Sara shrieks. "This is *exactly* what you need to get your groove back. You can use the sun and salt water to bleach your energy of all things Farquaad."

"Really?" I deadpan.

The server arrives at the table before Rebecca can chime in. Sara makes a quick order to go before turning back to me. When her eyes meet mine, they're filled with an enthusiasm that feeds my excitement.

"I need a travel buddy," I tell her, leaning forward. "Rebecca can't. That leaves you."

"Oh, I'm so excited to take the opportunity considering I was the second choice."

Rebecca scoffs. "You know she was going to ask you whether I said yes or no. You're way more fun than I am."

"This is true," Sara says, swiping a chip from the basket. "And I would if I could."

I gasp. "What do you mean *if you could*? You have to come. I can't go alone, and you love to travel."

She takes a bite of her chip. "I'm meeting with executives from a distillery that I've had a hell of a time scheduling. I'd be fired on the spot if I canceled. *And*," she says, scooping some guacamole on her chip, "I swore hand to heart that I would take my little sister to a concert that weekend. Like I can't go. *I can't*. No way around it. I'm sorry."

I never thought to consider that neither of my friends could go. Sara can always get time off work—perks for sleeping with her boss. Rebecca has enough sick days to cover the trip, and I know her boss at Smokey's would be more than happy to give her some time off since she works practically every day. I was sure she'd want to go too.

Now what am I going to do?

"You'll be fine," Sara says, running a hand through the air. "It'll be good for you. You'll have an empty bed in which to bring the hot pool boys and lifeguards. This can really be a true experience if you play your cards right."

I lean back in the booth and laugh. "Easy, there. I'm not doing this Sara style. I'd like to know a bit more about my hookups than *green eyes, great shoulders*. Or wait—how did you save that one guy on your phone? Scorpio Sex?"

Rebecca laughs too, angling her body toward Sara. "Or Blue Shirt Chris. Remember him? I can't imagine being reduced to the color of my shirt and first name."

"Trust me—being Blue Shirt Chris was doing him a favor. It differentiated him from Green Shirt Chris. *Huge* difference, if you get the picture."

"Oh, I got the picture," I say, my laughter fading into a fake cry. "I learned the hard way to never—*never, ever, ever*—look at the pictures on your phone."

Sara smirks. "It *was* hard, I'll give you that."

"I'm not opposed to some *hard*, that's for sure," I say. "But I'd like to tiptoe into that world. Dip my toe in, so to speak."

"Take your time," Rebecca says just as Sara speaks.

"Just hop back on and ride. It's like riding a bike." Her grin turns mischievous. "They both end with a sore ass sometimes too."

I snort as our server reappears. After learning we don't need anything else, she slips our bill onto the end of the table.

"I'm sorry I missed dinner," Sara says. "I'll make it up to you. Want to go out to eat this weekend? My treat."

I grab my purse and dig around for my wallet. "Maybe. I'll probably get my stuff together now that I'm fully committed to the Bahamas."

A burst of excitement streaks through me. Salt, sand, and sun—just what I ordered … when *I* bought the trip.

"I can't do dinner on Saturday. I have a late shift at Smokey's," Rebecca says. "I'm not sure how long I work Friday either."

Sara nods. "I'll text you guys later this week, and we'll figure it out."

"Perfect," I say.

I reach for the bill, but Rebecca grabs it first.

"It's my turn to pay," I tell her.

She shakes her head. "I'm the one who suggested we come."

My heart tugs for my sweet friend. Rebecca struggles, but she does it with so much pride. *I love her so much.*

"You aren't paying for dinner," I tell her. "You're letting me crash with you, for heaven's sake. I'm not your ward."

Our server comes back and immediately understands the situation. She laughs at our friendly yet serious debate. "I'll stand here quietly until you handle this amongst yourselves."

"I'm paying," I tell her, thrusting my card toward her hand.

"She's not." Rebecca extends her card across the table. "Take mine."

"Just let me pay for it and ignore these two," Sara tells her. "I'll leave you the best tip."

I stare at both of my friends.

"Keep glaring at me," Sara says, smiling brightly. "But you're still not paying."

"No, she's not," a playful voice says from beside me. *Because I am.*

CHAPTER 2

Ashley

Goose bumps ripple across my skin. Air laced with the faint scent of spiced cherries toys with my senses. Even if the smooth, flirty voice and *ga-ga* look on Rebecca's face didn't make it abundantly clear who was standing beside me, I'd know by the way the right side of my body tingles.

Maddox Carmichael's lips flicker into a half-smile, half-smirk. "Hey, Ash."

"Hey." I grin as a familiar warmth floods my veins. "I haven't seen you in a while."

And that's a shame.

His sandy-colored hair is cut close to the scalp, highlighting his ridiculous cheekbones. The angle of his jaw—one of my favorite things about him—is covered with a day's worth of stubble, and his neck slopes to his shoulders in a way that makes me melt.

It's not a bad look. *At all.*

He chuckles, the sound deep and smooth. "Miss me?"

"Oh, it was *unbearable*," I tease. "I didn't know what to do with myself. That's basically why I'm here—hoping to run into you."

"Sounds about right." He slips his wallet out of his pocket, and then, for the first time since he approached us, he acknowledges my friends. "Hey, Sara. What's up, Becca?"

Rebecca turns a bright shade of red.

"Hi, Maddox," Sara says with a cheek-splitting grin. "Fancy seeing you here since Ashley's car is parked outside and all."

I roll my eyes.

My friends don't understand my relationship with Maddox—a relationship that's a harmless, flirty friendship more than anything else.

The two of us have a strange, effortless connection. It started on the first day of first grade when I got a piece of bubble gum stuck in my hair. I wasn't supposed to have it but snuck it in like a rebel. Of course, it stuck in my hair while I was showing off, and I panicked. Maddox came to my rescue with his safety scissors and snipped the glob off in the back of the classroom.

He was a true hero that day.

Ever since then, we've been sort of stuck together.

We find each other in crowds without knowing the other is there. We've sat by countless bonfires and talked while our friends got wasted. If we're in the same room and someone says something funny, our eyes snap together, and we laugh at the same time. On occasion, we're the only ones.

Our friends have always given us hell, assuming we've engaged in other *extracurricular activities*. But we haven't. I've thought about it— *nearly every time I see him, how could I not?*—and we certainly joke about it.

But we've never crossed a line. *The line*. The one that leads to things that complicate friendships. *Why?* Because I know what a player he is. I've had a front-row seat. He knows how serious I take my relationships. He's wiped my tears a time or three. And I'd like to think we both respect each other's dreams and our friendship too much to entangle said lines.

Maddox hands the server his credit card. "Can I get six crispy tacos to go? And whatever this table ordered?"

Sara snickers.

"You are *not* paying for our dinner," I say.

He looks down at me, amused.

"I mean it." This time, I make my meanest face. "You can't just waltz in here and do whatever you want."

"That's cute. Now scoot over and hush," he says, elbowing me in the arm.

I move toward the wall until I'm directly across from Rebecca. "Why are you here, anyway?" I ask him.

He settles in beside me, his thick forearms crossed on top of the table as if he has nowhere else to be. His eyes are gorgeous, *an unearthly chartreuse*, and I struggle to pull my hazel-colored ones away.

"For dinner. *Obviously*." He licks his lips. "A little birdie told me that *someone* called off her wedding. So when I saw that someone's car out front as I was driving by, I had to stop."

"That little birdie would be correct." I wiggle my ring-free finger in the air. "This little birdie flew the coop."

"Are you okay?"

"I'm the one who called it off. I'm great."

His lips spread ear to ear. "*You were right, Maddox*." He laughs. "Go on. I'm waiting."

"Not happening."

The table quiets, our laughter slowly subsiding. I glance around at my friends, the people who are truly my found family, and my heart fills with warmth in places that had begun to feel cool.

"I'm trying to decide if we should throw her a divorce party," Sara says.

"You have to be married to get divorced," I point out.

She shrugs. "Yeah, but I don't know what other word to use." She turns back to Maddox. "Any ideas on what we should do to celebrate the demise of the worst decision Ashley has ever made?"

He looks at me and hums. "Well, I mean, I guess I could offer a striptease—"

"*Yes*," Rebecca says quickly. *Too quickly*. Her red face goes from cherry to beet. "I mean, I think Ashley would love that."

She wouldn't be mad about it. "Speak for yourself."

Instead of acknowledging Sara's mumble about me being a liar, I grab my margarita and take a long drink. My elbow brushes Maddox's arm. I ignore that too.

"Maybe I'll throw a small bash at Mega Pint," Sara says. "Wanna come, Maddox?"

I roll my eyes and set my glass back down. "I'm sure there are a million other things he'd like to do. Besides, we are not having a party for this. I have too many things to figure out, and … it's weird to celebrate a broken engagement."

"What's that supposed to mean?" Maddox asks. "The part about me?"

"The last time you were at Mega Pint with us, you and your brother Banks chased off the Marines who wanted to go back to my place," I say.

"And I'm still waiting for you to thank me for that." He holds my gaze for a long second and then turns to Sara. "What time are we going?"

I shove his shoulder, making him laugh.

"You're wounding me," he teases.

"Whatever. I'm not making you feel anything other than a little guilty for ruining our Marine fun."

"That's debatable."

"Behave, will you?"

Even though he's just my friend, I'm still a woman. A woman in the middle of a dry spell at that. Maddox flirting with me, even though I know it's just an extension of his personality, mixed with those ridiculous eyes and sexy dimples—I'm a powder keg ready to explode.

And, somehow, I think he knows that.

His grin deepens.

And I think he enjoys knowing it too. *Bastard.*

"On that note, I'm out of here," Rebecca says. "It makes me nuts to watch those two pretend they're not into each other."

I give my friend a pointed look as she shoos Sara out of the booth so she can get out.

"Here you go," the server says, returning to the table. She hands Maddox his card and a bag. Then she hands Sara a box.

"Thanks." He slides his card into his wallet. "Did you get their bill?"

"I did. That was so sweet of you," she says, batting her lashes.

Sighing, I dig around my bag and find some cash for a tip. I hand it to her before Sara can. "Thanks."

"No, thank you." Her eyes drag from mine across Maddox. "Let me know if you need anything else."

"We will," Sara says even though the server wasn't talking to us. *Only Maddox.*

She smiles as she walks away.

Rebecca clears her throat. "Thank you for paying for ours, Maddox."

"Yeah. Thanks for coming to see Ashley," Sara says. "I didn't have to do anything for my meal for once."

Rebecca stifles a laugh. But Maddox just shrugs … his eyes on me.

"Despite the fact I told you not to—thank you," I say as if it pains me.

"Was that so hard?"

"Yes, because you never listen."

"Last week, he came into Smokey's and bought a man's dinner at the bar after the man told him it wasn't necessary," Rebecca says, looking at him. "Do you always just do whatever you want?"

"Most of the time." He shifts in his seat. "Not always, though."

"*Right,*" I say. "Name *one time* you didn't do something you wanted to do."

He slowly places his wallet in his back pocket, holding my gaze steadily. The intensity causes a shiver to curl down my spine. Then just as quickly as the intensity came, it evaporates, and he smiles as if that whole moment didn't happen.

"I wanted to throw this dad out of the gym last night for being too hard on his kid at wrestling practice," he says, his eyes darkening for a quick moment. "But I didn't."

"Ah, so you do have self-control," Rebecca says.

"Clearly," Sara says under her breath, lifting a brow at me.

"Eh, kind of," he says, disregarding Sara. "I sent Banks over and let him have a talk with the guy instead."

I laugh as I imagine the youngest of the five Carmichael brothers—Foxx, Jess, Moss, Maddox, and Banks—*having a talk* with a kid's dad. Heck, even their baby sister, Paige, is a firecracker.

"Bet that went well," I say, giggling.

"The guy apologized before he left, so I think it's safe to say that Banks was effective."

"Oh, I bet he was," I say, ending it with a snort. "Probably politically correct too."

The fact that Maddox has always coached little kids in wrestling has always endeared him to me. He was a high school standout and had scholarships to wrestle in college. For whatever reason, he didn't go on to the collegiate level. But he did volunteer to be involved in the local youth organization. I love that about him.

Sara hoists her purse onto her shoulder. "I'm going to go. I left the house at five this morning, and I'm dead."

Rebecca nods. "See you at home, Ashley?"

"Yeah. See you there."

They give us a little wave and then make their way toward the exit. As soon as they're gone, Maddox turns to me.

The air between us settles into a familiar ease. He picks up a glass of water that's gone untouched in front of me and takes a sip.

"So ..." Maddox's eyes sparkle. "Are you leaving, or do you want to split these tacos with me?"

"So tempting, but I need to get to Becca's. As you can imagine, my life is in shambles, and I need to start picking up the pieces."

"I'll walk you out."

We exchange a soft smile as we rise from the booth. Maddox waits for me to grab my purse, and then we head toward the exit.

He walks beside me through *La Pachanga*. Patrons shout his name from the bar as we pass, and more than one table extends a hand to him as we walk by. He makes sure to bring me into every conversation. It's amusing. Watching him interact with each person—giving them his undivided attention and then expertly extracting himself from the chat—showcases his charm.

It's what makes him so likable. *I never saw Eton do anything like this. He ignored everyone who couldn't do something for him.*

Memories of uncomfortable dinners and receptions make my stomach twist.

Finally, after what feels like a hundred pauses, we make it to the door. He holds it open for me. I make a great effort to get around him without touching him. I'm not sure if it's intentional or not, but the way his body is positioned makes that difficult.

I manage. Somehow.

"Whoa," he says as we step into the heat. "I swear that it's gotten hotter since I got here."

"It's so hot it's offensive. Sometimes I wonder why I love this place."

The air is thick and humid as we make our way to our cars. His Jeep is parked next to my Telluride beneath a palm tree at the end of the lot. He checks his phone, and I use the time—and the privacy offered by his distraction—to check him out.

Brown dress pants hug his behind and highlight his muscled thighs and narrow waist. A white shirt covers his chest. It's tight enough to skirt the lines of his body but loose enough to keep prying eyes guessing about the rest. *Except I know all about the rest.* I've seen him shirtless more times than I can count.

"So you want to talk about it?" he asks, putting his phone in his pocket.

"What?"

He shrugs. "Fizzle-fuck. Elroy or whatever. That asshole you were going *to marry*." He says the last two words like they're bitter.

"Why? Fishing for gossip?"

We stop at my vehicle. The breeze picks up his cologne and envelops me, almost taunting me.

"I don't gossip—about you, anyway. And if I was fishing for information, Miss Thompson, you wouldn't know it. I'd be more discreet."

"Mr. Carmichael, there's not a discreet bone in your body."

Our laughter mixes in the air.

"His name wasn't Elroy. It was Eton Eldridge, as if you don't remember. And there's really nothing worthwhile to talk about when it comes to him. Honestly, I'd rather forget he existed."

"Okay. Just offering to listen. Sometimes you keep stuff in that pretty head of yours."

The kindness in the question and the concern in his eyes make my heart swell.

I open my car door and turn on the engine to cool the interior. Maddox's gaze is heavily on my back as I lean in. Although I don't want to talk to Maddox about my relationship with Eton, I find myself doing it anyway.

"I was listening to the radio, I don't know, two months ago," I say, standing back up. *What a light bulb moment that was. It prompted so much change ... before the revelations that demanded it.* "And this Reba McEntire song came on. It's about this woman who wonders if there's something more to her life—if there's a life beyond what she's doing."

"I know that song." He laughs at my surprised reaction. "My mom is a huge Reba fan. It's what she would blast on Saturday mornings at an ungodly hour to make my brothers and I get up and help her clean."

"Okay, well, that song got me thinking about *my life* and all the things I haven't done."

His bag crinkles as he switches the hand that's holding it. "So what do you want to do? Climb Mount Everest? Run a marathon? Skydive? You wanted to do that in high school, remember?"

"I remember." I chuckle at the memory. "But no, I was thinking more along the lines of swimming with pigs."

"*What?*"

"I want to do it. And I was thinking about how that's a thing you can do where we were going for our honeymoon, and I didn't even schedule it because Eton would've refused."

His eyes darken.

"It was the moment that led to the end of the engagement. If I couldn't swim with pigs on my freaking honeymoon, what else would I miss out on, you know?" I shrug. "*Pigs.* Who would've thought?"

"Hey, whatever it takes."

I smile. "It's just really easy to forget who you are and what you need if you aren't careful."

"You can always call me, and I'll remind you who you are." A smirk settles on his lips. "I can remind him who you are … and who I am too, if you want."

My laughter is instantaneous. His is too.

"What? He has one coming," he says. "Pulling up to the curb and asking me if I'd park his car for five bucks. Bastard. I mean, I would've at least charged him fifty."

His dimples settle deeper into his cheeks.

This is why I like you so much. You're such a good friend.

"It was good to see you," I say. "I need to get out of here and tackle my pile of responsibilities. I've put the hard stuff off, and I can't ignore it anymore."

"Same." Maddox steps back so I can open the door wider. "Want to have dinner sometime? No pressure. Or you can hang out with Banks and me. If you're lucky, we won't even have to see a judge afterward."

"Now there's an offer."

"That you can't refuse?"

I only laugh.

Maddox rocks back on his heels, his gaze lingering on mine. He's so ridiculously handsome in the most genuine, approachable way. *It's no wonder women lose their minds over him.*

"Thanks again for picking up our bill," I say.

"Of course." He clears his throat. "Are you moving back home or staying in Orlando?"

I lift my shoulders and then let them fall. "I'm going to stay here. *Stay home.* I can work from anywhere, and I miss being close to Mom. What do I have in Orlando to stay for now anyway?"

"Love it."

I ignore the smugness on his face and climb into the car. Then I gaze up at him.

"I'm sure we'll run into each other again," he says, strumming his fingertips on the edge of the door.

Each *tap* reverberates through my body. "Probably."

He smirks, taking a step back. "See you around, Ash."

"See you later. Thanks again for—"

I'm silenced by the sound of my door shutting.

"Picking up the tab," I say to myself.

Maddox walks around my Telluride to his Jeep. He waves at a passerby before climbing into the car. Then without a second glance my way, he drives off.

Yup. Friends. We'll always be friends.

"I can remind him who you are … and who I am too, if you want."

"Maddox Carmichael, I'm not sure anyone needs to be reminded of who you are."

I smile and pull out of the parking lot too.

CHAPTER 3

Maddox

THE PACKAGE OF TACOS SLIDES ACROSS THE COUNTERTOP, RATTLING THE bright pink bowl in the center of the island.

I drop my keys and sunglasses inside the dish. The system of depositing my things there as soon as I walk in the door has surprisingly worked to keep me organized. I laughed at my sister, Paige, when she plunked the bowl down in my kitchen and explained the process almost a year ago. But, given she let me borrow her car twice in one week—because I lost both sets of my Jeep keys—I had to give it a try.

If only I could get Banks to give it a whirl ...

The last rays of the setting sun filter through the kitchen. Remnants of my hurried breakfast, a peanut butter and jelly bagel, sit next to the toaster. I can hear my mother's voice in the back of my head, warning me that I'll get palmetto bugs if I don't get it cleaned up.

My right shoulder aches from an old wrestling injury as I shrug off my shirt and toss it onto the counter. I turn toward the toaster to clean up the palmetto bait when movement in the doorway leading into the living room catches my attention.

Banks walks into the room. His eyes are glued to his phone.

Fucking great.

"Hey," I say, a little more forceful than necessary.

He looks up and jumps, almost dropping the device in the process.

"Dammit, Mad," he says, sighing. He has the audacity to look annoyed. "Can't you yell or something when you come home?"

"Yeah. I'm about to yell right now, as a matter of fact."

He rolls his eyes. "It would be a little late for that considering I already know you're here."

Is he serious right now?

Banks hums as he sits on one of the stools that overlook the sink. "Please don't turn into Moss and Jess and get all … *persnickety* about me being here. You're my favorite brother for a reason."

"Persnickety?" I let go of my annoyance—it won't do any good anyway because this is Banks, after all—and grab a disinfectant wipe from beneath the sink. "Who were you talking to today? Did you screw up and wander into a library or something?"

He ignores the question.

"Persnickety." He enunciates every syllable. "A delivery guy used it when he was dropping off a *1954 Bel Air* for us to restore." He whistles between his teeth. "You should see this baby. I can't wait to get my hands on her."

I toss the chunk of bagel that I didn't eat into the trash. "Don't let Betsy hear you say that."

He fires me a look, warning and pleading with me not to tease him about his pet name for his Corvette—a name none of us knew until Jess stole the car out of Banks's garage. *What a mess that was.*

"Do you want to hit the gym?" I ask, needing to rid myself of the tension that I've carried since my client asked me if they could go through the house they are never going to buy *just once more.* "I—"

"You went to La Pachanga?" He grabs the bag of tacos and drags it toward him. Then he peeks inside. *"And* you got tacos? I fucking love you."

I hold my hands to the side again, as if to say *What the fuck?* but either the gesture is lost on my little brother, or he doesn't care.

Probably the latter.

Who am I kidding? *Definitely the latter.*

Banks is, by all definitions, my best friend. Only eighteen months separate us. And as the two youngest boys out of five—and the most talented and best looking—we had to team up to battle our three brothers and defend our little sister.

Banks and I have kept more secrets for one another, helped each other out of trouble, and had each other's back through thick and thin more than any two brothers in the history of the world. That being said, Banks is also a giant pain in my ass.

"Help yourself," I say as he crams half of a taco into his mouth. "Need a drink with that?"

"Please?" he asks, crumbs falling to the counter.

"I was joking."

"But now I want one."

His words are muffled through the food.

"You know where I bet you can get a beverage?" I ask, my energy levels falling. *Forget the gym. I just want to eat my tacos—if Banks doesn't eat all of them—take a hot shower, and pass out in front of the television.* "Your house."

"*My house?*"

"Yeah, *your house.*" I move to the window and knock on it with my knuckles. The sound echoes through the kitchen. "See that building over there? That's your house. *The whole thing.* You can put whatever you want in your fridge, and you can have it whenever you want. Cool, right?"

He swallows. "You think I have drinks? I don't think I've bought any drinks besides beer for myself in my entire life."

"Try it. It's fun."

He jams the other half of the taco into his mouth. I sigh.

"You don't really want me to go home, do you?" he asks through his mouthful.

"I'm just saying," I say, grabbing the lemonade out of the fridge, "that you do pay for utilities and real estate taxes. It would make sense for you to get some use out of it more than the garage."

He flinches. "So you're saying I should sell the house? Mom and Dad bought it. They would be pissed."

I roll my eyes and take out a glass, add some ice, and top it off with lemonade.

"I have to keep it. I need the garage. If I lived here, we'd fight over yours, and you don't have space for my tools," he says. "Unless you're going to let me—"

"You need to use your *whole house*, not just the garage. Think about it. Think about the privacy you'd have. All of your things would be in one spot. You could watch television, eat, and sleep in the same space."

"I do all of that here."

I take a sip of my drink and watch him over the brim.

Banks has always had a thing about being alone. From the day my parents brought him home from the hospital, he's been attached to me. There are pictures to prove it. Before he was old enough to move his arms, he would just stare at me. Once he could walk, my life without a constant shadow was over.

I can't decide if my constant presence in his life made him this way or if he was just born like this. Either way, I can't help myself. No matter how irritating he gets, I can't get too mad.

Lucky for him.

"So," he says, shifting in his seat. "I have an idea."

I groan, putting the lemonade back in the fridge.

"Don't act like that before you even hear what it is," he says. "Give it a chance."

"Your face gives you away. I see the bullshit written all over you."

He snorts. "Just hear me out. This is a good one."

"When you say it's *a good one*, that always means that it's going to be—"

"Fun?" His eyes sparkle with mischief. "It's always fun, right?"

I'm not about to admit he's right. It *is* usually fun—at least in some respects. But I don't have the energy for him and his shenanigans tonight, thanks to Ms. One More Glance at the Crown Molding.

I'm two seconds from threatening to toss Banks out on his ass when my phone buzzes in my pocket. I pull it out and unlock the screen.

> Paige: Any idea why your brother Banks asked me where to order stickers? Because I'm kinda worried. 😬

Oh, fuck.

My fingers travel swiftly over the keys.

> Me: No. Also, why is he MY brother tonight?

> Paige: Because I have a feeling that whatever he needs stickers for isn't going to end well— it's Banks and stickers, for crying out loud— and I don't want my name attached to this. So … he's YOUR brother. I'm tapping out on this one.

> Me: So you think you're tapping me in? No deal.

> Paige: Oh, come on, Mad. You'll be involved before it's over anyway.

I roll my eyes. But she's not wrong. Somehow, someway, I'll be wrapped up in some sticker scenario before the week is over.

I need to do something really nice for Jess so he'll take pity on me whenever this erupts into the nightmare that I can already tell it's going to be.

"Who are you texting?" Banks asks.

"Paige."

> Me: Point made. But I'd like the opportunity to call Not It sometimes.

> Paige: I don't make the rules.

"She told you about the stickers, didn't she?" Banks sighs from across the room. "Tell her she's a snitch, and I'm disappointed in her disloyalty."

"Stickers?"

He makes a face. "Don't act like she didn't tell you."

"She didn't say shit."

> Me: I told him you didn't mention the stickers, but he just let it slip. Don't cave when he pressures you to admit you told me first.

> Paige: Noted. Enjoy your brother tonight. I have to go make pancakes for dinner. Again.

> Me: You could throw some blueberries in there to keep it interesting.

> Paige: It's obvious you've spent no time with children. If I go screwing with Ryder's pancakes, I'll never hear the end of it, and he probably won't eat them either. Then he'll be hungry at bedtime, and we'll have to deal with that instead of … you know, doing what we like to do at bedtime.

> Me: STOP, PAIGE.

> Paige:

I reach for my glass of lemonade. I swipe around on the counter until I finally look up and see it. *In Banks's hand.*

"So just hear me out," he says, this time with a smirk.

God help us.

"I hate this idea already," I say. "I hate everything about it. All of it."

"You haven't even heard it yet."

"I don't have to. I already know that it's probably going to make one of our brothers pissed, and after the whole *you made Moss think he was getting arrested* bit, I'm tired of looking over my shoulder all the time."

"But that had nothing to do with you. So why are you looking over your shoulder?"

I narrow my eyes. "Because somehow my stupid ass always gets wrangled into helping you so you don't fuck everything up."

Banks beams. I don't know what to say to that.

Paige: One more thing—you didn't hear this from me, but Moss might have lost your White Sox hat today. Maybe lost as in it landed in a spot where concrete was being poured. Also maybe not totally on accident. So you know, there's that. Just some info to use as necessary.

Me: HE is YOUR brother tonight. Actually, you can have him forever. I bequeath Moss to you. You're welcome.

Paige: I'm so happy that I live far, far away.

Me: Liar.

Paige: Going to make pancakes.

Me: Love you.

I toss my phone on the counter.

Banks picks up the papers the tacos were wrapped in and drops them in the trash. *Weird.*

"Are you done talking about me with our sister?" he asks.

"For now. I'm sure you'll come back up again."

He leans against the sink. His lips curl into a Grinch-esque smile. "So Jess is always bitching about how I borrow shit from his house, right?"

"Well," I say, pretending to think about it. "I think it's more that you take it and don't return it—which is more like stealing and less like borrowing. But yeah. You're close."

"Whatever." He takes a quick breath. "Tasha was at work today talking about how she's having these custom stickers made for her daughter's birthday party invitations or some dumb shit. I was only half-listening until she said that the last time they had stickers made, her toddler got ahold of them and stuck them to every surface in the house."

His eyes twinkle in delight.

"*And they found them for weeks*," he adds, lifting his chin like he just solved world hunger. "Everywhere. In cabinets, on the dog, in the car ..."

My stomach drops. "Banks ... *no*."

"Maddox ... *yes*." He grins. "Jess is always giving me hell about taking stuff. The grill lighters. The applesauce in his pantry that he was never going to eat anyway, so that's really just him being greedy. His shaving cream."

"*His shaving cream?*"

"I was out." He looks at me like I'm out of line to even question such a thing. "What was I supposed to do?"

"Uh, go buy some? Or buy two and then you'll have a spare."

"I was already late for work."

"Then plan." I shake my head and refocus. "Look, if you're going where I think you're going with this ..."

He lowers his voice as if we're conspiring to rob a bank. "Instead of taking stuff, *I'll give him stuff.*"

I walk around the kitchen to the stool that Banks occupied earlier and sit. I need the support.

This is a terrible idea, even though I don't fully see where he's going with it. *What's he going to do—put stickers all over Jess's house?*

Jess will kill him. Throttle him. He might even murder him, and while I'll always do my best to save Banks's ass, I'm not sure I'll be able to save him this time. There's a line somewhere that Banks has managed not to cross. I think that line is just before stickers.

I run a hand down my face.

On the one hand, I appreciate Banks's antics. He keeps things lively. He keeps life entertaining. It's mostly fun because he doesn't fuck with me, but whatever. On the other hand, I understand why Moss and Jess

—because even Banks doesn't have big enough balls to mess with Foxx too much—get sick of him.

I get sick of him too.

The guy has no boundaries, no common sense, and fails to take any sort of responsibility for his day-to-day life. Yet somehow, he runs a hugely successful custom car restoration business. People trust him with vehicles worth millions. Hell, Banks is practically a celebrity in the car world, but he'd have his water shut off if the bill wasn't on autopay.

Which Paige set up for him.

"Tasha gave me the website of the place where she buys hers, but Paige knew a better place." He bites his lip and squints. "I might have ordered one thousand of them today."

I gulp, my eyes bugging out. "*A thousand?* You ordered *one thousand* stickers?"

"Yup."

"Of what?"

"*Of me.*" He smiles widely. "I may have had a small photo shoot to get the perfect shot. I thought we'd have a hard time getting something usable, but we ended up with fifteen that were print-worthy."

"Why does that not surprise me?"

He shrugs. "Probably because I'm one good-looking moth-erfucker."

I hop off the stool and make my way back around the counter. I grab another glass. This time, I head straight for the alcohol cabinet.

"They'll be here this week. I paid for express delivery," he says. "And this is where you come in."

"Banks, as your brother, and as *their brother*—"

"Oh, it's just *his* brother. Just Jess. I'm not about to fuck with Foxx. And after that whole breaking into Moss's back door thing *and* the thing about making him think he was getting arrested, I'm letting that sit for a while."

"Smartest thing you've said all day," I mumble.

He joins me at the liquor cabinet and takes out a glass too. "So let's brainstorm all the places we can stick my face." He smirks. "Besides the obvious."

The back of my neck pinches as I pour us both a shot of tequila—never mind that we chose full-size glasses. Together, we down it.

The tequila burns as it rolls down my throat. My stomach heats as the liquid pools inside it. I close my eyes and hope it eases the stress of a very long day.

But I don't hold my breath.

"You okay?" Banks asks.

"Yeah. It's just been a ..." My mind slips slowly through the day until it gets to the one thing I've avoided thinking about. "A very ... *unexpected* day."

Damn, she looks good.

Seeing her today did what it always does—it makes her hard to forget.

Her smile was brighter, warmer than it has been the last few times we've run into one another. She was rosier too. Ashley's laughter wasn't forced, and our banter flowed as easily as it ever has.

Of course, it doesn't hurt that she's downright edible. Every piece of that woman is perfection. Her eyes are kind. The way she listens to what you say is so damn attractive. The way my body flames when she brushes against me? It's undeniable.

If she wasn't the serious, marriage type, we could have a lot of fun. *God knows I've had to remind myself she's not into casual relationships a million times over the years.*

"What happened?" Banks asks, his curiosity piqued.

I set the glass down and then hop onto the counter beside it. The stone is cold under my ass. "Guess who I ran into today?"

He shrugs. "Do you really want me to guess, or is this a ... what do you call it? A rhetorical question?"

"*Ashley*," I say, her name falling from my lips before I can stop it. "She was at LaPa."

Banks grins, leaning against the counter beside me. "I thought it was odd that you brought home tacos. It all makes sense now."

"I saw her car parked there on my way home, so I stopped."

"To say hello?"

I look down at my brother. His grin turns devious.

"What else would I be stopping to say?" I ask.

"Oh, I don't know. *Ride my cock* is always a good one."

"Saying that to Ash is a good way to get your nose broken."

Banks chuckles.

I hop off the counter. This conversation can go a couple of directions, and I'm not interested in either one of them at the moment.

He reads me correctly and walks toward the foyer. "I'm going to head over to that building you call *my house* and take a shower. Call me if you get bored."

"Later."

I wait to move until I hear the door slam. As soon as it does, I let out a huge breath and glance at the tacos. *Yup, he ate them all.*

Bastard.

A shadow filters through the room as a tree outside sways in the moonlight. Suddenly, the kitchen is darker and quieter than before. This isn't good for someone trying not to think.

Ugh.

I run a hand over my head and picture Ashley sitting in the booth earlier tonight. A smile tickles my lips.

We share a unique friendship—a tight bond that neither of us works toward, nor do we prioritize. *It just is*. It's my easiest friendship.

Mostly.

The only ripple in our rapport is the fact that it *is* so easy. We have the same sense of humor. Enjoy the same foods. Like the same hobbies, for the most part.

We have similar outlooks on life … except one.

Ashley wants what most women want. She's wanted the whole shebang—a husband, house, baby, and dog since we were in elementary school. She wants to live in one of those books she's always reading.

I have no interest in being the shirtless guy on one of those covers.

Although I could be if I wanted.

Serious relationships simply aren't for me. They're time-consuming. Both partners end up changing who they are in order to make the other one happy—then no one is happy. The sex stalls, you start arguing over what you're having for dinner, and before you know it, the person you loved at one point is now your mortal enemy.

Unless you break up with them first, which is what I do.

I'm pretty certain that it would be impossible to end things with Ashley and that's why we can only be friends.

I sigh, drop my hand, and head to the shower ... and I will absolutely not think of Ashley Thompson there.

Liar.

CHAPTER 4

Ashley

"I love this bowl." I set the mustardy-yellow Pyrex dish on the counter. "It reminds me of the potato salad you used to make every year at our big Fourth of July parties."

My mom hands me a plate. "Those were good times, weren't they?" She shuts off the water and picks up a hand towel. "I used to love having everyone come over. Making the menu, getting the pool ready, all of you kids running wild …"

Our eyes meet and she gives me a sad smile. The pain in her eyes, the same shade as mine, is fleeting.

"And then those parties you'd have as a teenager with all your friends," she says, drying her hands. "I don't think we had a night where it was just us throughout your whole high school life."

"Do you remember the night that Sara told her dad that she was staying here?" I know this memory of the time Sara was fifteen will make her happy. It wasn't Sara's first time staying over, but it was the first time she actually *wasn't* staying over. "When you found out about that, you took off in your pajamas to her boyfriend's house and put her in the car like she was your own kid."

"*Oh, I remember*. She didn't speak to me for two whole weeks after that. She'd just show up for meals, give me a look, and then walk out."

She leans against the counter. "That girl just about made me grayer than you ever did."

"She loves you for it."

Mom nods. "And I love her. She's still a wild child, but she'll always be *my* child. Even though she's not."

Her gaze settles on something in the distance.

My mom and Sara's mother, Kathleen, were best friends throughout their lives. When Kathleen was diagnosed with pancreatic cancer and died when Sara was only three years old, Mom promised her friend that she would always watch over Sara.

And she has. Because Mom is one of the good ones.

How my dad had a plethora of affairs for so many years will never be something I understand. *She never deserved that. No one does.*

"How is it going at Rebecca's?" Mom asks.

"Good. It's cramped—*but with two bedrooms*," I add quickly. "I have the privacy I wouldn't have had here sleeping on your sofa like a child."

She huffs. "I still think it's a bunch of baloney that you aren't staying with your mother after such a … a big life event."

"Pretty sure going through with a wedding that would've ruined my whole life would've been a bigger life event than saving myself."

Mom beams, smiling smugly at me. "You did save yourself, and I'm damn proud of you."

"Thanks, Mom. That means a lot."

She goes back to wiping down the kitchen, lost in her thoughts. I work with her side by side, scents of rosemary and thyme perfuming the air.

I want to tell her that I'm proud of her too. That her choice to leave my father over his unfaithfulness helped me realize that it's not wrong to put your heart first. To prioritize respect in relationships. But I can't say that. If I did, I'd have to tell her that Eton was doing the same thing to me that Dad did to her, and I think that would break her heart.

I remember the exact moment at the age of sixteen when everything changed. When Dad stumbled into the house, reeking of whiskey, and had faint red lipstick all over his face and neck. He was casually cruel about it, so utterly brazen that my mother was forced to acknowledge his infidelities—something that I think she knew about and had chosen to ignore for a while.

Over the next two years, my father's drinking showcased a manipulative and degrading part of his personality that I'd never known. One that I never forgot. I'd also never be able to truly rectify the juxtaposition between the sweet, tender man from *before* and the manipulative monster that I knew when he died.

If I told my mother that she was the role model for my choice to leave Eton—because she left my dad as soon as I turned eighteen—she would put two and two together. She'd figure out how to blame herself. Because that's what mothers do.

We fold our towels and drape them over the edge of the sink. Then she leads me into the living room. I flip the kitchen light off as we pass.

"I picked up a couple of things for you today." She pauses by the table in the small entryway and gathers a stack of magazines. "No pressure, but I just thought you might find these helpful."

I flop on the couch. Mom sits beside me and thrusts a million real estate brochures in my hands.

"No pressure, huh?" I hold the stack up for her to see. "You just randomly found ... six, seven, eight of these just laying around Muggers this morning?"

Mom grins. "Some of them were at Muggers when I went by for a coffee this morning, yes."

"And the other six?"

She laughs. "Just take them and have a look and stop being snotty."

I laugh too. "You'll be happy to know that I drove around today and looked at some places that I might be interested in."

"Did you tour any?"

"No. I don't have an agent or anything like that, but I wanted to see what was available. The market has changed so much since I've been gone. I was going to buy a place before we got engaged, and I swear they were tons cheaper than they are now."

"Now you see why I have this one-bedroom."

Because Dad left you with practically nothing, and now Gemma, the stepmother from hell, is enjoying half of his estate—the half that I didn't inherit.

"Why don't you let me give you some of my—"

"Don't." Her voice is stern. "That's not mine. It's yours. All I asked for in the divorce was for you to be taken care of, and you are. I don't want anything from that man."

Well, I don't particularly either, but his wife shouldn't get it all after what he put us through …

I open one of the brochures. "Why don't you go with me next week?"

"Where to?"

"My honeymoon."

"You're going?"

I look up. Curiosity is etched on her wrinkled forehead.

"Yeah. I decided that I might as well go and have fun. I mean, I did pay for it," I say.

"Which still disgusts me."

"Eton didn't want to go to the Bahamas. The only way I could convince him to choose it over California was if *I* paid for it, which was fine because I got a great deal thanks to my connections." I tap my chin. "That really should've been a red flag in retrospect."

"You think? What about the red flag that was waving in the air when he never complimented you? When is the last time Eton told you that you were beautiful? Smart? When was the last time he acknowledged how well you run your business and what all you've accomplished on your own?"

"Anyway," I say, going back to the brochure. A pretty two-bedroom place within walking distance to the beach looks tempting—and a great alternative to her question. *How did she notice that?* "You should go with me. What do you think?"

"I think I would've gone to California, but there's no way I'm flying over the water."

"Mom."

"I'm not." She shakes her head vehemently. "I won't do it and there's no way you'll talk me into it. I've had a fear of dark water since your grandpa drowned. Go and have fun but I'm keeping my butt at home."

I sigh. After dog-earing the corner of the page, I flip it to the next section of homes.

"You know who I could ask?" I say, moving to the condo section of the brochure.

"Who? But why don't you just take Sara or Becca? You always do a girls' trip anyway. This would be the perfect excuse to get away."

"They can't. They have to work. Speaking of work, I booked a trip for a couple this morning to Bora Bora. There's a new resort there that I didn't know about until I started researching this trip for them. It's amazing." My eyes sparkle. "It makes me want to book more things in the Pacific."

Mom rests against the pillows. "How is your business going? It wasn't too affected by all of this, was it?"

"Oh, it's good. I had slowed down because of the wedding, which is nice because I need a little time right now anyway."

"Right. So who were you thinking about taking?" she asks.

I bite my lip and look at her. She reads the expression on my face and starts shaking her head. "Don't say it, Ashley."

"What's wrong with Warren? We dated so long ago, and he's single. He popped up on Social for me a couple of days ago—"

"No."

"He looks great, and we really did get along. We just—"

"No, Ashley."

"It was probably bad timing," I say, amused at the displeasure on her face. I wasn't *really* considering Warren, but this makes me want to continue for the entertainment value of it. "Warren was a good guy."

And fun as hell in bed.

"You can't be serious," she says. "Tell me you're joking."

I just stare at her.

"Ashley …" She sighs, irritation thick in her tone. "You just took a huge step forward by dumping Eton, and you are absolutely *not* taking six steps back by getting with Warren. He still lives with his parents."

I lift a brow. "You wanted me to move back in with you."

"That's different."

"Is it, though?"

"*Yes.* Yes, it is."

I hum. "I read on Social that he just sold his business—"

"Which is an incredibly nice way of saying that he owed his ex-girlfriend's parents a very large sum of money and, because of their ... *shady background*, he had to pay up or probably get whacked."

My laughter fills the small room. "How do you know this? And since when do you use the word *whacked*?"

"I've been watching a lot of television. That's how you fill the time when your only daughter moves away, and then moves back and refuses to stay with you." She lifts her chin. "But this is also a very small town and Sara still comes over for dinner once a week, so I know things."

I snort as my phone rings. I glance at the screen. "Her ears must've been burning."

"Hey," she says over the speakerphone. "What's happening?"

"I'm at Mom's. We just finished dinner and were just talking."

"What did she make?"

"I made her minute steaks and brown gravy," Mom says. "And potatoes, of course—"

"And those yummy Brussel sprouts with the bacon pieces," I chime in.

"Gretchen, you know that's my favorite! There better be leftovers," Sara says, much to my mother's delight.

Their interaction warms my heart.

"Do you know what this daughter of mine just told me?" Mom says, scooting closer to the phone.

"No. What?"

"She told me that she's going to the Bahamas, and she was thinking of taking Warren Cartwright with her."

Sara gasps. "No, you aren't, Ashley. I swear to all that's holy, if you take him, I'll never talk to you again."

"There are days when I might take you up on that," I joke.

She gasps again—this time even more dramatically.

"I'm kidding. I was only suggesting that I take him for a good time. I wasn't saying I wanted to get back together with him," I say. "Who are you to tell me not to have casual sex?"

"You've never been that person," she says. "And while I'm incredibly supportive of you having casual sex—"

"You girls do know that I'm sitting here, right?" Mom asks.

"Sorry."

Mom shrugs. "I've had casual sex in my life. Just because I haven't had any in a while doesn't mean I'm not on the hunt."

"Mom!" I laugh. "Let's not have this conversation right now."

"Gretchen, I'll come over tomorrow and we can put together your hunting plan. But right now, let's focus on your daughter and her horrific taste in men. It's the absolute worst. Worse than mine and I'm banging my boss three times a week and I don't think he even likes me."

Mom shakes her head.

"Anyway …" Sara gasps. "*Wait*! I have an idea."

I set the brochures on the couch beside me and cringe. "That's scary."

"No, this is good," Sara says. "*Use your turn signal, asshole!*"

Mom looks at me and sighs.

"Sorry, I'm driving," Sara says. "When are you going home?"

"She is home. She's at her mother's," Mom says, side-eyeing me.

"Sorry, Gretchen. I mean, when are you going to *Rebecca's*, Ashley?" she asks sweetly.

"Better," Mom mumbles.

"In a little bit. Mom just gave me a stack as big as War and Peace of houses for sale from Daytona Beach to Sunnyvale to go through."

"If I can get you to buy a home here, maybe you won't leave me again," Mom says.

"I wasn't that far," I protest.

"It wasn't that far *to you*."

"Well, call me when you get there," Sara says. "No—I'll meet you there. This must be done in person."

"Okay, but I'll be a half hour or so," I say to Sara.

She groans. "Hold on. I can't come tonight. I forgot I'm having brunch in the morning with someone from Petterson Label Wines at Shade House. They rescheduled last minute. I have a ton of information to peruse for that and I'm swamped at work. How about I'll come by Friday night? That will give me more time to iron out the wrinkles in my idea."

"Fine. See you then," I say.

"All right. Bye, Gretchen. Love you."

"Love you, sweetie," Mom says to her.

I hang up the phone, not sure what just happened. But I have no time to replay it.

"It's getting late. You better be going," Mom says.

Instead of getting up, I fall into the cushions and give her a puzzled look. "It's seven o'clock."

"That's true. But I have a new bottle of sangria waiting on me and a bath bomb that I got out of the box you brought back from Orlando. So run along so I can relax."

"Are you kicking me out?"

She stands, a playful smirk on her face. "If you wanted to stick around, you could've moved in."

"You're playing dirty. But fine. I'll go."

We say our quick goodbyes and I'm out the door.

The early evening sun hits my face. It's hot and sticky and reminds me of seeing Maddox at this time yesterday.

I've never compared my boyfriends to Maddox. It would be like apples to oranges, mostly because I don't think of Maddox in a romantic way. But I did find myself comparing him to Eton more than once.

It wasn't fair to my ex-fiancé, really, but his coldness to me after he put a ring on my finger wasn't fair to me either. I found myself realizing slowly but surely that I was signing up for a life with a man who never laughed, never teased, and never ate food in bed. A life that would never be effortlessly joyful.

Why did I ever say yes?

I'm almost to my car when my phone buzzes.

> Maddox: If you're serious about sticking around, I listed a place today that you might be interested in. Seller is flexible on the price too. No pressure. Just trying to help.

I stop at my car and read his message again.

I watch the screen and a few seconds later, a listing appears in our text box. I wait a minute, and then two, to see if he says anything else. But he doesn't.

I shrug. *Typical Maddox. Always off to the next thing.*

With a smile, I get into my car and head to Rebecca's.

CHAPTER 5

Ashley

I park across the road from the listing that Maddox sent me yesterday. Then I turn down the air conditioner because the sound is distracting, and I can't multitask worth a crap.

The sun is high in the sky, practically baking everything on the ground. It was too hot for the beach, the wrong time of day for a casual stroll in Florida, and I was too antsy to sit alone at Rebecca's. So I decided to do a little house hunting so I can get out of Becca's guest room.

I've been there long enough.

"It's nice," I say, taking the house in. "Except for that hideous door."

The dark gray, two-story is tucked between old-growth trees on both sides. The landscaping appears low maintenance, and the neighborhood seems quiet and friendly. A man and woman waved at me a couple of houses down when I passed.

I reach for my phone, then find his name and touch it. Immediately, it begins to ring.

Shifting in my seat, I exhale—only to stop mid-breath when the ringing stops.

"Hey, Ash. Can you hold on for just a second?" he asks.

"Sure."

"No, Tati. That's fine. Just send them the contract and let them figure it out," Maddox says, his voice muffled. "If they have questions, they can call." He pauses. "Hey, can you close that door for me? Thanks."

A bead of sweat dots my forehead. I turn the vent up one notch.

"Sorry about that," he says. "You caught me mid-conversation with my assistant."

"You could've called me back, you know."

I can almost hear his grin through the line. "*Ha.* So what do I owe the pleasure of your call?"

I wonder if he can hear me smiling too. "Well, I happen to be sitting outside a certain gray house on Orange Street and I was wondering if I could get some more information on it. It's pretty cute."

"Except for that door? Did you see that thing?"

Laughing, I relax in my seat. "You're supposed to be talking the place up, not pointing out the flaws."

"I'm fairly certain that one's obvious." Papers shuffle in the background. "Let's see … I can show you that next week if you're really interested. The owners cleared us to show it, and then the husband decided to paint a bathroom. So we're on hold for a week—which is stupid, but people are stupid, I've learned."

"That they are."

"Or you could come by the office today, and we could talk about it …"

I hum, catching my reflection in the window. "I read the listing. What else is there to talk about?"

"I have other houses, you know. Or we could talk about what you're doing this weekend. Or why the sun is shining. Whatever gets you over here."

Maddox, you flirt. "Would you stop?"

"Stop what? I just want to see my buddy."

I roll my eyes.

"What's it gonna take, Miss Thompson?"

The warmth in his words heats my cheeks. *If someone walks by and sees me smiling like this, they'll think I'm a wacko.*

"I'm waiting," he says.

I have so many things I should be doing, and visiting Maddox at work isn't one of them. It's a time suck waiting to happen.

But it is about a house that I am interested in, so …

"See you in fifteen minutes?" I ask.

"Perfect."

"Bye."

———

"Go on in. I think he's waiting for you." Tati, Maddox's assistant, winks as she waves her hands toward the hallway. "It's good to see you again, Ashley. You look fantastic."

I stop at her desk in the lobby. *What did she say?*

"Oh, um … thank you," I say, glancing down at my shorts and old AC/DC T-shirt that I got at a garage sale a couple of years ago. The fabric is ridiculously soft … and thin. "Can you see through this?"

She laughs. "No. No, you cannot. I wouldn't let you go back to Maddox's office if your shirt was see-through. I wouldn't get any work out of him the rest of the day."

I blush.

"How have you been? I haven't seen you in a long time," she says.

Tati Melo moved here a few years ago—the same year as Rebecca. She's my age with long, silky hair and a body to die for. And if Maddox doesn't stay in line, she'll bury his body on the beach. She gives zero fucks. She's married to the love of her life with two beautiful children. She isn't mesmerized by Maddox's cheeky grin and dimples like most of humanity. That's why they're the perfect work team.

"Well …" I tuck a strand of hair behind my ear. "I ended my engagement with Eton, if you hadn't heard."

I don't know what kind of reaction I expected. The one I get is not it. I might as well have told her that I had breakfast this morning because she's *not* shocked.

"Girl, congratulations. I met that man one time—at your birthday party at Shade House last year, remember? And he stood in the corner and sulked the entire night. I went home and wondered why someone as bubbly and sweet as you would be with someone that dull."

Was it really that obvious that we were a mismatch?

She grins. "Now, go in there, you single woman, and see Mr. Carmichael."

I start toward the hallway. "Don't grin at me. It's not like that."

"Sure."

The bun on top of my head wobbles as I laugh quietly. *Guess she doesn't know Maddox as well as I thought she did.*

I knock on the door at the end of the hall, one that I'm sure has had many female visitors. Once Tati vets them, that is.

Maddox tells me to enter before my knuckles pull away from the wood.

"Hey," I say, stepping foot inside his space.

"Well, look at you busting out the old rock music T-shirt. The girl who doesn't even like rock music."

I make a face. "It's not about the band. It's about how soft this fabric is."

He leans forward, stretching a muscled arm over his large, dark wooden desk. "Let me feel."

I slap his hand away as I sit across from him. He chuckles and falls back into his chair.

Maddox's eyes are unusually bright, filled with light and mischief. They sparkle in the light streaming in from the windows that overlook Beachfront Boulevard.

"So you went by the house," he says, running his thumb over his bottom lip. "What did you think?"

I think I need to stop watching you play with your mouth.

"I love that neighborhood," I say. "And those arched windows are gorgeous. What's it like on the inside?"

He grabs his computer mouse and clicks around on his computer. "I have a video if you want to see it. I haven't uploaded it to YouTube yet."

I stand and walk around his desk. The closer I get, the more of his cologne I breathe in.

He looks at me over his shoulder. "Wanna sit?"

On your face. Yes … maybe.

My eyes go wide, and I scramble to swallow as if that will somehow hide my reaction to my very private thought. But it won't. Not when I think that Maddox was thinking the same thing.

"I'm good right here. I'll stand," I say.

He pulls his gaze away from mine as if it's been anchored there and it takes every one of his muscles to move.

Get yourself together, Ashley. Don't let your hormones get the best of you.

He presses play and we watch a quick walk-through of the house. The floors are beautiful and the kitchen is fantastic. The two bedrooms and two updated bathrooms would be perfect for me.

"And here's the outside," he says, shifting in his chair. His shoulder brushes lightly against my forearm. If he notices the goose bumps that scatter across my skin, he doesn't acknowledge it. "This pool is two years old. Saltwater and heated. Low-maintenance landscaping with all the pavers back there and a top-of-the-line, sophisticated surveillance system."

The screen goes dark.

"That's it," he says.

I should take a step away. No, I should go back to my chair. But my feet are frozen in place.

Maddox turns so that his knee is against mine. The contact sends a shock through my body, the waves pooling in my groin. My lips part and I haul in a quick breath.

"What are you thinking?" he asks.

I free my feet. I'm back in my chair in a second. "That you're a terrible cameraman." *So lame.*

"You should see some of my other work."

His lips twist into a smirk. He's obviously not talking about other real estate work. My mind starts to run, wondering if Maddox has sex tapes floating in the interweb, when he laughs.

"I don't have sex tapes, if that's what you're wondering," he says.

How does he do that?

"Moving on," I say, flustered. "I would like to tour that house. I'm not completely sold on it but it's worth a look."

"Absolutely. But don't feel pressured. I only sent you that link yesterday to get you to text me."

I grin. "What? Did *hello* stop being an icebreaker?"

"No, but *hello* is overused. It's simple. Basic. I needed something … *more*. Something that you couldn't resist replying to." He bites his lip. "I was trying to be polite. The last time I tried to get fancy you—"

"You sent me a picture of your abs when I was out to dinner with Eton." I try to be serious, but I can't. "What the hell?"

"You obviously hadn't seen a nice body for a while, so I was doing you a favor. Trying to brighten your day." He looks at me innocently. "I've never gotten such a blasé response to a picture before. Or since, really."

"Most of the recipients don't know you as well as I do."

"True. But the nice thing to do would've been to appreciate the picture—I even used a ring light to get a better quality."

I start laughing.

"You were supposed to send one back, you know," he says. "That's how it works. It's a trade. A pic for a pic."

"Poor you. I'm sure your messages are devoid of pictures."

He shrugs. "I mean, they're not, but that doesn't mean I don't want one of yours."

"I have no interest in being in your fangirl collection, sir."

He lifts a brow and leans forward. "You'd have your own collection. I wouldn't dare put you with the rest."

"I'm flattered."

Fire burns in my stomach as I watch the same flame flicker in his eyes. *What's happening right now? And why is Maddox turning up the heat on his flirting lately?*

Not that I'm mad about it …

"Well, for the record, I might've accidentally not deleted your picture," I say coyly.

"You were looking at it to get off, weren't you?"

"No!" I laugh in disbelief. *Although, I thought about it.* "But I bet that's why you wanted mine, huh?"

I don't know how to read the look on his face. I only know that it sends shivers down my spine.

"Why do we do this?" I ask, fanning my face. There's no sense in hiding it.

He exhales and reaches for a pen. "Because we are two good-looking people who know each other well enough to play around."

If only …

The space between us thickens, making it harder to breathe. I fidget with the arm of my chair.

"Do you want me to schedule some properties for you to look at next week?" he asks. *How can he seem so unaffected?*

"No, actually." I clear my throat. "I'm going out of town. But the week after would be great."

"You're going out of town?"

I nod.

A question lingers in the air. I can read the thought bubble over Maddox's head—*Where are you going, Ashley?*

There's no way I'm telling him that I'm going on my honeymoon alone. No way in hell. For one, it would bring Eton into this conversation, and I'm over talking about him. And for two, telling Maddox that I'm going to the Bahamas solo is a bit embarrassing. I don't know why. It's fine, and I know he wouldn't think anything of it, but he'd start quizzing me about being careful and drive me nuts. I don't need any more stress.

"Hey, how's Paige?" I ask. "The last I heard, your sister had moved to Savannah. Is she still up there?"

Maddox groans. "Yeah. She's shacked up with her boss and his kid."

"I take it you're not a fan?"

"Yeah, well, he's not a *terrible* guy. No felonies or restraining orders. She's happy. Dad likes him. So …" He shrugs.

"How do you know all of that—the felonies part?"

"Remember Skylar Schultz? He was a year younger than us in school."

"Yeah. He stuck a paperclip in an outlet in fifth grade."

"That's him." He grins. "Well, he's a cop now and Banks and I had him do some digging."

"Of course, you did. Poor Paige."

We exchange a simple smile. Once his dimples begin to settle in his cheeks, it's time to go. His dimples and my starved libido isn't a good mix.

I'll just go to Becca's and use that picture.

"I need to get going," I say. "I'm finalizing a trip for a couple to Bora Bora, and I need to pack."

"You just got here."

I glance at my watch. "Thirty minutes ago."

"Really?" He checks the time. "Too bad you can't just sit in here while I work all day. Time flies when you're around."

"So charming," I tease. "Thanks for making time for me today."

"It's my pleasure."

I start to respond when another voice rings through the room.

"Oh, we're talking about pleasure with Ashley. This should be fun."

I whirl around to see Jess, one of Maddox's older brothers, standing in the doorway. His jeans are filthy, and the way his white T-shirt is stretched over his barreled chest should be illegal.

He's almost as hot as Maddox.

"Nope. You aren't invited into this conversation," Maddox says, making Jess and me laugh. "Don't you knock? Or call before you come?"

"You know, I'm truly sorry. It took you guys, what, almost thirty years to admit that you want to pleasure each other?" Jess asks.

Maddox's face twists, so I hop in before he can get angry.

"*No, Jess,*" I say, scoffing. "We admitted that years ago."

I blow Maddox a kiss, watching with amusement as his eyes go wide and then dark.

Go. Now.

"I'll leave you guys to it," I say. "Talk to you soon, Mad. Bye, Jess."

I think I hear Maddox threaten to slice his brother's throat as I shut the door behind me.

CHAPTER 6

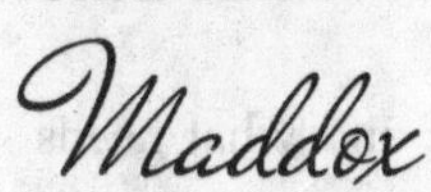

"SHE'S GOT A NICE ASS ON HER," JESS SAYS, WHISTLING BETWEEN HIS teeth. "And when she says my name with those pouty lips …"

I glare at him. He holds his hands up in front of him in defense. "Sorry."

"Did Dad send you over?" I ask, hoping to pivot the conversation away from Ashley. *I can't have a conversation with my brother with a hard-on.*

Jess takes the bait and yawns. "He did. My crew is just about finished with our last renovation for him. We'll have to go help Moss out with a couple of things, but we should be ready for you soon. A couple of weeks max."

"Good. I have something for you. Gimme a second."

I dig around my desk and pretend to search for the file that's next to my phone. I need a minute.

Ashley's perfume lingers, and I can still feel the place where her arm touched mine while she stood next to me. It's so fucking stupid to fixate on these things, but I'm having a hell of a time shaking it off like I usually do.

I didn't sleep worth a shit last night. I kept replaying our conversation from La Pachanga.

"It's just really easy to forget who you are and what you need if you aren't careful."

That line keeps rolling around in my head. It's so fucking true. I've noticed that in my own life lately—how you eventually accept things just because you forget to contest them. You get too busy going with the flow, too unwilling to rock the boat, and before you know it, you become this person with this life that you didn't really plan. You have thoughts and assumptions about the world—and yourself—and you can't even remember why.

It makes me wonder what part of her she forgot and what needs weren't being met.

I'm so curious. I'm also irritated that I don't already know.

"Oh, here it is," I say, acting like I found the file. "This is going to be first, I think. The contract gets signed at the end of the month. Dad looked at everything and approved it."

Our parents, Kix and Damaris Carmichael, are two of the hardest-working people I've ever known. How they created a mini-empire and raised six kids is beyond me. *And most of us didn't turn out so bad.*

Foxx, my oldest brother, and Paige, my baby sister, are the only two that don't have some connection to the family businesses.

Laguna Homes was started before Foxx was born. My brothers Moss and Jess fell naturally into place leading the construction and renovation of homes the company purchases. Although Banks owns a car restoration business, he jumps in every now and then when someone gets in a bind. I use my real estate license to help Laguna find and sell properties, as well as working on my own projects.

From time to time, I'll have a buyer that wants a custom renovation. I hook them up with my father and our businesses merge.

Benefits of having a large family.

Jess and I yawn at the same time.

"You didn't sleep either?" I ask.

"I stayed up watching Netflix and completely overestimated my ability to run on three hours' sleep. There wasn't coffee strong enough this morning."

"I think I got two solid hours before the alarm went off."

"What kept you up?"

Before I can answer, my phone buzzes with a text. Even though I don't know the number on the screen, I unlock it and read the message.

Flamingos can sleep standing on one leg.

What?

I look up at Jess. "Flamingos can sleep standing on one leg."

"What the hell?"

"I have no idea," I say, laughing. "That was just texted to me."

"From whom?"

"Fuck if I know."

Me: They must not skip leg day.

I wait for a response. None comes.

Me: Who is this?

Still, nothing.

"Who was it?" Jess asks.

"I don't know. They didn't answer." I shrug and toss the phone back on my desk.

Jess leans forward, resting his elbows on his knees. "I heard Ashley is a runaway bride."

And, just like that, my body temperature rises two degrees.

Unable to sit still, I shift in my seat. "Yeah. How did you know that?"

"Moss. He ran into her at Smokey's this morning." His grin makes the corners of his eyes wrinkle. "He said she's looking good. I'll have to tell him that I concur."

I picture her clear eyes and friendly smile. The curve of her hips and the fullness of her breasts. The way her hair shines in the light.

Fuck. I adjust myself under my desk.

"That's for damn sure," I mutter.

He stares at me, unblinking. *Only grinning.* It makes me shift in my seat again.

"*What*?" I ask, irritation growing.

"Nothing." He tries to stop smiling. "Just wondering how you felt about it and all. You weren't thrilled when she got engaged."

No. I fucking hated it. "Because that guy was completely wrong for her and, obviously, I was right."

"And that has nothing to do with some unrequited crush you've had on her for the last, well, I don't know—*your whole entire life*?"

I scoff, picking up a pencil as a distraction. "If I wanted to make a move on Ashley, I would."

"And you don't?" He slides his phone out of his pocket. "Shit. Hang on."

His momentary distraction gives me a second to breathe for the first time since Ashley walked into my office.

It's getting harder and harder to pull back from her when we get going. Before she came back from Orlando—before she got engaged—it felt more like a joke when we would flirt or tease. And it was. It still is.

I think.

I know all the reasons it should be. I need to pull my head out of my ass and tattoo it on my forehead before I fuck this up.

"So do you?" Jess says. "Do you want to make a move on her?"

Nice, easy transition back into the conversation, brother.

"No, I don't," I say, tapping the pencil on my desk. "I like my life just the way it is. I can go to bed without brushing my teeth. If I'm hungry, I can take a whole jar of cashews with me to bed and eat them while I watch *Gladiator* for the millionth time. I can … I can get a dog if I want to."

Internally, I cringe. *That was stupid.*

"Totally stay single for the dog," Jess says, laughing freely at my ridiculous words. "Smart. Good choice."

I blow out a breath. "You know what I mean. Relationships are the best way to ruin anything good. You put a label on it, and it can't breathe. Besides, Ash and I aren't like that. We're on opposite pages, and we know it. We're grown-ups." *Sadly.*

"I hope you get invited to her next wedding," he says, getting up.

I narrow my eyes at him. He ignores me.

"You know, she'll be looking for a rebound," he says, heading for the door.

A rebound? Ashley?

My brain processes quickly. *Of course, she'll need a rebound. Every broken relationship gets a rebound.*

She'll want to boost her confidence—although I don't know why it would ever be shaky to begin with. She's a great woman.

Will she ease back into dating? Maybe. She might be nervous about it.

But why would Ashley be nervous? Because she winds up with assholes every time. That's why. She's never found someone who's even close enough to being good enough for her.

Hell, that guy might not even exist.

Jess faces me at the door. A shit-eating grin splits his cheeks.

"I hate you. Do you know that?" I ask him.

He bursts out laughing.

"I do. Foxx is a dick but keeps to himself. Banks is Banks. Moss is usually pretty cool, but when he's a prick, he makes it clear, and you have to respect that. But you … you sneak it in and get under my skin," I say. "There's no redeeming quality there."

"My tactics are the most sophisticated."

"That's not what I said."

He winks. "Okay, I'll leave you with that little thought. See you tomorrow."

Jess gives me a cocky grin and then heads down the hallway. His voice trails behind him as he says, *"He shoots and misses. The opponent rebounds. Look at that rebound. So smooth. He's definitely going to score with those moves."*

"Fucker."

I get to my feet. I don't know *what* makes me so pissed off, but something does.

Maybe it's because he's intentionally trying to make me mad. Or that he thinks I care in the first place. Or maybe I'm pissed because Ashley might have a rebound ... and it won't be me.

What the fuck am I thinking?

I exhale harshly and pick up my phone again. I have no idea what to say, so I start typing.

> **Me:** Did you know that flamingos can sleep standing on one leg?

I grimace, knowing that was stupid as hell but not sure what else to say. It just came out. But I'm relieved that something was sent—even if it wasn't the best thing ever.

Her response is immediate.

> **Ashley:** Guess they don't miss leg day. 😛

My laughter fills my office, and my shoulders loosen.

Relax, Maddox. Everything is okay.

CHAPTER 7

Ashley

I LAY THE TWO SUNDRESSES IN MY BAG ON THE BED AND TAKE A STEP BACK.

I really should've packed better. Then again, when I left Orlando, I didn't plan on going on this trip, or I would've kept more of my things out of storage.

I grip my forehead.

Why do I constantly overestimate my abilities? I had a matter of days to pack everything I owned and get it into a storage unit before my landlord changed his mind about letting me break my lease early. I figured it'll be okay. *Orlando isn't that far. I can come back and sort through things if I really need them.*

Clearly, I didn't factor in gas prices. Or how hot storage units could get in the summer in Florida. Or the idea of climbing through piles of boxes with no room to move to find, what—a specific dress?

Yeah, no. I glance at the bed again.

Four days in paradise isn't going to work with a few shirts that were packed for comfort and not to impress, four shorts, two sundresses, and a bikini.

I sigh and sit on the chair in the corner of the bedroom.

The room is a mess. My entire bag is dumped on the comforter. Files, my computer, a notebook and pen are on the floor in the corner that I've turned into a pseudo-office space. Worst of all, sticky notes are stuck in random places for things I need to do and can't forget.

Except I probably will forget because they keep falling off the surfaces and getting thrown away.

I close my eyes. *I'll get it all sorted after I come back.* My eyes pop open. *But first, I'm going to need clothes.*

A knock on the door makes me jump. Sara's head pokes around the corner. She surveys the mess and makes a face.

"How do you live like this?" she asks.

"Carefully." I stand. "This isn't my idea of a good time, though. I'm in limbo, remember?"

"True. Now come into the living room where there's a place to sit so we can discuss my genius idea. Grab your computer."

"Why do we need my computer?" I grab my device and follow her down the short hallway.

"Patience."

"We're discussing patience?" I tease. "Let's start with yours."

"Don't be snarky."

She would've been proud of my snark yesterday.

My mind sashays its way to Maddox and our interaction in his office. And to the innuendos. And to the flamingo text. *What the hell was that?*

"What are you grinning about?" Rebecca asks as we walk into the room.

"Nothing."

I sit on the sofa next to Rebecca as Sara takes a chair across from us. On the table between us is a notebook. I set my computer on top of it.

"This is very *Baby-Sitters Club* of us," I joke.

"Obviously, I'm Kristy," Sara says. "So let this meeting begin."

We all laugh.

Rebecca tucks her legs up under her bottom. "For once in her life, Sara has an idea that I can fully get behind."

My stomach tightens. "That makes me very, very apprehensive."

"Oh, shut up," Sara says. "When have I ever lured you into something bad?"

I lift a brow.

"Don't answer that." Sara crosses one leg over the other. "Let's stay focused, please. We don't have much time."

"Really? *We don't have much time?*" I smile at her dramatization. "Are we saving the world from monsters from outer space or what? Have you called Jeff Goldblum?"

Sara slow blinks.

"Never mind," I say. "Continue."

"Great. I would like to begin by saying that I talked to my boss and tried to get out of work to go with you on your honeymoon."

A bolt of hope fires through me. *That would be amazing.* "You did?"

When she looks at me, the drinks in my imagination spill into the sand.

"I can't get off." She rolls her eyes. "Okay, that was proven by my boss today to be a lie. *Twice.*"

"*Sara.*"

She laughs. "But I can't get the days free to go with you. I tried, Ash. I really did. I even took my boss to lunch and offered … Well, let's say I offered things he's had before but really enjoyed." She winks. "But even that can't get me out of the meetings."

"While I appreciate your efforts," I say, as Rebecca snorts behind me, "I would like to speed this conversation up to the point where I find out what you've been plotting behind my back."

She bites her lip, then lets it pop free.

"We know you're okay going alone," Rebecca says calmly. "And we know you'd probably have a good time. But apparently, Sara heard that you were considering asking Warren Cartwright to be your travel companion."

Sara gags.

I'd forgotten about that.

"I don't know why everyone is all against the idea," I say, even though I'm against it too. "It's not like I was going to marry him. But he would be fun and help me get rid of this sexual frustration that's making me nuts."

The same frustration that's making me want to take things to another level with Maddox, for crying out loud.

We texted on and off last night—well into the morning. Our

exchanges were fun and playful. We talked about flamingos and the real estate market and stories from high school. He told me about Moss almost getting arrested, and I told him about the night when *I* almost got arrested, courtesy of Eton's mother—a woman as sour as her son.

It was such a fun night. I haven't had a textathon like that in ages. I had to smother my laughs behind pillows so I didn't wake Becca.

Will he text me again tonight or be out on a date? What's his normal routine? His habits? I'm *so* curious, but it's none of my business.

"You're *not* taking Warren," Sara says in a no-nonsense tone. "But we do have a solution to solve your problem."

I chuckle. "Let's hear it."

"We're going to have a contest." Sara throws that line into the room and sits back as if her work is done. "We're starting it tonight."

What? "Whoa, *whoa.* Hold your horses. *We're gonna what?*"

"Have a contest." Rebecca scoots to the end of the sofa and plants her feet on the floor. "I know it sounds a little unconventional, but it's honestly brilliant."

I must be hearing things.

"So let me just ..." I start again. "You're having a contest to—what?"

"To find you a honeymoon date."

I stare at them.

"You're untrustworthy when it comes to picking men for yourself —hence Warren and Eton," Rebecca says. "So Sara and I decided to do you a huge favor and pick one for you."

Pick one for me?

Rebecca smiles sweetly. "Let us run a contest for a date to your honeymoon."

I need a drink for this.

I'm on my feet. Before I know it, I've gone into the kitchen, poured a shot of the only liquor Rebecca has on hand—rum—and downed it.

"Just think about it," Sara says, appearing at my side.

The alcohol burns my throat. "Oh, I am."

The scary part about this whole thing is that it's not a bad idea.

Does it smell a little desperate? Yes. Impulsive? Also, yes. It teeters on the edge of looking like a scorned lover, too, if I'm not mistaken.

But on the other side of all of that is an altogether different vibe—one that's playful and carefree. One that shows I'm not heartbroken over Eton or hiding in my room with a pint of gelato.

One that I don't exactly hate.

"Think about it," Sara says again. "You don't want to go alone—not really. And you're not sure whom to ask, probably because you're even scared of your choices."

I give her a look.

"So live a little," she says. "Have some fun with it. It's a four-day trip. What can it hurt? It's not like we'll pick some rando you don't know or dislike."

"We have it all figured out," Rebecca says. "We wrote a little paragraph that we can put on Social—"

"What?" I yelp, cutting her off. "You want *me* to make a post on social media for a date to my honeymoon? For the world to see? Are you out of your mind?"

Sara sighs. "What are your options here? Do you really want to stay in some expensive room by yourself and have all that space to think about Eton?"

"We know you, Ashley, and you think you'll come home reinvigorated to take on your life. But you'll really come home sad. *Somehow.* Because only you could turn this opportunity into a sad fest," Rebecca says.

I narrow my eyes. "Thanks a lot."

"Truth hurts," Sara says with a shrug. "Now, are you in or not?"

She crosses her arms and stares at me.

I hate that they're right, but they honestly know me well.

I'm not like Sara. I'd avoid sexy cabana guys instead of being open-minded and on the prowl. I'm not a quiet soul like Becca. I won't find peace and revitalization by sitting alone and freeing my mind from toxic energy.

Nope. I'll be using those few days to scrutinize the past two years and feel angry about all I lost with Eton.

Does that mean I would come home sad rather than proud of my choice to end things? Ugh. It might. Sadly, it just might. And if it did, it wouldn't just set me back six steps like Mom said Warren would—it would set me back a whole mile.

Fuck that.

I lift my chin.

"Just read what we wrote," Rebecca says, shaking the notebook in her hand. The pages rattle in the air. "Then let's talk."

She thrusts the notebook at me. I take it while giving her the stink eye.

I sit at the table. My friends scramble into chairs too. They're practically holding their breaths while I peruse their chicken scratch that's slanted across the page. *What kind of animal writes like this?*

"'Contest. Win a date to my honeymoon,'" I read aloud. I look at them. "This is ridiculous."

Sara taps the paper. "Keep going."

I sigh and look down at the paper again.

Contest: Win a Date to My Honeymoon

I realize that a social media post isn't the usual way of securing a date to your honeymoon—for obvious reasons—but here we are.

The wedding was canceled. But what's not canceled is the nonrefundable, ten-thousand-dollar all-inclusive vacation at a luxury resort, and I'm not about to let it go to waste.

I'm packed and ready to hit the beach. But I can't deny that it might be more interesting to honeymoon with someone.

Since my track record of picking dates isn't exactly golden, I've done something that I hope I don't regret. In a moment of weakness—mixed with panic and fueled by margaritas—I agreed to let my friends choose someone to go with me.

It'll be a blind date / postnuptial vacation—without the nuptials. A few fun days in paradise with no expectations. No obligations.

Before you say, "pick me for a free vacay!" there are a few things to consider ...

The perfect candidate will be single. He won't talk too much on the plane. And he'll be able to leave town quickly.

He will also be okay with sharing a bed. It's a honeymoon suite, after all.

If you want to be considered, email Rebecca and Sara your application at the address below. (Get creative. There's a free vacation on the line!)

Wheels up next week!

Godspeed, honeymooners.

I slowly lift my eyes to Sara. "It says I've had margaritas. That would've helped."

She sighs. "You've had rum. Same difference. I had one—okay, two margaritas—as I was scheming this ingenious proposal, so it was technically fueled by them."

I rise from the table and pace the room slowly.

Some internal voice—the sensible shoulder—tells me that this might be dangerous, but then the *other* shoulder tells me that traveling alone could be dangerous as well. *Cheeky bitch.* And I've already bailed on a wedding this month. If I'm worried about anyone's opinions of me, it's a little late for that.

Not that I care anyway.

I turn toward the table. They both look up at me.

"Your mom loves the idea," Sara says. "She called me yesterday, and I told her everything. She said she trusts me implicitly."

"Of course, she does." I sigh. "How do I know that you'll choose someone who I can actually stand to spend that much time with?"

"Because we know you better than you know yourself," Rebecca says.

Sara makes a face. "I don't know if that's technically true, but I do know that we know better than you who you *should* get to know. And if you don't believe me, then I present to you your dating history."

"Look at yours," I say. "That doesn't fare well for your abilities."

She pretends she didn't hear me. "Let's just post it and see what happens. If we don't get anyone to respond who's a great match, then we'll forget the whole thing."

My defenses wane.

I think back to something my grandma used to say to me. *You can't make an entrance without making an exit.*

I thought about that line in the days leading up to my conversation with Eton that ended our engagement. The only way to enter a place where I had the potential to be happy was to exit that one.

That morsel was tucked in my brain—alongside the emails of Eton's hookup locations with many different women around the country—when I walked into the restaurant to have what would be our final conversation. The stupid asshole had never been faithful. Why the hell did he propose to me in the first place? I don't know. For control, I suspect. Regardless, *good riddance.*

You can't make an entrance without making an exit.

Here goes nothing … "How do you know that anyone will even be able to go? I leave on Monday. That's not much time."

"We don't," Rebecca says simply. "We just want to try."

"If a day before I leave arrives and you've picked no one, then I can ask Warren," I say.

I won't ask Warren, but I need a concession on their part.

Sara rolls her eyes. "What do you think, Bec?"

"I think that's fair."

"Fine," Sara says. "Do we have a deal?"

I nod. "Yes. We have a deal."

My stomach twists and I can't tell if it's due to excitement or fear. Maybe a little of both.

I'm really doing this. Holy cow.

"We'll take care of everything," Rebecca says while Sara dances around the kitchen in celebration. "All you have to do is post it on your Social account and show up at the airport. We'll pick the guy, get the ticket—all of it."

"I'll pay you back for the ticket," I say. "Hard limit."

"Fine," Sara says, clearly unhappy to have to give in.

We sit again. It takes a second to get logged in to Social because I forgot my password.

"Want me to type?" Sara asks. "I'm faster."

"Be my guest." I shove the computer toward her. "It'll give me an out when I regret this later. I can just tell myself that you took my computer and posted it."

Sara's nails clatter against the keys. "Whatever helps you sleep at night."

Rebecca pats my leg. It's her way of reassuring me that everything will be okay. It's one of my favorite things about Rebecca. She has a protective nature and a sweet, methodical approach to life.

"There," Sara says, turning the screen toward me. "Want to proof it?"

Seeing the words on the screen hits harder than reading them on paper in the privacy of the house. When they're in the text box of a program that can reach millions or billions of people, things become a bit more overwhelming. Vulnerable. *Real.*

"Sara ..."

"Looks good to me," Rebecca says over my shoulder.

Sara holds my gaze. "Look good to you?"

"I mean, it's grammatically correct but—*Sara!*"

Her finger clicked the mouse, and the post delivers to the world wide web.

I gasp, my back hitting the wooden chair rails, and stare at the screen. But with each passing second, my panic eases.

What do I really have to lose? The people who love me—Rebecca,

Sara, Mom—all think it's a good idea. And to be honest, I know I'm in good hands.

I exhale slowly.

"I need to get this," Rebecca says, looking at her phone. "Be right back."

She steps through the back door and onto the small patio to take the call.

I stand. There's too much nervous energy floating around my body to sit still much longer. Sara follows suit.

"I need to go," Sara says. "I just wanted to come and do this, but I need to finish a few spreadsheets that will probably take me most of the night. Tell Becca that I said goodbye."

"Okay."

We make our way to the door.

"I'm not going to thank you for doing that just yet," I say. "But I'm hoping you're right about this whole honeymoon date thing."

She taps the tip of my nose. "I'm your fairy godmother. Just watch." With a quick wink, she's out the front door.

I stand alone in the foyer with my head spinning. *What just happened?*

I dig my phone out of the sofa to call my mother. As soon as I unlock the screen, I see Maddox's last text—one that must've come in while I was dealing with Sara.

My smile is instantaneous, and I don't try to fight it. Nor do I fight the warmth that I feel when reading his name.

This whole thing with Maddox lately is weird. I don't hate it; I'm just not sure what to think of it. He's been a part of my life for so many years. He's just *been there*. But now he's consistently there—every day. Multiple times. In different ways.

Sure, we've texted before but not like this. We've flirted our whole lives but not to this level. I've looked at him and thought how hot he is a million times, but I've never actually wanted to strip him naked like I have since I've been home.

I've only been back in Kismet Beach for two weeks, and it feels like something has shifted. I'm more … aware of him. Interested rather than amused. His awareness of me is peculiar now as well. In a way, it's as if we've just met and have that fun magnetism you get after a meet-cute.

But we're not strangers. We're old friends.

Am I just feeling the effects of freedom, or is this dynamic new? Is he aware of the same shift?

I sigh.

Maybe I'm reading too much into this. I'm probably reading way too much into this. He's still Maddox Carmichael, playboy extraordinaire. The man who declared himself a proverbial bachelor in our eighth-grade yearbook. Nothing has changed.

You know he flirts with everyone like this. Stop overthinking. Don't make it uncomfortable.

> **Maddox:** I don't think I told you, but you looked very pretty in my office yesterday. I was just thinking about it so I thought you should know just in case you needed a little boost of confidence.

> **Maddox:** Not that you need it. Just saying.

> **Me:** A girl can always use a boost of confidence. Especially when she's feeling like she might have just lost her marbles.

> **Maddox:** Everything okay?

> **Me:** I think so. Sara's a bad influence.

> **Maddox:** We should hook her up with Banks and see who can out-bad influence the other first.

I laugh.

> **Me:** That would be fun fireworks. Almost as fun as watching your face when I send you this pic in a minute.

Maddox: REALLY?

Me: No.

Maddox: ☹

Maddox: Quick question—do you like basketball?

Me: No. Why?

Maddox: No reason.

I furrow my brow. *What is that all about?*

Me: A little odd but okay.

Maddox: I'll tell you for a picture.

Me: I'm not that worried about it.

Maddox: Figures. If you need a new one of me, just let me know. I've been doing pull-ups all night to get a pump just in case.

Me: 😑

Maddox: That's what I usually get. Eyes rolling in the back of heads.

My smile is unstoppable. The small laugh that topples from my lips can't be halted either. It feels good. Free. Fun.

I've missed this.

Me: Don't take this the wrong way, but I missed you. Thank you for always making space for me in your life, you know?

It takes him a long couple of seconds to respond. But, when he does, my throat pulls tight.

> Maddox: There will always be room for you in my life. You have a permanent place, Ash.

My eyes grow cloudy as I read the words a second, then a third time. I didn't realize it until now, but I don't think I've ever heard, or read, a man communicate that to me. That I matter *that* much. And that I always will.

Maddox Carmichael, you're a charming bastard.

> Me: 🖤

> Maddox: 🖤

I clutch my phone to my chest and head to my room to make a packing list for the trip.

CHAPTER 8

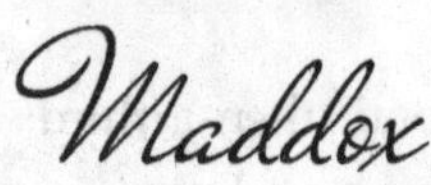

"I CAN'T BELIEVE YOU WANTED CHICKEN NOODLE SOUP WHEN IT'S THIS HOT outside," Mom says, handing me a bowl. "Do you want any, Banks?"

My brother shakes his head. "Nope. This sweet tea is all I need. That and your love, Mama."

She rolls her eyes at him.

The kitchen at my parents' house is bright and airy, thanks to the wall we took down a few weeks back. It was a messy job—and Foxx and Moss almost came to blows over it—but we got it done, and it doesn't look half bad.

I stir the soup, watching the carrots and celery swim around in the broth.

"What did you two do today?" Mom asks. "When I talked to you, it sounded like you were at a party." She turns on the water at the sink but watches us over the island.

I grin. "We were. It was a total rager."

"You should've seen it, Mom," Banks says, twisting in his chair so he can watch her reaction. "Wet T-shirt contests and these big t—"

"Banks," she warns. "*Don't*."

We laugh. She's not sure whether to believe us or not, which is hysterical.

"Who goes to parties at four in the afternoon on a Saturday?" I ask.

Banks looks at me over his shoulder. "We have before."

"That's true."

Mom shakes her head and sighs. "You two are going to be the death of me. Especially you, Banks."

"Why especially me? Why is it always especially me?"

"Because you, you little shit, broke my cookie jar."

She levels her gaze with my brother.

I dip my chin toward my soup and fill my mouth with the still-too-hot liquid. *Fuck.* My mouth opens and I blow out steam toward the ceiling.

"Your cookie jar is broken?" Banks asks as if he has no clue. "Which one?"

"The shoe."

"The one Dad bought you for … your graduation, I think?" he asks.

"For Foxx's birth, but yes, that one." She places a hand on her hip. "Why didn't you tell me that you broke it?"

"Um …" He looks at me over his shoulder. "Because I didn't do it?"

The last sentence sounds more like a question than an answer. If Mom had any hesitation that Banks broke the jar, she doesn't anymore.

I glance at her to start trying to deflect her attention from the subject, but she gives me *the look*—the one that I know better than to screw with.

"Okay, in Banks's defense," I say, ignoring his dropped jaw, "that thing has been broken for months now, and you just noticed."

She rolls her tongue around her mouth. "So it was Banks."

"See? She didn't know for sure," he says to me. "You snitch."

"Banks, shut it. Everyone knew for sure that it was you, just like she already knows I'm the one who glued it together. It was only a matter of time."

Banks lifts his chin and turns back to Mom. "If you're just noticing, I guess that means you don't bake enough. You might want to reevaluate your mothering skills."

"You better watch your mouth, little boy," Mom tells him.

I snort and sip more soup.

"So where were you heathens?" Mom asks. "Are you avoiding the question?"

"I taught the bitty kids this morning," I say.

"Didn't you opt out of coaching this quarter?" Mom asks. "I thought you were stepping back from wrestling for a little while."

I sigh. "Me too. Chris took one of the junior wrestlers to a competition in North Dakota and asked me to fill in today."

Mom comes around the island and pulls out a chair at the table between Banks and me. "When is the last time you took a day off?"

I shrug and take another mouthful.

Staying busy is a Carmichael family trait. We're always into something, doing something, plotting something else. But, according to my mother, I'm going to work myself to death.

"Why don't you ever ask me that?" Banks jokes. "Why is it always *Banks broke this* and never *Banks needs some time off*?"

"Because you're here so much that I know all the days you take off, the time you go to work, when you get home …" She grabs his chin in her hand. "I love you, son, but you need to find a wife."

I chuckle. "You think someone is gonna take him? Good luck with that."

"And *you*, Maddox Anthony, need to take a break," she says, her voice no-nonsense. "I appreciate your work ethic—especially considering that I didn't think you had one through college."

"Gee, thanks."

She smiles. "But now you don't know the definition of a vacation. It's good for the soul. You should try it."

"Yeah …"

Dad walks in the kitchen, whistling an old game show tune. "Hey, boys."

"Hey," Banks says.

"Hi, Dad." I lift my spoon toward him like a toast. "What are you up to today?"

"Talking your mother out of buying a couch for the hundredth time this month," he says, making a point to glare at Mom before winking at her. "She's hell-bent on getting a new one."

She pushes her chair back and stands. "It's disgusting, Kix. It's time. Hell, it was time when the date still started with a one-nine."

"A little dramatic."

She sighs. "One of these days, I'm going to just buy one. I'm trying to be reasonable and let you help me pick it out, but you're pushing my limits."

Dad puts a pod in the coffee maker nonplussed. When nothing happens, he taps his palm against the front. "Looks like we're going to have to get a new machine."

"You get a new coffee thing more than I get new sheets," I say, rolling my eyes.

He smirks. "My *coffee thing* probably gets more action than your sheets."

I burst out laughing. Mom, too, tries to hide her giggles.

Banks throws his hands up and groans. "Can we not go there? Please?"

"I can guarantee that's true for Banks since he *never goes home*," I say, annoyed that I found him on my couch again this morning.

"I do go home, asshole. But then I wake up and need a snack or I'm bored, so I come over to see if you're up and wind up falling asleep. Not my fault."

"Should've saved our money on Banks's house," Dad says before kissing Mom loudly. "I'm going to go find some coffee."

"It's late afternoon, Kix. You'll never sleep."

"Guess we'll have to find other things to do then." He wiggles his brows before disappearing around the corner.

I sit back in my chair, leaning so that I'm in the sun. As Banks and Mom discuss him helping her with her landscaping tomorrow as repentance for the cookie jar—something my brother does with her all the time anyway—I let my mind wander.

If I took a day off, what would I do?

I do some sort of work every single day. It took me a long time to figure out what my passion was—real estate, not marketing like I went to college for—and I've had a hard time walking away from the office ever since.

My intensity with my business took the place of my obsession with wrestling and then partying.

I lived wrestling, breathed it. I was pretty fucking good at it. But there's no real future in wrestling, so I gave it up before college. Then I partied most of the time to fill the hole. Now, I work.

"Ooh," Banks says, drawing my attention back to the table. "Look at this."

I glance down at his phone. A tracking number is printed on the screen.

"*My stickers,*" he says, smirking. "They shipped."

I set my spoon down. "Are you really doing that?"

He nods.

"Banks, really. Jess will kill you if you break into his house and stick your face all over the place."

"He won't kill me if he doesn't know that I did it."

I give him a look. "It's going to be *your face.* What do you think he's going to think? That Moss had stickers printed of you and then plastered them all over? Come on."

"Hey, that would be a good alibi. Why would I use *my face* if I was going to do it? It'll throw him off. He won't know it's me."

"Of course, he'll know it was you. Just like Mom knew you broke her cookie jar."

"She didn't know. You told her." He crosses his arms over his chest. "You basically owe me now."

"Banks, honest to God, you owe me already for the rest of your life. Just take it off your tab."

I get up and carry my bowl to the sink.

"Hey, look at this," Banks says a little too loudly.

If his enthusiasm is this high, I don't even want to know.

"Nah, I'm good. I think I'm gonna head home and return a few calls," I say.

"*No.*" He looks at me with a mixture of somberness and mischief that makes me both worried and curious. "*You have to look at this.*"

I rinse out my bowl and stick it in the dishwasher. Then I make my way back to the table.

I stop behind Banks and peer over his shoulder at his phone. The

Social app is on the screen—an app that I mostly detest. Nothing on there is real, nor is it healthy.

"You see this?" Banks asks.

"What are you …" I flinch. *"What is that?"*

I rip his phone out of his hands and sit beside him.

He chuckles. "You have your own account on your own phone."

"And you have your own couch in your own house."

I hold the phone in front of me and re-read the headline beside Ashley's profile picture.

CONTEST: WIN A DATE TO MY HONEYMOON

A slow smile slips across my lips. "What the hell is she doing?"

"I don't know. Is it a joke?"

"Maybe?"

I read the post again—slower this time.

But what's not canceled is the nonrefundable, ten-thousand-dollar all-inclusive vacation at a luxury resort and I'm not about to let it go to waste.

Okay, that sounds like Ashley. It's logical. Makes sense.

… it would be much more fun to go with someone …

Probably true. But what does that have to do with a contest?

I'm letting my friends choose someone to honeymoon with me …

She's what?

No way.

… okay with sharing a bed …

I suck in a breath. Goose bumps ripple across my forearms as I hand Banks his phone back.

She's going on her honeymoon with someone that Sara and Rebecca are choosing from applications?

I have to laugh. That's a total Sara thing to do. I'm just surprised Ashley is going along with it.

This is what she was talking about in the text—that Sara was a bad influence. And this is the trip she's been talking about. Why didn't she tell me?

"What do you think about that?" Banks asks, setting the phone on the table.

"I don't know." A chuckle escapes my lips. "I'm a little shocked. A little curious."

"Same. Sounds like it could be a good time for the right candidate."

"Are you guys talking about Ashley's Social post?" Jess walks in, tugging his shirt over his head.

My brows pull together. "When did you see it?"

He grins. "Five minutes ago, when Banks sent it to me."

I look down at my younger brother and catch his grin. Instead of saying something to him about it, I press my elbow into the back of his neck as I walk to his other side.

"*Ouch*! Fucker," he says, rubbing his palm beneath his hairline.

"Are you guys applying?" Jess asks, taking a bottle of water out of Mom's fridge. "Because I agree with Banks. Looks like it could be a good time."

My jaw sets as I watch him take a drink. Even though he's tipping the bottle back, I still see his smirk.

"You know, I do have all of those pictures ..." Banks's eyes go wide as he catches himself from spilling his secret to Jess. "I mean, *I have* a lot of pictures."

He looks at me, pleading with me not to say anything and foil his plan.

"Didn't you just tell me you took a bunch of new pictures at work?" I ask. "That there was a photo shoot or something."

"No. I didn't." He glares at me before turning to Jess. "I'm applying."

I scoff, triggered by his announcement. "The hell you are."

Jess laughs. "See? Banks can be her rebound."

"Fuck off, Jess."

"Yeah," Banks says, smartly getting up and walking to the other side of the kitchen next to our brother. "I'll be her rebound. I can imagine her on a beach, in a bikini, rebounding on this dick."

I roll my eyes, trying desperately not to let my annoyance bleed through to my face.

"I might apply too," Jess says, taunting me. "I saw her checking me out the other day in your office."

You wish.

"Go ahead," I say, even though it pains me to utter the phrase. "She wouldn't pick either of you anyway."

Banks shrugs. "I don't know. I've always felt a connection with her."

"You are such a liar," I say, my jaw tensing again. "Stop fucking with me."

Jess leans against the bar. "Why would Banks saying that be fucking with you, Mad?"

I face them and think. *Why would it be fucking with me?*

It's fucking with me because I've been thinking about her since she got home. Because I'm texting her randomly throughout the day and I check my phone to see if she's texted me. It's fucking with me because *she's* fucking with me—even though she doesn't mean to.

Ashley doesn't need those two goofs screwing with her vacation. She just broke her engagement, for fuck's sake. She doesn't need their bullshit too.

But she doesn't need some random guy sharing her fucking bed either.

"He's scared she'd pick one of us over him and he'd have to watch his little crush board a jet to paradise with a bagful of bikinis on our arm," Banks says, mocking me.

"You want to fight?" I ask.

He grins. "If you're feeling froggy, leap."

I chuckle, running a hand over my jaw.

Those two fuckers will send an email to Becca and Sara. They'll do it just to spite me.

"Tell ya what, Banksy," I say. "Instead of breaking your nose like you're asking for, I'll send an email myself. We'll just see who she picks. Cool?"

"You both realize that she's not picking, right? It's her friends that are choosing her date," Jess points out.

Banks and I don't pay any attention to him.

"Game on," Banks says.

"Go grab those selfies you took last week," I say as I head for the door. "I hear you got some good shots with Tasha."

I grin as I listen to Jess ask, "Why was Tasha taking your picture?"

The door slams behind me.

CHAPTER 9

Ashley

"Hey, how are ya, Charlie?" I smile at the man across the counter. "The pump on three isn't taking my card. Can I pay in here?"

"Sure thing. Where have you been hiding?"

"Orlando. But I'm back now so no worries. I'll be in to torment you on the regular."

"I'm glad to hear it. The town isn't the same without you." He grins. "How much gas are ya putting in there, kiddo?"

"Give me seventy-five dollars' worth. I need to fill it up so I don't have to worry about gas on the way to the airport."

He punches numbers into the register. "If it doesn't take that much, it'll just go back on your card. You don't even have to come in here."

I slide my card, sign the screen, and take my receipt. "Thanks, Charlie."

"Take care, Miss Ashley."

I push open the door and step out into the heat. Sweat dots my skin as I make my way back to my vehicle. Slowly, my pace stalls.

I see him well before he sees me.

Maddox is parked on the other side of the row of gas pumps. He's busy filling his Jeep and unaware that I'm ogling him.

And ogle him I do.

It's no wonder that the man doesn't want to settle down. His phone must ring off the damn hook.

His pants, a light color that might be gray, cling to his thighs. A black short-sleeved button-up highlights his biceps. The last button is undone, giving me a peek of a white tee underneath.

Tease me, asshole.

I begin walking again. The movement must catch his eye because I'm no more than three steps when his eyes flip to mine.

A slow, sinful smile slips across his cheeks.

Despite the scorching Florida sun, my body heats even more.

By the time I reach my car, he's headed that way too. He takes the nozzle off the pump.

"Hey," I say.

"Hey."

The word is low, quiet, loud enough for only me to hear. It sounds like a secret, like a promise between the two of us.

Maybe I should trade pics with him because damn.

"This pump never works. Did you have to pay inside?" he asks.

I nod.

He smiles and sticks the nozzle into my car. *Oh, the puns that could be made.*

"Did you do some shopping today?" he asks.

Huh? My brain is still back on the sticking the nozzle into the hole thing.

He reads my expression. "Bags. You have shopping bags in the back seat."

Oh. "Yeah. I needed to pick up a few things. I left most of my stuff in storage like a fool."

I unlock the door and find my purse. Replacing my wallet gives me enough time to get my bearings.

My body tingles and I'm not sure if it's because Maddox is so close, and smelling so divine, or if it's because I'm keyed up from the contest and the trip.

The contest? I snort. *I still can't believe I'm doing this.*

"Anything specific?" he asks.

I lean against the door, confusion written on my face. "Anything specific what?"

"Did you need to pick up things for a specific reason?" he asks.

"Not really. Just some … things." *For my honeymoon hookup that we aren't talking about.* "What about you? Are you out doing anything *specific* today?"

He grins cheekily. "I'm filling you up."

I roll my tongue around my mouth. "Well, thank you for doing that. It's been a while since someone *filled me up*. I was starting to forget what it felt like."

This is what spending time with Sara produces.

He laughs. "I'll fill you up any time you need it."

I laugh too. "Seriously, thanks for doing this. *I hate pumping gas.* I hate getting the oil or grease or whatever on my hands and then having to smell it all day because it doesn't wash off."

"Must be hard adjusting to single life again."

"Are you kidding me? I don't think anyone has ever pumped my gas in my life."

He lowers his chin. "For real?"

"Yup. You're getting my *filling me up* cherry."

He lifts a brow but doesn't say anything. *Is he pissed off? Amused? I don't know.*

The pump stops. Maddox replaces the nozzle and then screws the cap back tightly.

A gentle breeze ripples through the parking lot, carrying with it pieces of sand from the empty lot next door. Maddox steps in front of me, effectively blocking me from getting pelted by a thousand small pieces of dirt.

I smile at him. "You are quite the gentleman when you want to be."

"I have all kinds of tricks up my sleeve."

"You should make sure that you're wearing sleeves longer than this when you say that," I say, tugging on the sleeve of his shirt. "It would be more impressive."

This was a massive miscalculation on my part. My fingers brush against his arm—skin to skin—something that I take huge precautions to avoid. His eyes turn a bold green as he holds completely still. I pull away. *Out of necessity.*

"What's Sara up to today?" he asks, fighting a smile.

A flare of jealousy streaks through me. "I don't know. Why?"

"You said she was a bad influence. I just wondered if something happened. If she was causing mayhem."

There's a sparkle in his eyes that makes my stomach flip-flop.

"Sara's always up to something," I say, studying him.

He knows I'm onto him because he smiles. *Big.*

What? What does that mean?

He glances at his watch. "Shit. I have to run. I have a couple looking at a beachfront condo in thirty, and I'm probably going to be late."

"Better hurry."

"I'll see you later. You look smokin' today, by the way."

He jogs back to his Jeep before I can respond and takes off.

My head is swimming as I climb into my car and head back to Rebecca's. Something was off about Maddox.

What was it?

For a split second, I consider that he might've seen my post on Social. But he's never online. He's online less than I am, and I'm never logged in. And, sure, his brothers have Social accounts, and I suppose they could've seen it. But we never interact there. So what are the odds that my post popped up for them? It's not like it went viral or anything.

I turn onto Rebecca's street and let my mind wander. *What would it be like to take Maddox with me?*

He'd swim with pigs. We'd laugh the entire time. He probably wouldn't shut up on the plane, but I could live with that.

And his hands, dripping with sunscreen, running down my back …

I shiver as I park the car.

After gathering my bags, I head to the door—still trying to pull my head out of my daydream.

"How was your day?" Rebecca asks from the couch as soon as I walk in. "Did you get anything done?"

"Yeah. Hang on," I say as I haul ass to my room. I deposit the heavy bags on my bed.

I sigh and then go back into the living room, still confused by Maddox.

"I had a very … *terse* conversation with Eton's mom, Ester, today about this crystal bowl that her mother got me for the wedding," I say. "I really think Ester picked it out and wanted it but whatever."

"What's so special about a bowl?"

"It's crystal and sits on this pink crystal stand. *Thing*. I don't know. It cost almost a thousand dollars." I grin. "Want to know how I know?"

"How do you know?"

"Because Ester *accidentally* sent me a link for it a week after we got it." I roll my eyes. "She just wanted me to know it was expensive because that's how that whole family is. It's all about the money."

Rebecca makes a face. "What did you do with it?"

"Well …" I bite my lip to keep from smiling as I sit beside her. "I wrapped it up nicely and had it sent to Eton's grandma with tracking and insurance. Mostly because I didn't feel right keeping it, but also just so Ester would have to ask her for it if she wanted it. And they *don't* get along." I shrug. "Petty, I know, but Ester told me I better not gain too much weight before the wedding if I don't want to look like a porker. I figure she had it coming."

She gasps. "Are you freaking kidding me?"

"I wish."

The door swings open, and Sara sashays in. She kicks it closed with a red heel.

After a groan and exaggerated sigh, she sets a shopping bag and an oversized leisure tote beside the couch. "Girls, it's been a day."

"In red heels," Rebecca says.

Sara holds a finger in the air. "Watch it, Becca. I got you a present and I won't give it to you if you're mean."

"You got me a present?" Rebecca's eyes light up. "Why?"

"Because I love you, and I immediately thought of you when I saw this last week. I just forgot to bring it over." She hands her the bag. "Here."

Rebecca's bottom lip quivers as she pulls a cornsilk-blue dress out of the bag. She stands and holds it to her body. "Sara …" She turns the tag over in her hand and then drops it like it's on fire. "No. That's … *No*. You spent that on this dress?"

"I got it on sale as far as you're concerned. Take it. I want you to have it. I love you but don't make this mushy." She tosses a strand of hair out of her eyes. "We have other things to discuss, and I can't be emotional."

I snort. Rebecca and I exchange smiles. *Under that detached exterior, Sara is such a sweetheart.*

Maybe Maddox has realized that too … and he's interested in her.

I gulp. *That can't be right, can it?*

He did ask about her …

What do I care?

"Now for the good stuff." Sara lowers herself onto the sofa beside me. "We had some great applicants."

My stomach wobbles. "Are you going to let me see any of them?"

"We talked about this, and we'd rather you be surprised," Rebecca says. "But because we know you're a worrier, we thought we'd let you see *some* of the names in the hat to make you a little less anxious. At least you'll know we picked from a good crop."

"Okay. That's fair."

Sara digs into the tote bag and pulls out a folder. She hands it to me.

"Here," she says. "Becca and I weeded out the weirdos and these are some of the guys who were left in the running."

The blue folder is thick—much thicker than I anticipated. I glance up at Sara.

She shrugs. "We had two apply with a video."

"And they were ruled out immediately. Don't ask why," Rebecca says, pretending not to hurl.

My eyes go wide.

"Go ahead and flip through those if you want," Sara says. "Your lothario might be in there, and he might not. We won't tell you."

My hand trembles as I open the front cover. Staring back at me is the face of a guy who I went to college with.

"Henry applied?" I laugh. "He was in my communications class my freshman year of college. I forgot he existed."

"According to that application, he didn't forget you," Rebecca says.

Flipping through the pages, my anxiousness eases and, in its place, is excitement. Some applications, so to speak, are formatted like an employment résumé. Others read like a letter. There's a poem and a Haiku.

There are guys I grew up with, men I've worked with, previous clients, and even a guy who used to cut and color my hair. *He was the best.*

"All of these people could actually go on such short notice?" I ask. "I have a hard time believing that."

"The guy we chose certainly could," Sara says. "I mean, you did put it in the post."

"Yeah, but they probably thought it was a joke. Not everyone can just go … like … *that.*" I lift my gaze to Sara's. "*Jess Carmichael applied?*"

My voice is squeaky as I utter his name.

Sara licks her lips. "Keep going, baby."

"I feel like I need a minute here." I laugh in disbelief. "I mean, he's freaking *gorgeous*. I just saw him a few days ago, and I think you could get pregnant if you looked at him too long."

My friends laugh.

"But I can't go on a honeymoon with Maddox's brother. It would be weird."

"Flip the page," Rebecca says.

I swallow. "Why?"

"Flip. The. Page," Rebecca says, smiling.

I lift the corner of Jess's one-page sales pitch and burst out laughing. "Banks? You have to be kidding me." I turn another page of the stack that is stapled together. "What are these pictures? Is he really shirtless with a wrench?"

Sara giggles. "He literally sent a PowerPoint presentation. It had his sister's name on it, so I think he had help."

"This is hilarious." I turn the sheet around and am overcome with laughter again. "He's lying shirtless on the hood of a freaking car. What the hell?"

Rebecca fans her face. "I call dibs on that printout. I'll just make that clear now. I haven't had a boyfriend in far too long."

"Oh, you can have it," I say. "He's such a dork. I love that he did this, though."

Sara hums. "Can you imagine that man all wet and sandy? His abs glistening in the sunlight. His hands, all rough from the engines and whatever cars have, sliding oil all over your back and legs?" She shivers. "Maybe I will go in your place. Fuck my job."

I lean back and laugh. "I'm sure Banks would go with you wherever you would like." *And maybe Maddox.*

I stifle a groan.

My friends get into a verbal sparring match over who is the best catch—either Jess or Banks Carmichael. I don't get involved because my answer wouldn't be either one of them.

Even though Maddox is not the perfect match for me, and even though he'll probably never settle down at all, he would make a great catch for someone.

My heart tugs a bit that his name wasn't in this pile. I hadn't even realized that I'd started to hope that his application would be next after seeing his brothers.

I set the papers on my lap. "I have to say—you guys actually have some good choices here." I sort back through the papers again, trying to convince myself that I'm not looking for Maddox's name. *Why bother? It's not realistic anyway.*

"Just know that I'm prepared to take this trip all by myself. If your pick doesn't show up, it's not the end of the world," I say, trying to tamper my excitement at this whole charade.

"I'm getting a drink. Do you guys want anything?" Rebecca asks.

"Nope. I'm good," I say.

"Trying to preserve this lipstick for later." Sara pushes her lips out to display her mouth that's the same color as her heels. "I'm meeting someone from a dating app after this. We've met a few times. He's not *the one*, so I keep seeing him."

I just shake my head. She never totally makes sense. *And her boss clearly doesn't seem to mind her choices either.*

She reaches over and takes the folder. Then she puts it back into the bag.

"Can I ask a favor?" I ask.

"Sure."

I bite my lip. "Please don't pick the Carmichaels?"

"Did you just say *not* to pick Jess or Banks?" Rebecca comes back into the room and takes her seat on the chair. "Did I really just hear you say that? What's wrong with you?"

I shrug. *I don't know what's wrong with me.*

"Just … I think it might be awkward since Mad and I are friends. I don't know. Maybe it's fine too." *I'm talking too fast.* "You know what? Just do what you want. Just … it's fine. It'll be fine. I'm overthinking."

Sara and Rebecca exchange a look that I can't quite place.

"Are you guys going to tell me what that look is about?" I ask.

"No." Sara stands up and grabs her bag. "You're imagining things. I'm going to go and meet Fine As Fuck Freddy at a hotel on Maribella. We're calling it Happy Hour because we'll both definitely leave happy."

"Enjoy," I say as she walks to the door.

"I'll call you later," Sara tells Rebecca.

"Thanks for the dress, Sara," Rebecca says as Sara shuts the door.

The room is quiet, *almost too quiet*, once Sara is gone. Rebecca takes her new dress back out of the bag and admires it.

And I admire her.

"Hey," I say, getting up. "Let's get out of here."

She looks up at me.

"Let's go grab something to eat. Want to go to Shade House and have some Cajun fries?"

She stands. "Always. Let me hang my dress up. Be right back."

As I wait on Rebecca, my mind drifts to the things I bought for my trip. A few new sundresses and a couple of cute tops. I found a cover-up that doesn't really cover anything up but is pretty sexy—just in case they pick really well.

I imagine standing on a beach with one of the applicants. With Henry or Jess or even Banks. But as soon as I try to see their face, my stomach tightens into a knot.

I only see Maddox. And there are so many problems with that.

"Ready?" Rebecca asks.

"Let's go."

CHAPTER 10

Ashley

Why are airports always so cold?

I roll my eyes at myself.

Sure. It has nothing to do with your overwhelming desire to stand and scream, "Who is here for me?" Nothing to do with that at all.

I tug the sweater that I borrowed from Rebecca tighter to my body.

Getting to the airport three hours before takeoff was a horrible choice. There are only so many things you can peruse in the Newsstand, so many times you can walk the length of the concord, and your bladder can only hold so many iced lattes.

And to think, it's all to keep your mind off a mystery man you're about to spend a few nights with.

Who hasn't shown up.

I pull out my phone *again* and text my friends' group chat.

Me: Still no one.

Rebecca: I love you, Ash, but if you don't stop texting us this every ten minutes, your stuff will be on the lawn when you return.

Me: It's just as well because, while I'm fine to go alone, I'll already be humiliated that someone I know stood me up ON A HONEYMOON. 😕

Rebecca: You do realize it's not your honeymoon with them, right?

Sara: Relax and read a magazine. He's coming.

Me: Just tell me who he is so I know when he arrives.

Sara: You'll know him. He's ridiculously handsome, which will be unusual for you to spend time with, we know. Do your best. He's also excited to come. It's been adorable, and quite frankly, we're jealous. And, again, you know him. I promise.

Rebecca: Now stop with the freak-out. I'm trying to wait on tables, and you're driving me nuts. 😫

Me: Then put your phone in the back.

Rebecca: I'll have your stuff in a box tucked against the garage.

Me: 🙄

I pull my hands into the sleeves of my sweater.

This was a lot more fun when I wasn't sitting at the airport, staring at a jet through the window with just a little while left until boarding. *Why did I agree to this?*

A man approaches the terminal looking confused. I sit up in my seat, my heartbeat picking up. *Do I know him? Did I take a random class with him at some point in my life?*

Look at me, dude.

He checks his phone and then looks at the departure screen. After a quick glance at the seats, giving me a good look at his face, he turns to the desk.

Not him.

Shit.

> Me: He's not here, you guys. We board in like ten minutes.

Their responses come in quickly.

> Sara: Relax. I just talked to him. 😒

> Rebecca: STOP IT. 😑

> Me: I'm starting to think this was a mistake. 😰 Who waits until ten minutes before boarding to get to the airport? Do I even want to vacation with someone like that? Really shows how excited he is.

> Me: I think I dislike both of you right now. 😒

> Me: I'm getting twitchy. 🙈

> Me: Why did I let you talk me into this? It's embarrassing. 😳

"Good afternoon, passengers. Will BlueSky Passenger Thompson please report to the check-in desk?"

I freeze. *That's me.* I look around and find no one else looking specifically worried about the announcement and head to the desk.

Why do they want to talk to me?

I grab my bag and make my way through a maze of feet, bags, and one person reclined on the floor. I have half of a notion to stop him and let him know that a mother changed her baby's diaper there two hours ago, but I don't. I can't save the whole world, and right now, I need to focus on my sanity.

"Hi," I say, coming face-to-face with a pretty attendant. "I'm Ashley Thompson."

She smiles brightly. "Yes. We wanted to let you know that you've been bumped into first class. You can board with the first group shortly."

What? "I'm sorry." I move my strap around on my shoulder and slow blink at her. "I'm not … Are you sure it's me? That's Ashley with a -*ley*. Not a -*leigh* like a lot of people do these days."

"Yes. You were upgraded a few minutes ago."

Dammit, Sara.

I force a smile. "Thank you."

Of course, Sara upgraded me. She probably feels terrible about me getting stood up when this was all her idea anyway.

She should feel bad.

A behemoth of a man with muscles the size of my head sits in the seat I was in before, so I take one across from him. As soon as my butt hits the plastic, I pull my phone out again.

> Me: FIRST CLASS?

> Me: First of all, SARA, I don't want to know what favors you're doing for your boss in order to afford that ticket. GOOD GRIEF. Second, I know you guys feel terrible AS YOU SHOULD, but this is overkill.

> Me: And I'll pay you back.

> Me: I'm not happy about paying you back because I'm scared to look up the price of that ticket, but I can't stomach letting you do this.

> Me: This was a pity ticket. Do you know what I'm feeling right now, knowing that you guys bought me a first-class ticket out of pity? Defeated. I'm defeated.

> Me: You are the reason I'm sweating right now.

I grin.

> Me: Guess I'll cool off with a nice cold beverage in first class. 😎

I wait for a response. *Crickets.*

Static buzzes overhead before a monotonous voice comes over the speakers.

"Good afternoon, passengers. We are pre-boarding Flight 1868 to Nassau. We are now inviting those passengers with small children, any passengers requiring special assistance, and active-duty military personnel to begin boarding at this time. Please have your boarding pass ready. Regular boarding will begin in approximately ten minutes. Thank you."

> Me: We're boarding. I'll text you when I land.

I reconsider my outburst earlier. Maybe *I* was overkill.

> Me: Thank you for trying to help me. I know your intentions were good, and I love you for loving me. 🥺

I start to put my phone back in my pocket, but I can't help myself.

> Me: You're obviously shit matchmakers, though. Let's remember this going forward. xo

> Sara: 🙄

What the heck is that?

I do a quick check of my carry-on items. Everything is where it's supposed to be. I slide my phone next to the magazine I purchased after I used the restroom for the third time and sigh.

A bubble of pure excitement forms in my belly. It slowly overtakes my frustration from moments before. Whether he comes or doesn't come, *I'm going*. And that's still pretty great.

I'll have lots of quiet reading time.

And I can swim with pigs!

"Now boarding BlueSky Elite members and first class."

I head for the short line to board. Quickly, I sweep the area one final time to see if I happen to recognize anyone.

Not surprisingly, I don't.

Who cares? This is going to be fun. And someone else would've just been a pain in the ass anyway. They would've wanted to talk. I couldn't eat what I wanted at every meal. What if I wanted to nap, and they didn't?

I won't even have to shave my legs.

I grin. *And I could totally have a vacation fling instead. It would be super hot, and it would also drive Sara batshit crazy that she doesn't know him.*

Yes, the universe took care of me with this one.

I show my pass to the agents, and in a few short moments, I'm taking my seat at the front of the plane with the other posh passengers.

"*Wow*," I mutter under my breath as I sit comfortably in the wide seats. I retrieve my phone and then slip my bag easily under the seat in front of me. "This is nice."

I try to act cool like I fly first class routinely. It really doesn't matter because the other people on this part of the plane don't pay any attention to me. After getting buckled and nestled into the seat, I slide my phone into airplane mode and pull up my Kindle app.

A cover depicting a beach and a hot guy with tight abs is awaiting me. I downloaded it last night in preparation for this moment. But instead of reading, I close my eyes and *breathe*.

The last few years stream through my consciousness like a farewell parade. I replay meeting Eton, dating him, the night we got engaged.

None of my emotions are happy or nostalgic. The only thing I feel is a deep, deep relief.

I open my eyes as the line of passengers filing back to the main cabin thins.

"Welcome aboard Flight 1868 with service to Nassau. We are currently fourth in line for takeoff and are expected to be in the air in approximately eleven minutes. We ask that you please fasten your seat belts and secure all baggage underneath your seat or in the overhead compartments. We also ask that your seats and table trays are in the upright position for takeoff. Please turn off all personal electronic devices, including laptops and cell phones. Smoking is prohibited for the duration of the flight. Thank you for choosing SkyBlue Airlines. Enjoy your flight."

A lady across the aisle gives me a measured smile between a screaming child and a man dressed all in pink. She looks at me as if I'm one of her people. Suddenly, I'm out of my element, and I wish that I had someone with me. One of my people.

I consider texting Maddox but decide against it. Maybe this trip will help me get back to reality and stop toeing the line with him.

My attention goes back to a safer place—my Kindle app. Just as I'm about to focus on the words, a pair of jeans encasing muscled thighs comes into my peripheral view.

My throat constricts as my gaze slowly trails up the lean body dropping into the seat next to me.

Every cell in my body wobbles. Every hair on the back of my neck stands on end. Every muscle in my stomach clenches as I prepare myself for what I think is coming.

I skim up a pair of broad shoulders and a thick neck. And then to the best thing of all—to his gorgeous, chiseled face.

A megawatt grin splits his cheeks.

"Sorry I'm late. Sara gives shit instructions."

CHAPTER 11

SHE PARTS HER LIPS LIKE SHE'S GOING TO LAUGH, BUT NOTHING COMES OUT.

"This is the most speechless I've ever seen you," I say, sliding my backpack under the seat in front of me.

"I …" She closes her eyes and shakes her head. *"What are you doing here?"*

"Ladies and gentlemen, on behalf of the crew, I ask that you please direct your attention to the monitors above as we review the emergency procedures …"

I lean toward her and whisper, "Right now, we have to listen to the emergency procedures."

"Oh, screw that," she says a little too loudly.

A lady across the aisle bends forward to see who just made the outburst.

Ashley makes a face and slinks down in her seat. Her sweater balls up around her neck, and I would laugh if I didn't think she'd hit me.

"I apologize for her," I tell the gawker. "She's never flown before, and she's scared out of her mind."

Ashley smacks my arm.

"*Oh.*" The lady sits up and straightens her shirt. "I'm glad you're here to comfort her."

"Me too. It's our honeymoon."

Ashley smacks me again—harder this time. "I'm going to kill you," she whispers.

It takes everything I have in me to keep a straight face.

"How lovely," the woman says, touching her chest with her fingertips. She's downright enchanted with the idea. "How long have you been together?"

"Since we were kids. We had a little spat, and she wanted to go explore the world. And I had to let her go." My voice breaks, and I pause for dramatic effect. The woman is hanging on my every word. "I knew if she was meant to be mine, she'd come back to me. And she did. My little birdie came back to me."

"Maddox Anthony Carmichael, you're dead to me," Ashley hisses. "What are you doing?"

The woman tries to peer over me at Ashley again but pulls her eyes right back to me. "I'll let you get back to your wife. Congratulations."

"Thank you."

I twist in my seat to face Ashley. She looks at me slightly bewildered and ready to throw me out of the window.

"Birdie?" she deadpans.

"That's what you took out of that conversation?"

She glares at me as she sits up. She pulls the sweater back to a normal configuration and runs a hand through her hair. I reach over to tuck a flyaway behind her ear, but she swats at my hand.

"Tell me that you have business in the Bahamas," she says.

"Okay. I have business in the Bahamas."

I chuckle at her reaction. *At least I'm amused.*

"Flight attendants and crew, please prepare for departure."

She sighs. "I take it that it's too late to get off this plane?"

"I'm fairly certain it's a felony. Also, you have no parachute, and that traditionally doesn't work well unless you're D.B. Cooper. Even if you just kinda fall from here, it's a long drop to the ground. Planes are really tall."

She stares at me like she's still adjusting to this situation. Lip between her teeth, narrowed eyes, shallow breath. *She really is surprised to see me.*

I stretch my legs out and try not to disturb the person sitting in front of me. "I've also watched Banks jump off the hood of a car and break his shoulder. While I'm no aerospace expert or anything, I'm pretty sure this would be worse."

"Depends on what kind of outcome you're looking for." She takes a deep breath, appearing to gather her wits, and then looks at me dead-on. "Why are you here? Cut the crap."

"I happened to win a contest—*a very competitive contest* from what I've heard. Naturally, I won."

Her eyes search mine. "At the gas station—you knew about this already, didn't you?"

I grin.

"Oof." She sits back in her seat as the plane turns onto the runway, picking up speed. "Why didn't you say something?"

"Why didn't *you* say something? I'm a little offended that you didn't even give me a heads-up, and I had to hear about this from Banks, of all people. Do you know how humiliating that was?"

"Too bad. I'm offended that you didn't tell me you knew. Talk about humiliating."

"Guess we're just two offended, humiliated people then, aren't we?"

She tries not to smile. She also fails. "I hate you sometimes."

"There's a fine line between love and hate. Gotta keep the balance."

She crosses her arms over her chest and tugs her sweater around her. "I guess I better get over it, huh? You're here. There's nothing I can do about it now."

Oh. You want to play that game? Let's play.

"Hey, if you don't want me here, I'll find a desk when we land and get a ticket home. I'll never leave the airport," I say. "Just say the word, and I'm gone."

I've called her out—called her bluff. *Will she play or fold?*

Ashley focuses on her phone. She never swipes, so I know she's not reading anything. *She must be thinking.* I grab a magazine out of the seatback in front of me and flip through it like I give a shit about SkyBlue's new routes.

Rebecca said to give her some time, that Ashley would be reluctant —*her words, not mine*—when she saw me. "*But this is what she wants,*

Maddox. She wants you there. She needs you there. We're her best friends. We know. Trust us."

I'm trusting you guys. Not sure it's going well.

Finally, after what feels like forever, she sighs and sets her phone on her lap. She looks at me, resolved.

"What?" I ask.

"Truth?"

"Always."

The corner of her lip quirks up. "I had a very specific idea about what this trip was going to be. And now that you're here, I'm not sure what to do. Okay?"

What does that mean?

Before I can ask her, the pilot comes over the intercom.

"Good afternoon, passengers. This is your captain speaking. First, I'd like to welcome everyone on SkyBlue Flight 1868. We're currently cruising at—"

"Can I get you two a drink?" The stewardess stands to my right.

I turn to my left. "Ash?"

"Can I order alcohol yet?" she asks.

The stewardess nods.

Ashley gives me a lingering look before sighing. "Forget it. I need to stay sober for this conversation. I'll have a Coke, please. Thank you."

"Same," I say, giving the attendant a grin. Once she's gone, I turn back to Ashley. "So what's the problem? How did I screw up your plan?"

She bites her bottom lip. Her cheeks turn a rosy pink. "You just did."

"Nope. Not a good enough answer."

"Maddox."

I spot the stewardess with the drinks, so I pull my tray up and out of the armrest. Ashley watches me and copies my movements.

"Here you are." The Cokes are handed to me. "I'll be back with a snack shortly."

"Thank you," I say.

I set Ashley's drink on her tray. She lifts it immediately and takes a long drink.

"This is going to be a long, awkward trip if you don't talk to me," I say.

She takes a slow breath and blows it out even slower. When she's done with her calming routine or whatever it is, she twists as much as she can in her seat and faces me.

"All right, Mad—let's start here. Why did you come? Did you want to come? Did you think it was a joke and then got roped into it by Sara? Did Sara and Rebecca say anything about this other than what was in the post on Social? What? Explain it to me."

She begins to nibble on her fingernail. *She's nervous.* I place my hand over hers, feeling her smooth skin beneath mine, and tug her fingers away from her lips.

Her entire body stills at the contact.

My heart begins to pound.

"Okay. First of all, breathe when you ask questions. It helps." I smile at her and ignore her glare. "I wanted to come so I knew you weren't out gallivanting with some asshole who would take advantage of you." *It's the truth. Mostly.* "Jess pointed out that you might be looking for a rebound, and the thought of some Eton-like motherfucker preying on you made me want to hit people." *Complete truth.* "Hard."

Her lips twitch. "Rebound? Like basketball?"

I don't say anything, but she grins anyway.

"*Well,*" she says, her grin turning smug. "I'll have you know that Jess was right."

"*Excuse me, ma'am*?"

No fucking way. *There's no fucking way.*

She wants a hookup, and her friends knew this, and they sent me

…

She laughs. "Yeah. You wanted to know how you screwed up my plan, so I'll tell you. I haven't had fun in a long time—both … intramurally and interpersonally if you catch my drift. And I had this trip booked, and Sara got the contest idea when I threatened to take Warren to help dispel my dry spell, if you will."

I glare at her. She only grins harder.

"So due to my terrible taste in men, my friends were going to pick someone who responded to my call to action that was obviously interested in me so I could have a few days of casual sex without having to select someone myself before going on about my life. Kind of like a palate cleanser, so to speak." She nods as if she's pleased with herself. "Now do you understand?"

Nope. And how do you say all of that in one sentence?

I shift in my seat. My entire body was just hit with a shot of adrenaline, and due to federal law, I can't act on it.

"Let me get this straight. You were trolling those responses—or having your friends troll them—for a hookup?"

My brows lift higher and higher as each word slips out of my mouth.

"Yup." She pops the p. "And here you are. I'm sort of wondering where my friends and I got our wires crossed."

Fuck, fuck, fuck.

I run a hand down my face and laugh in disbelief. "Well, this is wild."

"You think? See why this is a little awkward? Why I didn't tell you what was going on?"

I adjust myself as discreetly as I can. "Honestly ... no. I don't."

"Seriously?"

"Okay, I get why you didn't tell me. We've pointedly avoided talking about hooking up our entire life—for good reason."

She nods cautiously.

"But ..." My heart pounds. Palms sweat. *Can I really say what I'm thinking?*

In one way, it feels stupid to rock the boat. What Ashley and I have is consistent and good. But we're here, and her friends knew what she was after ... *And my lord, I want her.*

I move my hand closer to hers—not quite touching it, but close enough that if she didn't like it, she'd move it away. But she doesn't. She holds still, holding her breath as if she's waiting to see what I'm going to say.

Like she wants me to say the words on the tip of my tongue.

Fuck it. You only live once.

"Look me in the eye and tell me you don't think about fucking me, Ash."

She struggles to swallow. Her breathing shallows, and she is absolutely still.

"I'm about to be *really* honest with you." I lean forward so the other passengers don't get an earful. "I think about fucking you every day. Every. Single. Day. I wonder what you taste like, what you sound like when you're coming—what you'd feel like wrapped around my cock."

"Mad …"

"Am I fucking everything up by admitting this? Maybe. But you can't tell me you don't already know. You can't tell me you don't think about it either. Ever since that day in La Pachanga, it's been different between us. Tell me I'm wrong."

She doesn't move. Doesn't speak. She sure as hell doesn't tell me that I'm wrong.

I take a deep breath. *I've already gone over the edge. What's there to lose now?* "If you want a hookup, I'm here. I'm here, and I'm all too happy to give you what you want."

She's frozen in her seat, completely unmoving. Her eyes are as big as saucers as she watches me.

I don't know what I expected her reaction to be, but it wasn't this.

Fuck. "I'm sorry," I say, taking my hand away from hers. "I shouldn't have said that."

Her chest rises and falls in bigger movements. Slowly, the rosiness comes back to her cheeks. She heaves an exhale and drops her shoulders just before a smile tickles her lips.

It's my turn to wait, to watch—to sit quietly.

I hold my breath as a bubble of anticipation forms in my stomach. I have no idea if she's going to tell me to screw off or if she'll laugh in my face.

As long as she doesn't tell me she hates me for this.

Her head falls to the side. A decision has been made.

"*Well*, which is it, Mad?" she asks, a teasing lilt to her voice.

"What do you mean?"

"Do you want to give me what I want? Or are you sorry you said anything?" She gives me a cocky grin. "Can't have it both ways."

What? Is she for real? Is this for real?

"I'll give you whatever you want," I say, the words adding gas to the smoldering flame inside me. "And I mean *whatever*."

She licks her lips. "Okay." Her eyes narrow playfully. "*Okay*. Screw it. You're right. I do think about you all the time. I always keep you at arm's length because we're friends, and I don't want to risk that, but I trusted Sara and Becca to use their judgment. To set me up with someone they think would be good for me because I can't. And they picked you."

Thank God.

"What can it hurt?" she says, working her thoughts out. "I mean, this isn't a relationship, right? It's a hookup. We have fun and then go home. If it turns out to be a bad decision, it's par for the course for me. At least I'm consistent."

"You're serious?"

"I'm as surprised as you, but yeah. I'm serious. *Why not?*" She laughs. "I mean, we've admitted that we're attracted to each other so we can't take that back now. Might as well get some use out of it, right? Besides, if it feels like we're kissing a family member or it gets too weird, we can just call it off. Right?"

Holy fuck. "Right."

I'm going to get to touch Ashley?

Kiss her?

Make her come?

What in the world just happened, and what will I have to do for Sara to repay her for this? Because ... damn.

"I feel like we need a safe word, though," she says, the lines around her eyes slowly fading.

"I like where this is headed already."

Her laughter is music to my ears. "Well, I meant so if either of us wants to walk away and go back to the way it was before we boarded this plane, we can. No questions asked."

"Okay. Pick it. What's our safe word?"

I just asked Ashley what our safe word is going to be. Mind. Blown.

She thinks. "How about ... *turquoise*?"

"Random as hell."

"We're going to the Bahamas, and they're known for their turquoise waters. So turquoise," she says with a shrug.

I grin. "But what if I'm like—*that water is so turquoise*? It's a pretty common term on an island. *Look at her turquoise necklace.* I mean, who knows what we might be in the middle of … and if one of us just offhandedly makes an observation? Things could get sticky."

Her eyes twinkle. "Well, in that situation, I think the problem is more that things *wouldn't* be sticky."

Damn you.

"It's turquoise," she says, satisfied with herself. "Take it or leave it."

"Take it. Done."

We exchange a smile that grows slowly until we're both grinning ear to ear.

"So now what?" She blushes. "I mean, that was a conversation I didn't expect to have with you, and now I'm not sure what we're supposed to do."

I lift a brow.

"Oh, *I know what to do*." She laughs. "I mean, what do we do *now*? It could get a little uncomfortable if we just sit here and look at each other."

No. Don't start overthinking this.

I relax back in my seat in hopes that she takes the cue and relaxes too. "We drink our Cokes, and you read your kissing book, and then we see what happens when we get there. We're still us."

"Right." She nods, satisfied with my reply. "This will give us time to think."

"Maybe you. After that conversation, I'm going to have to *not* think, or they'll have the Marshalls waiting for me in Nassau."

She laughs again as she shimmies around in her seat. "Good plan."

"I'm full of good plans today."

"Can't argue with that. But now that's settled, I'm going to read my kissing book, and you are *not* going to talk to me." She rests her head against my shoulder. "No talking on the plane was in the contest rules."

I chuckle.

"Don't touch me either," she says. "This is not the time nor the place. If you do, that poor lady to your right might die because you'll end up naked."

I growl. "This will be the longest plane ride of my life."

"You could've waited and had this conversation with me at the resort. You chose this."

You're right. I did, and I'm not sorry.

"Whatever you say, Birdie."

"You're pushing it already," she says.

She thinks I'm pushing it now? I laugh. *Just wait, Miss Thompson. This will be a honeymoon that you'll never forget.*

CHAPTER 12

Ashley

I didn't know that I could play it this cool.

Sara would be so proud.

Maddox sits beside me on the back seat of a golf cart and listens to Otis, our chauffeur, explain things we'll probably need to know about the resort. I'm glad he's paying attention. I'm not.

There's been a current moving dangerously just below the surface since our plane landed. It's taking everything in me not to cause a scene every time Maddox looks at me—because he doesn't just look at me anymore.

He sees me. He undresses me with his eyes unabashedly. He promises me things without saying a word.

Each touch lingers. Every smile is solely for me. Somehow, in the middle of the busy airport, in the van to The Royal Paloma, in the reception area bustling with guests—Maddox has made it feel like it's just me and him. Even as Otis goes in-depth about the available excursions and Maddox's attention appears to be centered on the information, his palm lies heavily on my thigh.

I shiver.

While Maddox chats with Otis on our way to our suite, I slip my phone out of my bag.

> Me: We will be discussing this when I return.

Their responses come without delay.

> Sara: YOU ARE DAMN RIGHT WE WILL 😄
>
> Rebecca: I'll let you in the house long enough to give me all the details.
>
> Rebecca: If you give me enough, I might let you stay. 😊
>
> Sara: ✏ I told you that I'm your fairy godmother.

I laugh. Maddox looks over his shoulder and smiles. *He's so handsome.*

> Me: We're almost to the suite. I'll text you later.

> Sara: ENJOY.
>
> Rebecca: How can she not?
>
> Sara: Excellent point.

> Me: I'm still here.

> Rebecca: That's your fault. Turn the phone off and go.
>
> Sara: 🍆 🔥 🌷 😳
>
> Rebecca: 🤭

> Me: 😏

• • •

I turn off the ringer and slip my phone back into my bag.

The champagne in my flute, given to us by Otis before we loaded up at the resort to be delivered to our suite, sloshes back and forth. It reminds me of the state of my stomach—turbulent and energized, yet bubbly in its own way. Even after agreeing to this arrangement with Maddox, I'm at ease.

I lean my head back against the headrest. The warm breeze tosses my hair playfully, and the smooth *hum* of the golf cart is relaxing. Maddox's voice from beside me—warm and strong—is the icing on the cake.

This is the most content that I've been in a very, *very* long time.

I'm so glad I didn't tell him to book a flight home—because I almost did. Panic had taken over and the fear of making the wrong step, of the potential regret of doing what I wanted, was starting to overtake me. And what I truly wanted was Maddox.

You have to make an exit before you make an entrance.

As I sat on the plane and looked at the man who was telling me exactly what I wanted to hear—and meaning it—I realized that if I told him to go home, I would be living the exact same life I was before I got on the plane. Nothing would change. And I still wouldn't be living my best life.

Wasn't that what leaving Eton was about? Living my best life?

Repeatedly cracking the same eggs, and choosing the same kind of man, isn't giving me a different omelet, or one with a happy ending. *Pun intended.*

Sure, the happy ending in this scenario won't be a happily ever after, but I'm not even shooting for that here. I'm shooting for temporary happiness. It's better than always being suspended somewhere between joyful and miserable. It's a decision and one that I can live with.

Especially with Mad.

"Do you have any questions, Miss Ashley?" Otis asks.

"No. You've done an amazing job explaining things. Thank you."

"You weren't even listening," Maddox whispers in my ear. The stretch

of skin at the back of my neck tingles. It sends a shot of heat straight to my core. "Want to tell me what you're thinking about?"

Your hands in my hair. Your tongue lashing at my clit. Your cock pounding—

"Ash?"

I flush. *I'm in so much trouble.* "I'll let you use your imagination."

He chuckles as I turn away and try to appear engrossed in the beautiful landscaping and crystal-clear sky.

If this is a dream, let me sleep.

"Here we are," Otis says, stopping the cart in front of a beautiful small house. "Welcome to your suite."

Wow.

The one-bedroom structure is both impressive and quaint. Tall palms sway on either side like guards to paradise, their fronds fluttering beautifully in the breeze.

Maddox steps off the cart with confidence that makes my mouth water. He offers me a hand. His eyes twinkle as I lay my palm in his.

He wraps his fingers around mine and helps me to the ground. But as soon as both feet are on the pavement, he lets go.

I frown at the loss of contact. He winks. *Asshole.*

"This is James," Otis says, gesturing to the man walking toward us. "He will be your butler for the duration of your stay." He pauses until James reaches us. "James, this is Maddox and Ashley Thompson."

I snort. *What do I say to that?*

"I'm sorry," Maddox says, ignoring me. "My *gorgeous wife* made the reservation before we were married. We're the Carmichaels. Maddox and Ashley Carmichael."

Ashley Carmichael? I giggle and start to move my elbow into Maddox's side. He captures my arm, slides his hand down my forearm —leaving a trail of heat behind—and laces our fingers together. *All without looking at me.*

I blow out a shaky breath and wiggle my fingers. He squeezes my hand tighter. The pressure cascades through me and pools in my stomach.

This isn't a good sign for my willpower.

I've made it two decades without losing my self-restraint. If I don't watch it, I'll be a puddle in minutes. I need to play a little hard to get.

"It is very nice to meet you, Mr. and Mrs. Carmichael," James says. "I'll be taking care of you for the next few days."

I think it'll be Maddox taking care of me, sir, but thanks.

Otis quietly turns back toward the car.

"Thank you for the ride, Otis," I say.

"It's my pleasure."

I try not to laugh as I remember our conversation with Jess about pleasure. Maddox glances at me and grins. *He remembers too.*

"How would you prefer that I address you?" James asks.

Maddox looks down at me. I was going to offer our first names, but the intensity in his eyes steals the words. *Speak for me. My brain-to-mouth connection is faulty.*

His lips twitch as he turns back to James. "Maddox and Ashley would be great."

"Perfect. May I show you to your suite?" James asks.

We follow him up the short walk and through a set of oversized doors. Maddox's hand is in the small of my back with just enough pressure to make its presence known. I glance at him over my shoulder.

"Behave," I whisper. "There are people around."

"I can fix that."

I laugh and face forward—*and gasp.*

The far wall is nearly all glass doors, framed by buttery-hued walls. Pale blue sky, bright blue water, and pale colored sand present like a painting on the other side.

"This is beautiful," I say.

Maddox and James talk animatedly behind me as I move deeper into the space. I practically float to the doors that showcase the water and feel my soul just pause.

This is perfection.

A pool with a small yard has been built below the house so it doesn't obstruct the view. There is a living room to my left, decorated in creams and browns, and a dining table to my right. I turn toward the table and spot a kitchen through a doorway. And as I keep turning, I land on the most attractive thing in the room—my pretend husband.

"Miss Ashley," James says, moving toward me with Maddox at his side. "I've given your husband a phone for you to use if you need anything during your stay."

Maddox holds up the device.

"I'm all but a push of a button away. Should you need dinner reservations, transportation, a book to read on the beach—whatever it is—it's my job to ensure you have the best experience at The Royal Paloma."

"That's great, James. Thank you," I say.

He nods. "We've unpacked your things while you were checking in. You'll find everything in the closet in the bedroom right up those steps." He points at a staircase that I didn't notice next to a door in the living room. "The kitchen has been stocked with the items on your pre-arrival form and you'll find a list of the restaurants, bars, and venues that are available to you on the kitchen counter. There is a list of excursions there as well. Should you need any suggestions, please ask."

He pauses. When it becomes apparent that we don't have any questions, he continues.

"It is mid-afternoon now," James says. "May I make dinner arrangements for you?"

I look at Maddox. "I ... I don't know."

"If I may make a suggestion," James offers.

"Please," Maddox says, walking across the room and standing beside me.

His arm wraps around my waist, his fingertips only dusting my side. I can't stop myself from leaning into him and basking in the warm wall of his body. *It's scary how nicely I fit into this spot.*

My heartbeat pounds in my ears as I try desperately to focus on James.

"Since it's the first day of your honeymoon, would you like a candlelight dinner on the beach? Many of our couples enjoy it, and the weather tonight is supposed to be perfect."

A candlelight dinner on the beach? I look up at Maddox. He doesn't flinch, doesn't appear flustered at all.

"Sounds great," Maddox says. "Thank you."

"Of course. Do you have any dinner preferences?" He smiles proudly. "If not, I'll create a menu based on your pre-arrival form."

Inwardly, I cringe. *I filled that out based on Eton.*

"That works," Maddox says.

Let's hope it works, and we aren't delivered ridiculous entrées because my ex-fiancé was a snob.

"Then I shall leave you. Dinner will be on the beach directly in front of your suite at seven fifteen. It'll allow you to witness the beauty of the golden hour." He bows his head. "Enjoy the rest of your afternoon."

The door clicks softly behind him.

Maddox takes a step back, removing his arm from behind me.

"I think you misunderstood the assignment," I say, laughing. "You touch me when people are around, and I can't do anything about it. And then once we're alone, you step away."

His grin is mischievous. "I have to touch you in front of people, or else they won't think we're married. Because, trust me, no man with you as his girl will manage to keep his hands off you."

"Well, it's a good thing the staff wasn't predominantly female then. You don't want to know what I'd have to do to you to make it believable."

"That sounds like a good time."

"It might be. Who knows?"

He steps in front of me. He's so close that a piece of paper would barely fit between us.

My breath hitches, and my heart thunders. *This is it. This is the moment.*

He places a finger beneath my chin and lifts my face. He bends forward until his lips are inches from mine.

I shiver, trying my best to hold my ground and not fall into him.

"For the record," he says, licking his lips. "I understood the assignment perfectly. And I *will* touch you when we're alone. I'll touch every inch of your delectable little body with my hands and my tongue."

I gasp. *Yes, please.*

"But before I do that, I need to know that you didn't agree to this on the plane because you felt pressured. You were my friend before this, and you will be my friend after. We can have a lot of fun while we're here, but not until I'm absolutely sure that's what you want."

"It's what I want. I promise."

He grins and drops his hand. "I hope so. But for now, let's get settled and explore this place."

My brain malfunctions. *This isn't what's supposed to happen. He's not supposed to tell me no—because that's basically what he's saying.*

Anger and embarrassment begin to rise inside me, but that stops when I look into his eyes.

They're clear, free of mockery.

He's not trying to put me in my place.

The man is trying to take care of me, putting me first.

So that's what this feels like.

Okay, then.

I smile at him and then face the glass. The waves roll gently into the beach a stone's throw away.

"Isn't this amazing?" I ask.

"Is it everything you dreamed it would be?"

One corner of my mouth dips as I remember the day I booked the suite. "It's more than I dreamed, really. Considering the day I booked it, I did it out of spite."

Maddox stands just behind me. I don't have to look to know it. The attraction of his body to mine is undeniable, like two magnets drawn together.

"Why was it out of spite?" he asks.

I close my eyes and breathe in his cologne, a scent that I realize calms me. It somehow dilutes my stress and makes me feel like everything will be okay.

"I don't want to talk about Eton," I say. "He has no place here."

"I don't want to talk about that jackass either. But I don't think you're talking *about him*. I think you're telling me how you felt *because of him*. And that matters to me. How else am I going to learn what makes you happy?"

My lips twitch. "That's pretty deep."

"I'm a middle child. I've had a lot of time to think."

"It's also pretty charming, Mr. Carmichael," I say, turning around and catching him grinning. "You're playing this husband role well."

"Mrs. Carmichael, we're just getting started."

"Sounds like there's a promise there."

"I took vows to keep you happy," he says, laughing when I do. "I promised in front of our friends and family. I don't take that lightly."

Humming, I start toward the kitchen. "I wonder what I swore in my vows. I bet I wrote my own."

We enter a large, bright room filled with state-of-the-art kitchen equipment. Stainless steel appliances and a built-in refrigerator make the space stunning.

"I love this, but who cooks on vacation?" I ask, laughing. "Who books a honeymoon suite and thinks, 'Man, I'm going to stay in that kitchen the whole time'?"

He opens the fridge and takes out two Cokes. "My mother. I've seen her do it. It drives my dad nuts." He finds two glasses and fills them with ice. "Dad says she can't sit still. They're always bickering about it."

I yawn. "I have no problems sitting still. How are your parents, anyway? I haven't run into them since I got back."

"They're good. Currently fighting over a new couch."

"Fighting as in *one wants a new one and one doesn't*, or fighting as in *they have different tastes*?"

"Mom wants a new one. Dad does not." He grins. "But we all know Mom will wear him down. I often think Dad just does it to irritate her because he thinks she's cute when she's mad."

I laugh. "I love that they're still in love and so playful with each other. They used to crack me up when they came to your wrestling meets and your mom would start yelling wrestling moves at you and your dad would yell, '*Do not listen to your mother!*'"

"Her go-to was always the cross-face." He chuckles. "She would yell at me to cross-face everyone—or to get them in a chicken wing. One time, I had a ref tell me that if I listened to the woman on the bleachers, I'd probably get thrown out of the meet."

I laugh again, imagining Damaris getting thrown out of a high school gym.

"Dad would get so embarrassed …" His smile wobbles. "But as soon as anyone started to say something *at* her, it didn't matter what she'd said. She was his wife, and you didn't get away with being aggressive toward her or the old man would throw down."

"You would've come off that mat. Don't lie."

"Hell, yeah, I would've." He grins. "And we would've had Banks coming off the bench and Moss and Jess out of the stands. Hell, Foxx would've shown up if it would have lasted that long. He might be a dick, but you don't fuck with Mom."

The pride on Maddox's face hits me in the heart. Out of all the things I love about him, his love for his family comes first. I've never heard him say a bad word about any of them. Sure, he jokes around and whatever, but he adores all of them. Even Foxx.

I smile and then yawn again. *I hate early mornings.*

"Tired?" he asks.

I nod. "Yeah. You should've told me you were coming, and I would've ridden with you to the airport and slept all the way."

"Come on. Let's see what they did with our stuff."

We walk through the living room and then make our way up the stairs. The landing opens into a cozy bedroom with a balcony that overlooks the pool. A large bathroom with a copper-colored tile that's to die for hosts two sinks and a deep tub with a ledge wide enough to sit all the way around. A window just above the ledge allows for an unobstructed view of the water below.

"Holy shit," Maddox says. "Look at this."

I walk across the bathroom and peer into the closet. All our things are hung or folded and put away. Our shoes are on small shelves on the wall.

How did they have time to do this? And where is my lingerie?

"I don't know how I feel about people fiddling with my panties, but I could definitely use someone to help me get organized when I move into my new house," I say.

"I'll fiddle with your panties." He winks at me, making my knees wobble. "My house is usually a mess, but that's really Banks's fault."

"*Poor Banks*. He takes all the blame." I can barely keep a straight face. *It's never poor Banks. Ever.*

Maddox rolls his eyes, making me laugh, before walking out of the bathroom.

I follow and watch him slip off his shoes and then plop onto the bed. He sets the glasses down, then the Cokes, and then pops one of the cans open.

The king-sized bed looks like a cloud. The white blankets are a stark contrast to the dark wooden headboard. The sight of it alone makes me yawn again.

"Trust me," Maddox says. "Banks doesn't get near the blame he deserves. Do you know what he's doing right now?"

I open the French doors. The breeze rolls into the room, billowing the curtains.

"No, what's he doing?" I ask.

"He just ordered one thousand stickers with his face on them."

I move around the bed and then climb onto it next to Maddox. He hands me a glass of Coke.

"What's he doing with one thousand stickers?" I ask.

"If I tell you, you can't say a word to anyone."

"Deal."

He stretches back against the pillows, turning his head to look at me. "He's going to sneak into Jess's house and stick them on everything."

"*No, he is not.*" I laugh. "Jess will kill him, won't he?"

"He will. It's going to be brutal and ugly, and I hate that I'm going to have to be a part of it."

I set my drink on the bedside table and lay parallel to Maddox. "Why do you have to be a part of it?"

"Because that's how it works."

He looks at the ceiling with his hands folded on his stomach. I could easily curl up beside him and place my head on his chest. It *feels like* that's what I should do.

So that's what I do.

I squirm over until my front is against his side. He slips an arm under my head and pulls it onto his shoulder. I drape an arm over his barreled chest and exhale the most contented sigh in the world.

We lie quietly, listening to the sound of the ocean and our breaths syncing.

Before I know it, I'm asleep.

CHAPTER 13
Maddox

THIS WILL HAVE TO DO.

I take a can of black cherry hard seltzer and crack it open. It's the only alcohol in the house besides a bottle of tequila, which I find interesting. Ashley drinks tequila when she drinks. Who the hell drinks hard seltzer?

Surely not her ex. I snort. *Nah, probably was him.*

Despite being tired as hell, I slipped out of bed as soon as she fell asleep. She's yawned on and off all afternoon, and I didn't want to wake her. I didn't want to lay there with my hands beneath me to keep from touching her either.

I almost lost it when she lay with me. Having her next to me, feeling her warm breaths and her heartbeat against my side, was almost my undoing. It was too fucking good. *Right.* It took everything that I had not to roll her onto her back and lose myself in her.

But I didn't. I did the right thing. Somehow.

Every hour that passes and I manage to resist her is a feat. I'm not playing games with Ashley. I'm ensuring that she's had time to really think about this. I'm not pressuring her. I refuse. If we go down this street, we'll go together.

And I hope to hell we do.

I take a sip of the seltzer when my phone buzzes in my pocket. Glancing down, I see a line of texts from Banks.

Banks: How do you make macaroni and cheese?

Banks: Never mind. Jess and I are going for burgers.

Banks: I decided to wait until you get home for the stickers. Don't worry.

Banks: Why do you have two pairs of tweezers in your bathroom cabinet? That's weird.

Really, Banks?

Me: Why are you in my bathroom cabinet?

Banks: Hi. I was looking for peroxide. I cut my finger.

Me: You okay?

Banks: Yeah. Moss superglued it shut. Should be fine.

Okay, then.

Banks: How are things with you and your new wife?

Me: She's currently blissed out in bed.

Banks: LUCKY BASTARD

I wish.

Me: What's going on with you?

Banks: My shop is being featured on a YouTube show. They contacted me today to see if I was interested. Said they saw that Mustang we did for Larry Gerwald.

I smile.

Me: That's great. I'm proud of ya. What did Dad say?

Banks: Haven't told him yet.

Me: Oh. Where's he at?

Banks: I don't know. I wanted to tell you first. If you were home, we'd go grab drinks and celebrate.

Me: Damn right we would.

Banks: Go get back to your wife. Have fun.

Me: Will do.

Banks: Remember—if you can't be safe, at least be good.

Where does he get this shit?

I take another drink when my phone buzzes again.

Ashley: Where are you?

Me: Downstairs. I grabbed a shower and got ready for dinner. Having a drink.

Ashley: Were you going to wake me?

Me: No. 😒

Ashley: YOU LET ME SLEEP FOREVER.

Me: A little dramatic, don't you think?

Ashley: Dinner is in thirty minutes.

Me: I know. I can tell time.

Ashley: Do you think I can get ready in thirty minutes?

Me: It doesn't take thirty minutes to stand, put on your shoes, and come downstairs, does it?

Ashley: May I direct your attention to your first response to my question in this exchange?

Me: 💩

Ashley: YOU took a shower. Got dressed. Probably brushed your teeth and hair.

Me: You're welcome.

Ashley: MADDOX.

Me: What? I had time to kill. You could go to dinner with matted hair and dried-up drool on your face and still be the most beautiful woman on the beach.

Ashley: ☹

Me: You're just wasting precious time. Want me to come up and help you get ready?

> Ashley: No. I would have earlier, but you made me wait so now I'm making you wait.

I grin.

> Me: Oh, that's mature.

> Ashley: That's rich coming from you.

> Me: It's our honeymoon, Birdie. Don't be mad. I'll make it up to you. 😘

> Ashley: Maybe. I might not let you.

I burst out laughing.

The sun is low in the sky as I stroll back into the living room. This place has an element of tranquility that I've never felt before. It's like your worries and problems were checked at the airport. *I haven't thought about work once.*

True, I've had other, better things to think about. But it's unusual for me not to think about work at all.

I grab my phone to send Tati a quick email when I look up.

Ashley stands at the foot of the stairs.

I nearly drop the phone.

"*Wow,*" I say, my jaw hanging open. "I'd love to see what you could do with more time."

"Same. Quickest shower in the history of showers."

I walk to her and pick up her hand. She follows my nudge and twirls in a slow circle, allowing me a three-hundred-sixty-degree view of her. Once she stops, her eyes are full of hesitation.

"I take that back," I say, releasing her. "There's nothing you could do with more time because I'm not sure I can imagine you, or could handle you, if you were any more beautiful."

She smacks my chest. Her cheeks are pink as she moves through the room to the kitchen.

"You do look beautiful," I say, taking in her candy apple-red dress that swishes against the floor. The front scoops down, providing a glimpse of her cleavage, and the back forms a V that shows off her sexy shoulders.

She's all mine.

She pulls out a bottle of water from the fridge. "Thank you. You cleaned up well yourself. But you did have more than thirty minutes." She glances at me over her shoulder. "Are you drinking a seltzer?"

"Yeah. It's awful."

"I know." She takes a long drink of water. "We should probably just have James take them tomorrow."

She puts her water back in the fridge. When she turns back around, our gazes collide.

The air between us crackles—I can almost hear it rippling with energy. Ashley must too because she grins.

"Ready for dinner?" she asks, sensing that I'm weakening.

"After you."

We move through the house, down past the pool, and through the gate. The soft sand on the other side is warm against our bare feet. Ashley gathers the bottom of her dress as we make our way to the table set up for us. A few other tables are down on the beach, but they're not close enough to hear conversations.

I pull out Ashley's chair and then sit across from her.

A black linen covers the table, decorated with a single long-stemmed red rose in the center. A candle flickers on either side of the vase.

"You look very, *very* handsome," she says, her voice soft.

She sits across from me with this insane mixture of innocence and sexiness. Her features are delicate and refined. *Smooth skin. Slight, slender nose. Cheekbones that hug her eyes.* But her body is curved, full— the edges rounded in all the right places.

It's enough to make me crazy.

I'm going to unwrap her from that dress like a fucking present. Slowly. Methodically. Deliberately.

The low-hanging sun casts an amber glow over the beach. The waves crash gently not too far away. It's difficult to rectify the pure tranquility of the environment and the chaos raging inside me.

"Here comes dinner," she says, looking over my shoulder.

A cart appears, and two men dressed in suit jackets deliver an appetizer, salads, and champagne to go along with the iced water they place in front of us. They promise to return with the next course and then disappear once again.

Ashley lifts her water glass and takes a sip. Her red lipstick leaves an imprint on the edge. I try not to stare as I create a list of all the places I want to find that lipstick later.

"You know," she says, setting her drink back down. "I don't think I've slept that well in a long time."

"Becca's guest room uncomfortable?"

She shrugs. "Even before that." She places her napkin on her lap and picks up her fork. "I've always felt the weight of my life at night. The sun goes down, and it somehow removes whatever levity I've managed to find, you know?"

I watch her lips wrap around her fork. *Fuck.*

"It's because you have fewer distractions," I say, trying not to be distracted by her mouth. "During the day, you're busy with work, or solving problems, or just living. And at night, everything slows down, and you just lie there with nothing to block all the thoughts you haven't processed." I stab a piece of avocado. "You've always had trouble sleeping, haven't you?"

Ashley nods. "Well, not always. I think it began when I was a teenager and my dad started acting up. I'd go to bed, and my stomach would twist while I waited for him to come home and start a fight with my mom."

The lines on her face tighten, and my heart breaks for her.

I remember when she was going through that. One night in particular, at a party on the beach, while everyone else drank and danced, Ashley and I were sitting around the fire together, and she opened up to me.

It was one of two times that she's cried on my shoulder.

It was one of many times that I felt connected to her—*drawn to her*—in a way that confounded me.

"I'd stay up and listen to Mom cry after they divorced. Then I'd stay up worrying about her or whatever dumb stuff he said to me or … about aliens." She smiles. "There's always something to worry about, you know?"

"Well, there's nothing to worry about right now. There's not a damn thing to bother you tonight."

Her eyes soften. She places her fork on the side of her plate and reclines back in her chair.

"Tell me something," she says.

"Anything."

"What bothers you at night? What keeps Maddox Carmichael awake?"

I abandon the avocado and push a piece of mango around the plate. "Lots of things."

"Do you still have bad dreams?"

The tenderness in her voice hits my heart. *How does she remember that?*

The night she told me about her dad, I told her about the nightmare that routinely plagued me. I only told her so she wouldn't feel alone in her pain. So she wouldn't feel like she was the only one with fears about real things they can't control.

"Sometimes …" I say.

"About Banks?"

I set my fork down and take a deep breath. "It's the same one. I've had it for almost twenty years."

"Have you ever told anyone else about it?"

"Not in a long time." *No one cares anymore.*

I sit across from her, the day in question rolling through my mind like an old movie reel. "It was from when we were kids and had just gotten a pool. Thought we were big shit."

She doesn't move, just watches me.

"And we were all outside goofing off—all of us except Foxx. It was hot as hell that day." I take a deep breath. "Banks had just come out and didn't have his life jacket on. The kid couldn't swim."

My stomach twists as the memory comes roaring back.

I can feel the sun of that day. Taste the chlorine of the pool. Hear the splash …

"I was on the slide. I don't know what happened—to this day, I'm not sure what happened—but all I know was that Banks was in the middle of the deep end by himself. *Underwater*."

Ashley's eyes go wide.

My entire body chills.

"I remember making eye contact with him just as I shot off the bottom of the slide," I say. "His eyes were huge—*terrified*. Begging me to do something as he sank to the bottom. And he looked at me like … like … like he thought he was going to die, and I was his only chance."

She reaches across the table and touches my hand.

"He didn't, obviously," I say, stroking the side of her finger with my thumb. "I landed not far from him and pulled him up. My brothers helped me get him out of the water, and he was fine. Scared shitless, but fine. But I remember praying as I got my arms around him that if God just let him be okay, I'd take care of him." I smile sheepishly. "I know it's so fucking stupid—"

"It's not. It's really not."

I chuckle. "No, *it is*, and I've never told anyone that happened. I mean, do I think God is holding me to a promise I made when I was a kid? No. But that moment … *he's my brother*."

As if that explains it all, I shrug. Then I slip my hand out from under hers.

"Maddox … you must have been terrified." She searches my face with an empathy that makes it hard to breathe. "Crazy antics or not, I can imagine there is a sense of *need* to watch out for Banks. You can't just experience something so traumatic—kids accidentally drown every day—and then be on your way. It doesn't work like that."

"That's *exactly* how it works. You move on to the next thing. Every happening can't be a cataclysmic event with six kids in the family or else you'd be in panic mode all the time. You stand, brush yourself off, and keep going."

She forces a swallow. The way she looks at me is so tender. *God, she's beautiful.*

I push the avocado around my plate again, frustrated that I just made a fun night somber with my ridiculous confession.

Why the hell did I bring this up now?

Something is on the tip of her tongue, a response brewing inside her beautiful head, but she doesn't say it.

I raise my brows in hopes of lightening the mood. "Fun honeymoon conversation, huh? Sorry about that."

"Don't be sorry. I'm glad you told me. It helps me understand pieces of you I didn't know before." She smiles. "That's what honeymoons are for, right? To get to know one another."

I wink. "I think traditionally it's in a more physical way, but okay."

"Well, considering we're sitting on a beach with other people within eyesight and servers coming at any point, keeping it nonphysical is probably our best option unless we want to get thrown out of here. Besides," she says, pressing her lips together, "you had your chance."

"My chance? I only get one?"

She shrugs. "We'll see."

I chuckle. "Fine. Your turn. Tell me something about you that I don't know—something to help me understand Mrs. Ashley Carmichael."

I wait for that to make my stomach twist. But it doesn't. *Weird.*

She takes a sip of her drink. "Okay, I worry that I'm too afraid of being happy to actually let myself be happy."

"What? You're *too afraid of being happy to be happy.* Is that what you said?"

"Yes."

"Please, explain."

Ashley sets her glass down and scoots back in her chair. "I've wanted a family since I was a little girl. I wanted the dolls and dollhouses and started choosing baby names in the third grade."

"I know. I remember when you were going to name a boy Anthony, and everyone teased me because it was my middle name."

She blushes.

"Anyway ..."

"*Anyway*," she says, tucking a strand of hair behind her ear. "That's always been my dream. But every time I'm happy in a relationship, it goes to shit. Any relationship. I'm happy, it ends. It's like clockwork. The knife twists in my back or heart or, you know, wherever it would hurt the most."

My chest tightens. "That's probably the universe saving you from the wrong guy." *Like Eton, thank God.*

"Probably. But it was the guys before him too. Hell, it was the same with my dad."

"How so?"

"When I was just learning how to have a relationship with him, started to lean on him, began to appreciate having a dad when so many of my friends didn't—*he nuked it all.* He walked away and didn't talk to me for years. It was almost as if he was waiting for me to get to that point so he could destroy us because, if he would've done it before then, I wouldn't have been so devastated. That would've been easier on my mother."

I can't imagine having a father like that. Even more, I can't imagine hurting Ashley.

She sighs and fiddles with the end of the tablecloth. "It took me a very long time to even want *to try* to resolve some of our wounds. And then, just as things were starting to sort of scab over—when peace with the whole relationship was just within reach—he died. He died and took with him any chance of rebuilding anything good." She chuckles sadly. "If I thought he had the choice, I'd say he chose to do it that way. He did love consistency."

The pain in her eyes is tempered by her strength. Hearing her be so vulnerable, so open to me about this makes me want to pull her into my lap and hold her. Try to make it better.

I lean forward, the candle flames dancing across the table. "What matters is not who he was. Don't focus on him. What matters is *who it made you.*" I wait until she looks me in the eye. "And I have to say that the woman you are is pretty fucking amazing."

Our gazes lock in what feels like an embrace. It fills me with warmth, comfort, and a sense of everything being right. The risk of coming with her, of taking this step that could end in a disaster, is worth it if not just for this moment.

The cart returns. Our glasses are refilled, and plates are taken away. As the servers work, Ashley and I sit quietly, sneaking smiles at one another.

"We have hand-cut filets with béarnaise sauce, crispy fingerlings with herb butter, and cremini mushroom and kale with garlic cream and parmesan." Our entrées are presented to us. "Can we get you anything else at the moment?"

"This is great. Thank you," I say before they slip away.

The sun begins its final slide below the horizon. Ashley and I both stop to watch the sky show off in an array of colors that slowly melt and fade. It's a beautiful tribute to our first day on the island.

"I see why people come here on their honeymoon," she says, smiling.

"Are you happy you spite-picked it?"

"I am. I'm glad I stuck to my guns and did what I wanted, especially considering ..." She groans. "Eton wanted to go to California." She rolls her eyes. "Now I know it's because one of his girlfriends lives there, and he wanted to get double duty out of the trip."

"What?"

The fuck? He fucking cheated ... on Ashley?

My eyes nearly pop out of my head.

How dumb could this motherfucker be?

"Yup. I didn't know it then, obviously," she says.

But you found out at some point. That bastard.

"It was odd that he was so adamant about not coming here and only finally agreed if I paid for it," she says.

I hold up a hand. "Whoa. Wait. *You* paid for this trip?"

She nods.

"Your fucking ex-fiancé was not only cheating on you, but he made you pay for your honeymoon?" My voice rises. "Are you kidding me?"

"No."

"Ash ..."

I shake my head. I honestly have no words. None. None that would be helpful, anyway.

"You know you don't deserve that, right?" I ask.

She lifts her chin slowly until her gaze levels with mine.

My heart squeezes at the look in her eyes.

She needs to hear this. She needs to know how amazing she is … and I don't think anyone has ever told her.

The flame flickers on the table, sending shadows dancing across her pretty, pale skin.

"Look, I don't know what the hell was wrong with him." I shift in my seat. "But I can't wrap my head around even looking at another woman if I had you."

Her lips part.

"Hell, I don't look at them now if I'm with you and you're not even mine." My stomach knots. I push the discomfort away. "You are beautiful, but you're more than that. You're the full package. Intelligent. Strong. An entrepreneur. If someone can't see all that and be honored that you'd give them the time of day, that's on them because it doesn't get any better than you."

"Really?"

Really? How do you not know?

I take a breath, trying to keep myself calm. This shit is pouring out of my mouth like I've forgotten how to think before I speak, but I don't regret saying it. The longer I sit with it, the more natural it feels.

Because it's true.

"Really," I say.

"Maddox …"

"Yeah?"

She grins. "We're not on the plane anymore. And I'm still absolutely sure."

I lift a brow.

Slowly, oh-so-slowly, she comes alive.

She lifts her chin. Puts her shoulders back. A coy smile plays on those fucking lips that I want around my cock.

"You know that it's going to change things, right?" I ask. "We can say it's not, but it will."

"I know."

"And you still want to do this?"

Her pupils widen as she bites her bottom lip. The neckline of her dress dips, showing more of the roundness of her breasts, and I think I might explode.

I honestly can't remember the last time I had sex. Between work and family and life, there's not a lot of time. Ashley thinks I'm some kind of playboy because I've never been with one person steadily, *and* I've let her think it. It's never mattered before, but it's not true.

What is true is that it's been far too long, and having this bombshell in front of me is not helping.

I reach beneath the table and adjust myself. Fuck being discreet.

Her chest rises and falls quickly, matching the tempo of my own.

"Yeah, Mad," she says, her voice husky. "I still want to do this. I still want you to fuck me."

I push away from the table. "You're done with dinner, right?"

She giggles.

I stand. "Let me rephrase—*you're done with dinner*."

"Ooh, bossy." Her eyes twinkle under the moonlight. "I might like that."

"*Oh, you're going to like it*. There's no question about that." I motion for her to stand. "*Up*."

She gathers her dress and gets to her feet. The fabric is bundled around her body, showcasing the curve of her hip and the bend of her waist.

"So," she says, taking her precious time. "What are you going to do to me first?"

Is she serious right now?

"Where are you going to touch me?" she asks, her voice taunting me. "I've been thinking about this for so long, so if you'd like me to share with you what Dream Maddox does, I'd be happy to."

She stops to gain a better grasp of her dress.

"Fuck the dress," I say, waiting for her to get it together.

"It'll rip if I step on it."

"Then I'll buy you another."

"This was the last one in this color."

"*Oh my fuck*." I take her hand to hurry her along. "Let's go."

"I thought you weren't touching me if people weren't around?" She laughs, pleased with herself. "You have no self-control."

Against my better judgment, I stop on a dime. Turning around, I bring my face inches from hers.

Her breath is hot against my face. Her body trembles at the proximity. Every cell in my body screams for me to take her in my arms and have my way with her.

Right here. Right now.

Instead, I grin. "The fact that we've been on this island for five hours, and I haven't had my face buried in your pussy already shows more self-restraint than I knew I had."

She gasps.

"So if you'd like to stand out here and discuss this further, that's fine, but—"

"Stop talking." *She* jerks *my* hand and leads *me* to the house.

Ashley, you're gonna be the death of me. But at least I'll go out in a blaze of glory.

CHAPTER 14

Ashley

"I'm warning you," I say as we take the stairs to the suite. Maddox's hand is wrapped firmly around mine, practically dragging me to the door. "If we get in here and you pull another one of your—*ooh!*"

I'm barely inside the suite—the door is still open—when he spins around. His eyes blaze, the green overtaking their normal almost yellow hue. In their depths is a carnal need, a desire, that I'm quite familiar with.

He stalks toward me. I take a step, then two, back.

My heart races, frantically trying to do its job while the rest of me is freaking the fuck out.

My back hits the glass, but that doesn't stop him from coming forward. He sandwiches me between a window and his rock-hard chest. His cock strains the fabric of his pants as it presses roughly into my stomach.

I look up, panting. "This is a good start."

He shakes his head. "I didn't take you as someone who would be so easily impressed."

"Oh, I didn't say I was impressed."

"Challenge accepted."

His mouth crashes against mine. Somehow, I wasn't expecting it and gasp.

I'm pinned, unable to move, as he expertly explores my mouth. He teases, darting his tongue along my lip before nipping it with his teeth.

"*Ah*," I say, moaning just before he takes my mouth again.

His hands roam my body—squeezing my hips, running up my stomach before palming my chest. His fingers drift over my shoulders and up my neck, sending a flurry of shivers over my skin.

It's as if he must touch as much of me as he can. Like he's waited a lifetime for this moment.

And all I can do is stand there and try to kiss him back.

His hands are in my hair, holding my head in place like I would have the audacity to pull away. He presses kisses across my jaw and back again. I lift my chin, giving him access to my neck.

My knees weaken, threatening to collapse, as he licks a line down my throat to my collarbone. He nibbles my shoulder before leaving a kiss in the same spot.

I drag in a ragged breath and squeeze my eyes closed.

"Still not impressed." My voice is ragged, the words punctuated by my gasps for air.

He chuckles against my throat, the vibrations doing nothing for the pool of desire between my legs.

His hands are planted on either side of my head before he pulls away. His lips are wet, *plump*, and his cheeks are flushed as he looks at me.

"Well, I apologize," he says, shoving off the window. "Because I am very, *very* impressed."

He grabs the hem of my dress and bunches it at my waist. "Hold this."

It's not a request.

I swallow nervously and gather the fabric in my hands. He slides a hand between my legs as he kisses me again.

His mouth absorbs the moan triggered by the sensation of his fingers at my opening.

Fuck.

I dig a hand into his hair and moan again as he slides my panties to the side. His fingers dip into my opening.

This time, it's me that swallows his growl.

I smile against his lips, yelping as he bites down on my lip and tugs. It stings when he releases it, but I barely notice.

He steps away. "Lean back against the glass."

I rest my shoulders against the window. The glass squeaks as my skin moves against it.

Maddox grips my thighs and then sinks to the floor in front of me. *Holy shit.*

His eyes lock with mine from his kneeling position. I pant as he trails his fingertips from my calves, so fucking slowly, to the tops of my thighs.

I shiver as he loops his fingers through the fabric of my panties. The sheer mesh scratches against my skin as he draws them to the floor and then tosses them to the side.

"I have to admit," he says as he spreads my legs farther apart. "You looked beautiful earlier tonight. But this?"

He rocks back on his heels and makes a show of gliding his gaze from my feet—still dusted with sand, up my thighs, and over my exposed sex. I shiver as he bites his lip, taking in my cleavage—the top of my dress askew from his earlier assault, up my neck to my face.

"This is my favorite so far," he says, his voice husky.

I smirk. "I'm pretty sure if you're about to do what I think you're going to do—that will definitely be my favorite look on you."

His eyes flare.

I hold my breath as he leans forward and grips my hips. Nothing about what he's doing is gentle or permissive. *He's owning me.*

He tilts me toward him as he gets closer, planting kisses along my thighs.

My head falls to the glass, my eyes closing, as the anticipation nearly kills me.

He scoots closer and grips the backs of my legs. He presses another kiss to the inside of my leg, but this time, he places the pad of his thumb *there.*

My clit.

I tremble at the contact—just light enough to drive me wild. I groan, spreading my legs wider, giving him all the access that he wants.

He rubs the spot, varying the intensity, *driving me wild.*

"Are you impressed yet?" he asks, knowing damn good and well that I'm impressed.

"You're getting closer," I whimper.

He chuckles. "Let's try this then. I don't want to disappoint you."

"You—*ah! Fuck!*"

He flicks his tongue against my bud, sending a shock wave of pleasure ripping through me.

"*Mad*," I half-yell, half-moan. I lift my head to see he's watching me.

He grins as he licks all around my clit. *Soft.* Hard. *Rough.* So gentle that I nearly can't feel it over the throb.

A finger swipes through my slit before sinking deeply, deliciously, inside me.

I grind against his hand. "That's better," I say, gasping for air.

His tongue flattens against my nub as he adds a second, then third, finger inside me.

If it wasn't for the wall behind me, I'd be flat on my ass. My legs are no more.

I reach for his head, digging my fingers through his hair, as he sucks and strums—playing my body like an instrument. *He's so much better than my fantasies. So much better.*

I pull his face toward me, *into me*, encouraging him to keep doing whatever he's doing. I've lost track.

"Maddox," I say, struggling to even say his name. "Mad …"

He looks up from between my legs. I can see the smirk in his eyes.

My breath stalls as I take in the sight. *Maddox Carmichael kneeling in front of me with his mouth on my pussy.*

I slide the straps of my dress off my shoulders. He holds my gaze as I lift one breast, then the other, out. My nipples bead, ache—beg for attention too.

He slows, licking in longer, more pointed strokes. I pinch one nipple with one hand and run my other through his hair. My dress drapes off my waist and hangs behind me.

I scratch my nails over his scalp. "Make me come, Mad."

His eyes darken and a sound that comes from low in his throat ripples across my wet flesh.

It doesn't take long for him to get me to the edge. I roll my nipple between my fingers and bite my lip.

He shoves his fingers deep inside me, twisting them as he pulls out. He chooses this moment to flick my clit back and forth—and that does it.

My head thuds as it hits the glass. I drop both hands into Maddox's hair and pull him into me as I cry out.

The suite is filled with my release. My voice, my moans—my pleas with Maddox not to stop—echo through the room.

I scream as the most intense orgasm I've ever felt, like it was a grenade going off inside me, rips me in two.

"*Maddox*," I groan, clenching my teeth. My body shakes around his face. I can't stop the convulsions. *"Fuck it ..."*

The words fall roughly, as if I'm hitting speed bumps.

Finally, once he's licked and plunged every last ounce of pleasure from my body, he pulls away.

My dress falls to the floor unceremoniously. It's as if it's tired too.

I'm spent, weak, and unable to support myself. It takes monumental effort to lift my head and get my feet beneath me. Maddox must anticipate this because he wraps his arm around my waist as he stands.

We're face-to-face, my arousal soaking his face. His eyes shine, shimmering with satisfaction.

"That was some show, Birdie."

And that's enough to bring some life back into me.

I laugh.

He drops his head and licks a nipple, and then the other. "You're a playground, you know it? A fucking wonderland."

"Well, come on, Wonderboy. Let me return the favor."

CHAPTER 15

Ashley

I TUCK MY BREASTS BACK INTO MY DRESS AS WE ENTER THE KITCHEN. "SIT."
I point at the countertop by the sink.

Maddox, looking smug, starts to hop on the marble.

"Wait." *What am I doing?* "Don't move."

He lifts a brow. "Can I do something for you?"

My insides quiver. *I'd most definitely like a repeat of that last orgasm, thank you very much.*

He must see every thought in my expression because his smug smile sinks deeper.

"You can, actually, and I fully expect you to do every single one of them at some point over the next few days. But, right now, we have other measures to take care of."

He palms his cock through his pants. "This, I hope."

I stand in front of him and begin unbuttoning his shirt. I start at the bottom and, one by one, work my way up his chest.

I grin.

"What?" he asks, furrowing his brow. "What are you smiling about?"

"I've never undressed a man before. And I was just thinking that I always thought I'd be nervous but I'm not."

He snorts. "I'd hope not. I still have your pussy juices on my face."

My cheeks blush. "Take this off."

"Yes, ma'am."

He shrugs off his shirt and sends it sailing down the counter. *My lord, what a sight to behold.*

"You know," I say, taking his hand and twirling him around like he did me earlier tonight. "You could get laid just by having parts of this."

He laughs. "What are you talking about?"

I unfasten his belt and pants, making sure to drag my knuckles down his cock as I lower the zipper.

"Your abs, obviously, are great. But that's a given. Not *highly* impressive," I say.

"Gee, thanks. I put a lot of work into those."

"Oh, they're nice. But I just mean scientifically, women are more predisposed to find men with lower stomach fat attractive because more fat means lower testosterone." I shrug and tug his pants off him. "You don't get a bonus point for science."

He makes a face.

"I will, however, give you a point for the happy trail." I screw up my face. "I hate that term."

"It's like *rebound*. Fucking hate that word."

I grin. "Your shoulders are money." I drag my finger from the side of his face, down his thick neck, and over his broad muscles to his arms. "Strong muscles mean you can pick me up and have your way with me."

"I'm here for it."

"And the cuts on these arms are very nice but these forearms?" I pick up his arm, holding it at the wrist. "This makes me wet."

"Huh. I'll keep that info for later."

Like I'm not always wet for you. "Your back is also complete magic."

"Do you only like me for my body?"

I pull his boxer briefs down much less smoothly than he did my underwear. "No, I like you for your tongue now too."

And that. Holy shit.

His cock stands straight up. The shaft is thick, heavy, and the head is smooth.

My pussy clenches looking at it.

"Sit," I say, tapping the counter again.

He narrows his eyes and grips the base. He makes a point to pump it a couple of times before doing as I asked.

I find a washcloth and run it under warm water. My thighs sticky from my orgasm as I make my way back to Maddox.

"Come here," I say.

He leans forward. I grip the back of his neck to hold him still before I wipe his face with the cloth.

His gaze locks with mine as I clean him. The heat from before is tempered by a sweetness that would make me mushy if I thought about it too much.

I toss the washcloth across the kitchen. It lands in the sink with a thud.

"Look at that. No rebound needed," I say, winking.

I position myself between his knees. Tapping my fingers up and down his cock, I lean forward to kiss him. He wastes no time cupping my cheeks in his hands and dipping his tongue into my mouth.

I feather the back of my knuckles up and down his shaft before swirling my hand around the top and sliding it over his length.

He groans against my mouth, flexing his hips as I stroke him.

"You like that?" I ask against his lips.

He answers me by kissing me harder.

I bring my free hand to his balls and cup them, stroke them, squeeze them until he growls.

"You are so hard," I whisper as he kisses his way to my ear. "I really want to just sit on this."

"Be my guest," he says, bringing his mouth back to mine.

A bead of pre-cum sticks to my thumb as I roll it over the top. I pull back, ending the kiss much to Maddox's chagrin, and tremble from the pure heat he shoots at me.

He plants his hands behind him and watches me carefully, as if he's not sure what to make of me.

I flick the head with the tip of my tongue. His jaw clenches.

"You're already wanting to come for me," I say, eyeing another dot glistening at the head of his cock. "Look at that."

I keep my eyes glued to his as I dart my tongue out and lick his head. He hisses through his teeth.

I kiss the top before sucking the head into my mouth.

"*Fuck*." His breath is shaky. "Fucking hell."

Watching him react to me—what I'm doing to him—makes me feel more powerful than I've ever felt. If I can elicit this reaction from Maddox … *Damn.*

I drag my tongue up and down him, making sure to include the underside. He flexes, shifting his hips as I reach the top.

I take him into my mouth, rolling him around my mouth like a popsicle. He groans and the sound triggers another round of wetness to slip down my legs.

Blowing across the tip, I catch his eye again. "Do you want to come in my mouth, Mad?"

I don't give him time to answer. I wrap my hand around his shaft, cupping his balls with the other, and take him in as far as I can. Up and down, I pump him while swirling my tongue around his girth.

"If that's what you want, that'll do it," he growls.

Oh, fuck. The sound of him growling his pleasure is the sexiest thing I've ever heard. My body heats, my sex pulsing, begging for attention again.

He leans up, shoving the top of my dress down, and palms my chest in both hands. As I massage his balls, he does the same to my breasts.

I lick and tease, flick and squeeze. Once I find a rhythm that I know he likes, it doesn't take long to feel him swell.

My mouth waters. Saliva pools around the base. A hint of a saltiness begins to register on my tongue when he grabs my head and stills me. His cock is still in my mouth.

"Don't. Fucking. Move." His words are a command. "Don't move."

I can't help it. I swish my tongue against him.

"Ash …"

I watch as his Adam's apple bobs in his throat. His eyes are squeezed closed. Finally, he eases me off him.

"Um …" I say, wiping my mouth with the back of my hand.

He hops off the counter. "You almost had me."

"Wasn't that the plan?"

He chuckles. The sounds level up my libido. He takes my hand and pulls me through the house.

"If you think that I've waited this many years and I'm not going to come in your pussy first, you're out of your mind."

Oh.

We take the steps two at a time. My breasts are halfway in my dress and halfway out. My hair is stuck to the side of my face with spit, and the insides of my thighs are so wet that I can feel it inch farther down my leg.

"You could've fucked me downstairs, you know," I say, irritated at the delay.

We enter the bedroom and he heads directly to the bathroom. I roll my eyes and follow him.

"Condom." He rummages around the closet.

When he comes back out, he's already rolling it on.

When he looks at me, I'm already naked.

"Good grief, woman."

"What?"

"Lie down. Now."

We're both panting as I drop to the floor. Urgency fills the air. I lie on my back and Maddox falls to his knees. He brings my legs up and spreads them into a V.

I'm almost begging I want him so badly.

Our eyes lock. We grin.

"Can you hurry, please?" I ask.

As much as I love Maddox's smile, I need his cock more.

My pussy is wide open, angled toward him in the air. He lines himself up with me and, in one heavy thrust, he's deep inside me.

"Oh, *fuck*," I hiss. *He's so fucking big.*

"Holy shit, Ash." His hips lift and he thrusts again. "If I knew you felt this good, I would've skipped everything else and come straight to this."

"Did you have a—*shit!*—doubt?"

He chuckles.

"If I knew how fucking deep you were gonna get," I say, grimacing at the almost-pain, "I would've skipped the rest too."

He looks down at me as he continues thrusting. "You didn't like me eating you out?"

"I didn't say I didn't like it. Don't put words in my mouth." I grin. "Just your cock. *Dammit.*"

He pushes into me. Each push is harder, bringing me closer to the edge again.

I'm so close I can taste it.

My back, coated with sweat, scoots from the force, but it doesn't deter him. He drives his cock gloriously into my pussy over and over until my head is against the base of the bathroom cabinets. The sound of contact ricochets through the room. Maddox starts to stop.

"Don't you dare," I say through clenched teeth. "Fuck me."

He slows anyway.

"I'm so close," I say, almost angrily. "*Fuck me until I come.*"

Something about that works.

He pounds into me mercilessly. I sag as I explode around him, my muscles spasming around his thick cock.

Our bodies slap against one another as he finds his release. He slides as deep as he can into me and lets go.

I struggle to open my eyes, but I'm not about to miss this.

His chin tilted to the ceiling and his eyes squeezed shut—he's a dream. His neck strains as he groans.

What a picture.

He pulls back and pushes again, softer this time. His shoulders shake as he finishes.

When his eyes open, he's looking right into mine.

I grin. "I'm impressed."

He chuckles and then leans down and kisses me. It's almost … *reverent. Now that's new.*

"You're beautiful," he whispers against my ear. "Sexy as hell, but so damn beautiful."

I swoon. I have no words. He's literally fucked me silent.

He smiles, then slowly removes himself from me.

"Are you okay? Is your head okay?" he asks.

Oh. I run a hand over the spot that hit the wood. "It's a little tender, I think."

He gets to his feet and then helps me to mine. Then he surprises me.

Instead of walking away like I expect him to, he pulls me into his chest and holds me there.

His heart beats against my cheek. I don't move other than to wrap my arms around him too.

We stand there for a full minute before he presses a kiss to the top of my head. He checks the spot I touched earlier and once he's satisfied that my head isn't caved in, he turns to the giant tub overlooking the ocean.

"Bath then bed for you," he says, turning on the tap.

"Only if you get in with me."

He looks at me over his shoulder. The shyest smile I've ever seen on Maddox's face is printed on his lips. "Okay."

I'm not sure what just happened between us, but I like it.

CHAPTER 16

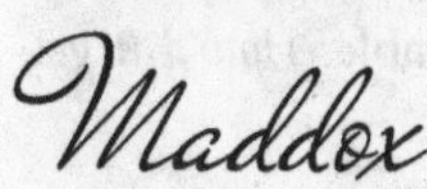

"I'M GOING TO GET A DRINK. DO YOU WANT ANYTHING?" I ASK.

Ashley lies in bed in one of my T-shirts because I didn't know which of her things she wanted from the closet. I would've been happy having her naked, but she asked me to grab her something. So I did.

She touches the towel still wrapped around her head.

The smile on her face is sleepy. Satisfied. Content.

"I don't want anything," she says, yawning.

"Okay. I'll be right back."

She nods, her eyelids getting heavy.

I walk down the stairs to the bottom level, and my feet smack against the tile as I make my way into the kitchen.

A grin slips across my cheeks as I pass the spot where I sat earlier. I stop and look at the place where she stood with my cock in her mouth.

Ashley Thompson had my cock in her mouth.

I'll remember that visual for the rest of my life. I chuckle in awe. *And her taste. I could've eaten her pussy all night.*

Her body was made to be worshipped and I'm the lucky bastard that gets the honor. Strangely enough, I'm not sure that anyone's ever showered her with the attention she deserves.

But I will. She's the most unbelievable woman I've ever met, and I'll make her feel like the woman that she is every time she'll let me.

I grab my cock and rearrange it. It's half hard again.

I look around the room and try to remember why I'm in here. *Snacks. I'm here for drinks and snacks.*

I busy myself making two drinks, just in case, then checking out the snacks. There are weird crackers, unsalted popcorn, and trail mix.

What the hell kind of snacks are these?

I check the fridge and find some uncured pepperoni. *Guess this will have to do.* I set it and the crackers by the drinks and then set out to find my phone. Eventually, I find it on the dining room table. *How'd it get there?*

It's surprisingly not too late, so I pull up my email and take a quick peek. My out-of-office response directed everyone to Tati who was more than thrilled to support these few days away. Like the gem she is, she emailed me a list of all the things she handled today.

It puts my mind further at rest.

Before I head upstairs, I do a quick check of my texts … and start laughing.

> **Moss:** You had a package delivered to my house today.

> **Moss:** Correction—it was your address but Banks's name. I'd be concerned if I were you.

> **Moss:** New correction—I'm concerned. I had Banks come and get it and he was pale. You know what that means. He's up to something. Fuck. Why do I feel like I have to be on guard now? And why didn't I look in it before I handed it over?

He's fucked.

Banks: Well, the mailman delivered my stickers to Moss. I got them and I don't think he's suspicious, but be ready. He's not as dumb as he looks.

I snort.

Paige: Please go home. Your brothers are driving me crazy.

Paige: Also, I hope you're having lots of fun. Love you.

I click off her name and go to the next message.

Dad: I had Jess go by your office today and get the file for Padawon. I think I want to pull the trigger on that one. Let's talk when you get home. Be safe, buddy.

"Glad that's sorted."

Mom: I went to your house. You left out that entire pot of soup that I dropped off last weekend. I dumped it and took my kettle home but you're going to get palmetto bugs if you don't watch it.

"Sorry, Mom," I mutter, wincing.

Unknown: Flamingo poop is not pink.

"What the hell?" I laugh and head back into the kitchen. "What is going on right now?"

I turn my phone off and set it on the counter. I have an exceptionally gorgeous woman in my bed. Everyone, and everything, else in my life can wait.

Then I gather the drinks and snacks and return upstairs. Ashley is barely awake when I place the snacks on the bedside table and then head to the balcony door. There's nothing like hearing the soft waves at night.

"Did you bring me a drink?" she asks, sleepily.

"No."

"Ugh."

As I open the door, the sound of the ocean drifts across the room.

"You told me you didn't want one," I say, sitting up in the bed.

"But you should always bring a girl a drink and a snack. Were you raised in a barn?"

I chuckle, thankful we left the bathroom light on so I can see. "I brought you a drink."

"You did?" She struggles to sit up. "You just keep getting better and better."

I hand her the glass that I made for her. "If a drink tops earlier, I need to try harder."

"Please don't try harder." She takes a drink and then puts her glass on the bedside table. "My head hurts."

My hand falls to my lap and I stare at her.

If she let me hurt her, I'll never do it again. I'll never trust her to tell me the truth.

"*Not that bad.*" She adjusts her pillow so she's sitting more comfortably. "It's like wearing fancy heels. Sometimes a little pain is worth it.

And believe me—that was worth it." She situates herself against the headboard. "Now, where's my snack?"

I snort. "Well, whoever ordered the snacks for this place doesn't know good snacks. There are no bed snacks."

"Bed snacks?"

"Yeah. Bed snacks." I put a piece of pepperoni on a cracker and hand it to her. "Bed snacks are the snacks you get for the sole purpose of eating in bed. For me, that's cashews, devil's food cookies, and Chex Mix. I won't eat it any other time, but if I get up in the middle of the night, that's what I want."

"Oh. Well …" She averts her eyes from mine. "There are no bed snacks because Eton didn't eat in bed."

I make a face.

"*I know.*" She shoves the cracker in her mouth. "He thought it was trash behavior and if you wanted to eat, you could go get a small plate and sit down in the kitchen."

Penny-pinching, controlling, cheater, and boring as fuck. It keeps getting better.

"Where did you find this guy?"

"At an art gallery."

I make myself a pepperoni cracker. "That was your first mistake."

"One of many. But I'll have you know that he didn't eat *anything* in bed."

I lift a brow. "Anything?"

"Nothing."

What. The. Fuck. Let's add beyond selfish to that fuckhead's list of alluring attributes. Asshole.

I shove the cracker in my mouth and then make us each another one.

Ashley is so physical. She enjoyed herself so much tonight—both being pleasured and doling it out. She fed off the connection, off the confidence, and off knowing how desirable she is to me.

Did she go all that time without that?

"So you're telling me that you were with him for two years and he didn't eat your pussy once?"

"That's what I'm telling you." She nibbles the edge of the pepperoni. "Our relationship wasn't physical. I mean, we fucked sometimes." She reconsiders. "I'm going to take that back. After tonight, what Eton and I did was not fucking. I'm not sure what I would call it."

I lift my chin. *That's not bad for the ol' ego.*

"I basically laid there, he'd get on top of me, and then he'd get off," she says.

"And you were okay with that?" I ask, looking at her out of the corner of my eye.

She holds out her palm and I put another cracker in it. "Let's just say that I wasn't quite myself during that relationship. He caught me at a bad time when I was questioning a lot of things. Questioning myself. Hurting in a lot of ways. Now I think that's precisely *why* he singled me out." She shrugs. "It was a power trip. I was weak and he got off on manipulating me."

"Fuck that guy," I say, chomping a cracker harder than necessary.

"What about you?" She elbows me in the side. "Who was your last girlfriend?"

I set the packages down between us and sigh. "I don't remember."

"Come on, Mad."

"I don't."

"You're such a liar. I tell you everything about Eton and you won't even tell me who she is? That's shady."

I blow out a breath and consider what to do.

Do I tell her the truth, even though she won't believe me? Then she'll think I'm lying. But if I make something up, she won't really know that I'm not out running the streets like she thinks I am.

"Just tell me." The wrappers crinkle as she moves beside me. "It's weird if you don't."

"Fine. I think the last person I actually dated, if you want to call it that, was a girl from Sunnyvale around Christmas. We were over before the holidays, but it was last winter." *And we didn't sleep together. There just wasn't a spark.*

She looks skeptical.

"I took Martie out for dinner a couple of times. Do you remember her? She works at the bank down by the causeway."

She nods.

"And …" I think. "That's all I really have for you. Honest to God."

Her arms cross over her chest.

"I mean it. I know you think I just plow through the women, but I don't."

"How?"

I laugh. "How what?"

"How do you not go through women? Look at you. Your phone must ring off the freaking hook."

"Well, thank you for that vote of confidence. And I'm not saying I don't get my fair share of offers, but that doesn't mean that I take them."

She narrows her eyes. "Why?"

I slide down the pillows so I'm lying flat. I stare at the ceiling. "Maybe I'm just fling material, Ash." I wink at her. "You can't deny that I'm pretty good at it."

She chuckles. "Yes, Mr. Carmichael, I do know that. And I'm looking forward to additional demonstrations of your fling talents."

As. Am. I.

We both laugh.

Although it may appear flippant, I have actually thought a lot about this—*I am a middle child, after all*—and I owe it to Ashley to be honest.

I take a breath. "Okay, here goes. Remember, I've given this a lot of thought."

"Teach me your wisdom, Master Yoda."

I roll my eyes. "Smart-ass."

She shrugs like that's fair.

"Most women, especially at our age, are looking for their person," I say honestly. "That's my experience, anyway."

"And you aren't looking for yours?"

Her voice is soft and tentative. *This is why I'm not looking at you.*

"You want to know what I think?" I ask.

"Yeah."

"I think that everyone probably does have a person for them. I've seen it too many times to say it's not true. Mom and Dad. Moss and Brooke. They aren't them without the other."

The room is quiet.

"But there's a lot of work that goes into that," I say. "There's compromising. There's putting someone else before yourself. There's the time all of that requires that takes you out of the things you want or need to do to survive."

I turn my head to look at her. She's watching me. I can't read the look in her eyes, but I give her a little grin anyway. *I know this isn't what you want to hear.*

"Before you know it, you can't eat in bed anymore or have fun sex or take the excursion you want on your honeymoon because the other person is a dick about it."

Subtly, she nods.

I shrug. "I think we all have a person and sometimes it works out. Again, Moss and Brooke are a good example, as are my parents. But most of the time it *doesn't work*. Or it works, per se, but no one is happy. What you're having for dinner is a fight and someone is withholding sex. You're stuck with the responsibility of making the other person happy and that's unfair."

"Yeah."

"Relationships are the fastest way to ruin something good, to take two people who got along and make them hate each other for taking the good out of their life."

Her brows pull together as she processes what I'm saying.

"Okay. Fair," she says. "But if something is good and you aren't in a relationship with them, how do you keep the good?"

"*Fair*." I sigh. "I guess … I guess you entertain it as long as it's good and enjoy it until it stops working—until the responsibility of someone else's happiness becomes too much. Then you walk away before you hate each other."

You can walk away before they walk away from you. Ashley knows that more than anyone.

What makes her so into relationships, anyway? And why, having come from such a solid marriage, do I fear it just as much?

She searches my eyes as if she's trying to read my soul. I don't blink or turn from her—I let her see what she wants. Because when it comes to her, I'm all about enjoying it until it stops working. But *especially when it comes to her*, I'll end it before it can go bad. I won't let what we have devolve into ruination.

"Well," she says, moving the crackers and pepperoni onto the table. Then she climbs out of bed. "That makes sense in some jacked-up way."

She disappears into the bathroom.

"I didn't say I liked it," I say after her. "I just said that's the solution that I've deduced from what I've seen in the world."

I listen to her rummage around. *What's she doing?*

"Hmm," she says from the other room.

I laugh. "What are you doing?"

She flips off the light and comes back into the bedroom. Instead of walking to the other side of the bed, she crawls onto mine.

I grip her hips as she straddles me. My cock instantly hardens.

The moonlight streams through the open door, illuminating her from behind. Her hair is down from the towel and falls just below her shoulders.

My God, she's an angel.

She leans forward and places a sweet kiss against my lips.

As she sits up, her pussy rocks against my cock. I can feel the heat radiating from her body and the dampness as she sits on me.

"Enough serious talk. I have you for a few days," she whispers. "I don't want to waste time."

I dip my fingers deeper into her skin. "Whatever you want."

She scoots off me. The tear of a condom wrapper breaks the silence. She palms me and then rolls the protection over my shaft.

How did I get this fucking lucky?

I guide her back over me. She lifts her hips, and I position myself against her opening.

She slides onto me slowly, inch-by-delicious-inch. Her moan tickles my ears.

"You're perfect," I whisper as she rocks against me in no hurry. *Like she has all the time in the world.*

Something inside me stills.

Neither of us says a word.

I let her take control. I watch her silhouette on top of me, circling my cock. Her head falls to the side, her hair falling in front of her face, hiding her features from me.

This isn't fucking. This is something else—something I'm not about to name.

"Kiss me," I say, lifting my head toward her.

She lowers her head and does what I did to her earlier—she says everything she wants to say with her body.

For as long as we can, we'll give each other everything.

CHAPTER 17

Ashley

HOW LONG DID I SLEEP?

I stretch, squinting at the light pouring in from the still-open door. It can't be too early from the looks of it.

Sitting up, I look and listen for Maddox. The blankets beside me are a mess and one of his pillows is on the floor. Something about that makes me smile. It's another thing that I've discovered about Maddox. *And I love discovering all the new facts.*

I get up and make quick work of brushing my teeth. My hair is proof that I slept like a rock after riding his cock. *I could get used to that.*

Smoothing it into a better bun, I begin to put on clothes but change my mind. I like being in his shirt.

I pull the fabric to my nose as I make my way downstairs. His cologne is faintly buried in the shirt, and I wonder if I can somehow slip it into my suitcase before we leave. Between the scent of him and his picture, it would help bridge the gap from honeymoon to reality that I know is coming.

"Hey." He's on the couch, feet propped up on the coffee table, with a book in his hand. "Hungry?"

I lift a brow. His abs hint at the six-pack that would be visible if he flexed. His legs are solid as hell and he's barefoot—*kill me now.*

"You're going to need to specify," I tease.

His eyes darken. He closes the book and stands. "For food. A woman cannot live on dick and pepperoni."

"I'd give it a try." *If it's yours.*

He smacks my ass and then plants a rough, noisy kiss on my lips. "Come on. Let's get some food in you before I'm in you."

How my body can still crave this man, still burn for him after having him three times in the last twelve hours, I don't know. *But it does.*

Maddox holds my hand and leads me into the kitchen. I admire the lines of his back and the broadness of his shoulders as we walk.

"I had James bring us some breakfast," he says as we enter the room. "I feel like a total fuck doing that though."

"Doing what?"

"Calling him and saying—*Hey, can you bring us some fruit and bacon?*—like I'm some kind of a dick."

I grin. "It's his job. He gets paid to do it."

"Doesn't mean I like it. And if you weren't upstairs asleep, we would've just gone out and gotten it ourselves." He turns and wraps his arms around me, cupping my ass in his hands. "*Maybe.* If you were awake, I might've been preoccupied."

I raise on my tiptoes and kiss him. He wastes no time returning the gesture.

So this is what it feels like to have someone want you. Wow.

He pulls away and lifts me up, setting me on the counter. Then he takes a lid off a tray beside me. He grabs a fork and spears a piece of pineapple.

"What do you want to do today?" he asks.

"I don't know. Want a beach day?"

He offers me the fruit. I open my mouth and wrap my lips around the sweet chunk. Maddox's eyes widen as I pull it off slowly.

"Behave," he says, tapping my nose gently with the fork.

I grin.

"There is a chance of storms today," he says, selecting a strawberry from the plate. "I was thinking maybe you would want to go to the shops we saw on the way here with Otis."

"You're going to willingly go shopping with me?"

"It's your honeymoon."

I grin, opening wide for the berry. He plays along, inserting his finger inside my mouth much farther than necessary to deposit a piece of fruit. I suck his finger as he removes it.

"What am I going to do with you?" He shakes his head, amused. "So shopping or not?"

"Shopping."

He feeds me another strawberry. "We have bacon too. Want a sandwich?"

"I *want* coffee."

He scoots the fruit tray toward me and then moves across the room. "Did you know a flock of flamingos is called a flamboyance?" He chuckles.

"What is it with you and your flamingo facts?"

"I keep getting these random texts with them. It's a different number every time, and they don't reply when I ask who it is."

I reach for the plate of bacon and steal a piece. "Mad ex-girlfriend?"

"Moss gets them too, but his are about penguins."

"Same numbers?" I bite the end of a slice of bacon. "Because what are the odds unless you guys signed up for some zoological text thing."

He looks at me over his shoulder. "Yeah. That sounds like us."

I giggle. "Then you know what I think."

"Nope." The buzzer on the coffee maker goes off. "Cream? Sugar?"

"Cream, please." I smile, in disbelief that he's waiting on me like this. "It has to be Banks."

He adds the creamer from the fridge and then replaces it. As he heads toward me, he's shaking his head. "Yeah. It does. Why didn't I think of that?"

"I dunno because it's pretty obvious." I take the mug from him. "You know, having you cater to my every whim like this is pretty nice."

"What else would I do with you?"

I take another bite. "On another note, I dreamed about the house with the ugly door last night, and I think it's a no-go for me."

"You haven't even seen it."

"I can't help my intuition. I feel like if I see it, I'll buy it, and then I'll have buyer's remorse."

He holds a strawberry. "And you know that from a dream?"

"Yup." I sip my drink. It's hot and wonderfully vanilla. "You did good on the coffee-to-creamer ratio."

He plants one hand beside me while the other holds his strawberry. His eyes are wicked. Mischievous.

I take another berry and nibble the end while watching him, trying to decide what he's thinking. *Why is it harder for me to know what he's thinking than it is for him to know what I'm thinking? So unfair.*

"Is that good?" he asks, a tease embedded in the words.

My body heats. "Yeah," I say, still unsure what he's doing.

He runs his hand between my legs, grinning.

I suck on the end just to mess with him. Naturally, he has the upper hand.

His strawberry touches the apex of my thighs. My eyes go wide, and involuntarily, I spread my legs farther apart.

He slides the berry through my slit, dragging it roughly across my swollen bud. *Fucking. Hell.* The fruit is soft but firm. Smooth but scratchy. His finger drags behind it, flicking my clit before he pulls away.

"I think I'll try one too," he says.

My stomach clenches as he stands again.

"What are you doing?" I ask, but I already know. I can finally read his mind, although it's not that hard this time.

He holds the berry to his lips. "Bet this one is extra juicy."

"Maddox, if you eat that ..."

He pops it into his mouth, chewing it slowly.

I can't take it. I reach between my legs and begin to touch myself—to find relief for the instant ache he just caused. He wraps his hand around mine, effectively stopping me, and covers my mouth with his. He tastes of the strawberry he just ate ... and a bit like me. *Why is that so freaking hot?*

He nuzzles his face in the crook of my neck, and I wrap my arms around his neck, closing my eyes. He drops a kiss behind my ear and then retreats.

"Have you had enough?" he asks.

"Of what?"

His lips twitch. "Food."

"Oh. Yes, then. I'm done."

He chuckles and helps me off the counter. "Then let's get dressed and do some shopping." He takes my hand and leads me to the stairs.

I drop my jaw. *Is he serious? Does he think he's cutting me off after that?*

He glances at me over his shoulder. "Don't worry. I'm going to get you on all fours when we get up here before we get dressed."

I smile. "Okay. Thanks."

He laughs, shaking his head as we go.

———

"Look at these."

Maddox looks up from the other side of the small shop and takes in the earrings and bracelet I'm holding up. "Um, pretty?"

"Yes, *pretty*," I say, inspecting the pink-hued jewelry. "These would be perfect for Becca. She loves dangly earrings like this and looks great in pink. Plus, this bracelet is conch shells on a cord, and she's always wearing cord bracelets."

"Sounds like a good fit."

My eyes flip to his, and he's waiting to catch my gaze. *Read your mind there, buddy.* "Lots of good fits today."

He chuckles and goes back to the miniature wooden sculptures.

"Are you finding everything okay?" A small man with grayish hair smiles at me from the register. "We have lots of jewelry if that's what you're after."

"I found these for my friend," I say. "They're so pretty."

"They are. We just got this in. Come. Look."

I stroll to the front, meeting Maddox on the way. Together, we approach the black velvet display the man pulled on top of a showcase.

"These are new," the man says. "A lady on the other side of the island makes each one by hand."

I look down at the myriad of pink rings in various shapes, bracelets of all sizes with the beautiful conch hue, and hair clips that look too delicate to touch.

"These are lovely," I say.

The man flinches. "Are you two married?"

"Do we look married?" I ask, laughing.

"Yes. Very much in love. You have that gaga look about you."

Maddox laughs. "It's hard not to look gaga at her. Isn't she gorgeous?" He presses a kiss on the top of my head—right in the middle of the spot he banged against the cabinet last night.

My heart swells. *This man.*

"She is very pretty," the man says, glancing at my hand. "But why no ring?"

Oh. Shit.

"It's getting sized," I say, thinking on my feet. "It's at the jeweler back in Florida. I'll pick it up when we get home."

"Oh, that's no good." He turns to Maddox, solemn. "You don't want another man to see her and no ring. She'll be at the beach with no ring and ..." He shrugs. "I'm just telling you the truth. I've seen it before. I've worked here for forty years, and I've seen it. More than once."

I giggle at his obvious attempts at making a sale.

"You're right," Maddox says. "Birdie, pick a ring."

I elbow him in the stomach.

"How about this one?" The shopkeeper points at a gawdy, heart-shaped monstrosity that would be the last ring I would pick. "Very elegant."

Out of the corner of my eye, I spot Maddox watching me. He's amused.

"What would my wifey like?" he asks cheekily. "I'm thinking the heart-shaped one."

I shift from one foot to the other, feeling uncomfortable. "How much are these? They might not even fit either. Then I'll have two rings that I can't wear."

"I will make you a great deal."

"Let's try this one." Maddox picks up the heart-shaped ring and slides it on my finger. "It feels just like the day we said our vows."

Laughing, I hold my finger in the air. It fits like a glove. *Of course, it does.*

"It's destiny," the man says. "That's forty dollars."

Maddox pulls out his wallet.

"Let me pay for it," I say, embarrassed that he's being pressured into doing this. "Besides, I have the stuff for Becca anyway."

He gives me a look not to mess with him and plucks the gifts for my friend out of my hands. Then he turns to the cash register.

"We'll take all of this too," Maddox tells the man, setting a few smaller objects that I didn't realize he was holding next to my stuff.

The man looks at him with a smile. "Good selections."

"I got my mom something," Maddox says to me. "They had these little sand hourglass things that my grandma collected, and she has them displayed in her office."

What a sweet thought. So absolutely Maddox.

Gah. That has to be the multiple orgasms talking. I don't normally gush about men. *Or while orgasming … Yet another Maddox victory.*

Could he be any more perfect?

The checkout process is quick. With a final goodbye, we're back on the sidewalk.

"You didn't have to buy me that—or Becca's stuff," I say.

He laces his fingers through mine and slides his sunglasses over his eyes. "Quiet."

"Oh, you think saying *quiet* to me will make me be quiet? If that's what you're after, you didn't choose your wife very well."

"I chose perfectly. Because I know if we were alone right now, this would end in a little back-and-forth, and you'd be naked within five minutes."

"You only want me for sex, don't you?"

"Obviously not. Sex is better when you're not married. Although …" He dips his head and looks at me over his sunglasses. "I'm not sure how that would be possible."

I wrinkle my nose at him.

"What's that?" He stops and points at a stand with metal sculptures of birds. They're bright colors and very abstract and also . . . very adorable. "We're getting you one."

"What am I going to do with that?" I laugh.

"Put it in your new house—but not Ugly Door House." He rolls his eyes. "Obviously."

My smile reaches ear to ear. "Obviously."

CHAPTER 18

Ashley

I DRAPE MY ARMS OVER THE RAILING AND STARE INTO THE NIGHT.

The ocean at this time has always fascinated me. If the moon is covered and the sky is dark, the water takes on a new identity. Its presence is even stronger than it is during the day when its expanse can be appreciated. After dusk, it becomes this invisible giant lurking just out of view.

I breathe in the salty air and hold it, letting it stretch my lungs.

Unlike my usual relationship with thinking at night—when my worries take the shape of concerns about whether my car doors are locked or if the oven is still on, tonight's mindfuck is slightly different.

Tonight, I can't just get up and ensure the oven is off.

Tonight, there are no answers.

I groan softly so as not to wake Maddox in the room behind me.

I laid beside him for hours and watched the moonlight flicker across his face. I studied him without fear of him catching me, without worrying if I looked like one of the girls who bat their lashes in the hope he might smile their way. I cataloged every freckle on his cheeks, every line around his eyes, the mole just under his hairline at the top of his forehead.

The slope of his shoulder. His birthmark, so faint, on his right pectoral muscle and the one gray hair hiding in the stubble dusting his jaw.

How did I ever miss all of the layers of this man? How did I not see just how kind, thoughtful, and patient he really is?

I hang my head, letting my hair drape over the rail.

Those thoughts are a distraction from the real thoughts taking up residence in my head. When I can tell I'm trying to distract myself, there's trouble brewing.

I know how I missed all of Maddox's layers, how I didn't see his wonderful qualities. There's not a big mystery as to why I didn't see his beauty under his sexiness or the sweetness beneath his goofiness.

It's because I didn't want to.

"Dammit," I whisper.

I pull my head back to the darkness and sigh.

When I frame my relationship with Maddox over the last twentysomething years, I see it all differently. The moments when we were almost *this*.

The nights around the bonfires, just the two of us while everyone else partied, sharing stories. The day he found me sitting in my car outside of Publix, drying my eyes from a heartbreak a few hours earlier. He sat in the passenger's seat, listening to me tell him how my life was over because some asshole dumped me to the background music of Toni Braxton. The week we had detention because we started laughing in Spanish and couldn't stop. *Disruptive when together, must be separated* is what the letter told my mother.

So many times, we could've found ourselves like this ... but we didn't.

He got out of my car and gave me a big hug. And then watched me drive away. I'd found solace in Maddox's friendship, and I vowed to never date another jerk for as long as I lived. I chuckled when my mom couldn't discipline me for our laughter, and we moved seats in class.

We were so close, so many times, to taking our friendship to a different level. Either on our own accord or due to the universe's interference, it never happened. And somewhere along the way, we decided that was the right answer.

And it might've been because taking down my self-imposed shield and allowing myself to see Maddox as a whole—all of his sides and truths—doesn't feel right.

It feels too right.

Yet nothing has changed. The circumstances are the same. Maybe I was wrong, and he's not a player—maybe I ran with that story because it fit my narrative. I don't know. But it doesn't matter because he's *fling material*.

I heard it from his own mouth.

So why does my heart feel so full when we're together, and why am I already regretting the end of this? Why does one part of me think that ending it might be ending something that I'll never have again, while the other part of me knows that it has to happen? *That it's going to happen.* That it's going to happen and I'm better off if it ends before I get too comfortable in this mess.

My happiness is at stake here. My happy ending. I can enjoy my time with him—enjoy it to the max. But I can't forget that I'll have to *exit* this fling if I'm ever going to *enter* a relationship for life.

I sigh. *Will I ever find someone as compatible, fun, selfless, and kind as Maddox?* That's probably the hardest part about ending this. The question of it all just peaked, and I'll find myself settling elsewhere.

Maddox's arms slip around me, and he places a soft kiss on the spot where my neck meets my shoulder.

"Come to bed with me," he whispers, his voice barely audible over the crashing waves.

I close my eyes and relish the moment. Remember this feeling.

I turn and look up into his sleepy eyes.

"Okay," I say softly. "Let's go."

CHAPTER 19

Ashley

"Wake up."

I groan and roll away from the voice.

"*Hey, Birdie, wake up.*" The mattress dips. "I have a surprise for you."

I make a face and look over my shoulder. The light is bright. "Surprises are better in the afternoon."

Maddox laughs and leans in to kiss me.

I bury my head in the pillow. "No. I haven't brushed my teeth."

"Kiss me."

"No."

He straddles me, making me squeal. His hand wraps easily around my wrist.

"If you don't kiss me, and then get up—in that order—we can't go swim with pigs today."

What? I roll over and gape at him.

I'd given up on swimming with the pigs. Booking an excursion this late was nearly impossible, and honestly, once the contest began, I forgot all about it. And then when Maddox showed up ... I hadn't thought about much else besides him.

"What are you talking about?" I ask.

His eyes shimmer.

"Don't screw with me, Mad." I sit up and brush my hair out of my face. "Are you serious?"

"James is a good man." He leans in and, although I wince the whole time, kisses me. "Now up."

I cup my hand over my mouth and blow. Then sniff.

"What are you doing?" He laughs. "Are you trying to smell your breath?"

"Yes."

"You're nuts."

I dash for the bathroom before he can sidetrack me. "If you're lying about the pigs …"

"What if I am?" he teases, his words dancing through the air.

I cover my toothbrush with toothpaste and shove it in my mouth, sticking it in my cheek. Then I pop my head around the corner to see him sitting on the edge of the bed. "If you made that up to get me out of bed, I'm never honeymooning with you again."

Dumb, but that's what came to mind.

He grins. "Good thing I'm not lying then."

I try to control myself so I don't look like an idiot, but it doesn't work. "Eeek!"

He chuckles. "I gotta go downstairs and make sure James got our picnic shit together."

"*And a picnic*?" The words are muffled because of the toothbrush.

"I told you this would be your best honeymoon ever." He stands and straightens his T-shirt. "Now hurry up. James will be here to get us in half an hour."

I groan, swallowing a lump of toothpaste. "Why do you always wait until the last second to get me up?"

He comes to me, standing just out of reach. He looks down and smiles. "Because if I get you up too early, we'll have time on our hands. And if we have time on our hands, we'll never make the boat."

Memories of last night—of Maddox taking me from behind on the balcony—flutter through my mind. I slurp a mouthful of spit and swallow.

"Exactly." He grins, letting me know he's thinking what I'm thinking. "Get dressed. I'll be downstairs."

He places a kiss on my forehead and then disappears down the steps.

———

"I'm Captain Jimmy. Welcome aboard."

"Good morning," I say, climbing carefully into the boat.

Maddox steps down behind me. "I'm Maddox, and this is Ashley. It's nice to meet you."

Captain Jimmy shakes Maddox's hand. "Nice to meet you both. Newlyweds?"

"Yes," I say, snuggling into Maddox's side. *My, how this has gotten easy.*

"Congratulations." Captain Jimmy smiles. "You've booked a private tour, so it'll just be the three of us today. Because of the weather, we can only do one stop. If the storm holds off, we might be able to sneak a second, but if there's one thing you're looking to do specifically, I think we should start there."

"My wife wants to swim with the pigs," Maddox says.

Excitement bubbles in my stomach. *I'm getting to do this after all.*

"The pigs are the most popular attraction, believe it or not," Captain Jimmy says. "Get settled. There are drinks in the cooler right here." He kicks a red square. "We'll take off in just a moment."

Maddox waits for me to choose whether to sit at the front or back of the boat. Because Captain Jimmy takes up shop at the wheel in the center, I choose the back for some privacy.

"Did you put on sunscreen?" I ask.

"Yup. Want me to put some more on you? I'll happily rub my hands all over you."

"Not if you want to keep this rated PG."

He chuckles and takes a seat on the bench.

Captain Jimmy shouts something that I miss, and then the engines start. I sit quickly next to Maddox as we start out to sea.

The sky is clear overhead, but the sky is dark in the distance. That's worrying. As I look out over the water, I can't believe how calm it is.

How glasslike. And when I cast my glance to the left, I can't believe how divine my husband is.

Green board shorts make his eyes look even more captivating. The white tee shows off the shape of his body. And the smile he's beaming, *the happiness he's radiating while doing something for me*, is my favorite thing about him.

"You're the best if I haven't told you that," I say, holding on to his arm.

"You haven't. Feel free to say it often."

I smile up at him. "You're the best kisser."

He lifts a brow in appreciation.

"You're the best in bed," I say.

"Good news for me."

I laugh. "You're the best guy to shop with. You lasted all day."

"I always last as long as necessary."

I giggle again. "That you do."

The boat picks up speed, racing over the water. I rest my head against Maddox's shoulder, and he extends an arm around my waist.

Closing my eyes, I enjoy the warmth of the indirect sunlight, the slightly cooler day, and the serenity of being with my fake husband.

"I'm going to hate going home tomorrow," he says in my ear, flexing his fingers against my side. He plays with the waistband of my bikini under my shorts. "I've had the best few days with you."

My heart swells and then sinks.

I want to look at him, to see whatever emotion might be in his eyes, but I don't. Because it doesn't matter. We leave either way.

"Thank you for coming," I say as he leans closer so he can hear me over the wind. I touch the side of his face. "You didn't have to come, didn't have to participate in Sara's silly game, but you did."

He twists his lips to my ear. "For you. *Anything* for you."

My insides turn to liquid as his words echo through my head. *For you.*

"Maybe we can come back," he says, leaning his head against mine. "You're a travel agent. Maybe you can book us for a whole week." I feel him smile against me. "Imagine what we can do with seven days."

I chuckle for reasons he'll never know.

I booked a four-day, three-night stay because that's all the time Eton could get away from work. Now that I know the extent of his bullshit, I'm sure there was another reason. But at the time, it made sense, and although I was sad my honeymoon would be so short, I took it.

I took the breadcrumbs that were given to me and excused away. The lack of care. The lack of commitment. The lack of interest. The lack of spark and friendship. *Like a fool.*

How was I so blind?

Never again.

But Maddox—Maddox wants longer. A man who I'm not even marrying wishes he could stay longer with me. *"Maybe you can book us for the whole week."* The difference between the two astounds me.

I want to ask him what will happen when we get home. Will we go back to being friends who see each other on occasion? Will we return as flirty friends like we were when we left? Are friends with benefits something I can really do? Would he even want to?

Is that healthy for our relationship? Because this, how we are right now, just feels so right. But can this last in Kismet Beach? Should we tempt fate?

I don't ask him because I don't want to know. *Just enjoy the day that you have and then figure it out later. The only thing you'll do by asking is ruin what you have now.*

The trip takes a little longer than I expected. By the time the boat begins to slow, I've nearly been lulled to sleep by the waves and Maddox gently stroking my arm. Every now and then, he takes my hand and plays with my wedding ring.

Each time he touches it, I smile.

"You two doing okay?" Captain Jimmy asks.

"We're great," Maddox says.

I lift my head from his shoulder.

"That island right there is where we're going," he says, pointing straight ahead.

Maddox and I get to our feet as the boat slows even more.

"How did the pigs get here?" Maddox asks.

"There's a little lore with that. Some say pirates or explorers brought them hundreds of years ago and left them on the island. Others say they were on ships, being transported to slaughterhouses, or being sold, and a ship or ships wrecked, and some of the pigs made it and survived. And still, others say that the locals on neighboring islands got sick of their smell, so they used this as a pigpen. They'd boat over and feed them, grab a pig if they needed it—that sort of thing."

I frown. "We're going to go with they were little survivors from pirates while I'm here, okay?"

Maddox laughs.

"When they hear our motor, they'll start swimming out to us," Captain Jimmy says. "There are some apple slices and pieces of bread in the cooler at the front of the boat. If you get in the water and want to feed them, use the apples on sticks. They're friendly, but they're animals. Don't have a finger between them and food."

"Sounds like Banks," Maddox says, grinning.

I laugh. "You're not wrong."

Maddox looks at me. "You want to swim with these things?"

"Yes." I look over his shoulder. "Look at them! They're coming."

The water gets shallower, and Captain Jimmy cuts the engine. We drift closer to the beach, meeting the animals halfway.

My heart leaps with joy.

We dart to the front of the boat and find pieces of apple.

"Just toss it to 'em," Captain Jimmy says.

I laugh at the sight of the pigs swimming around our boat. They snap up the treats we send their way, squealing with delight.

"Aren't they amazing?" I ask. "Seriously. Think how adaptive they have had to be to swim. Pigs don't swim."

Maddox tosses a piece of bread to a large black beast. "Clearly, they do."

We drift until we're almost to the shore.

"Got lucky today," Captain Jimmy says. "We're the only boat here. There are usually four or five at least."

"Can we get in with them?" I ask, my heart racing.

"Yeah. Go ahead. Have fun. I'll let you know if we need to head back."

We go to the back of the boat. Maddox removes his shirt and sunglasses. I shed my shorts and tank.

Maddox growls. "Did you have to wear that?"

"It's a bikini," I say, laughing.

He leans closer. "I'm going to get in the water, and they're going to think I have a banana in my shorts."

I cover my mouth and try not to draw attention to Maddox's attempt at being less interested in me.

"Want me to get a picture of you with the pigs in the background?" Captain Jimmy asks. "Might make a good souvenir."

"Yes. Please. That would be great," I say, grabbing my phone and handing it to him.

Maddox puts his arm around me, tucking me against him. I wrap my arm around his waist and dip my fingertips in the band of his shorts.

"Careful," he mutters under his breath.

"Smile," Captain Jimmy says.

He takes a few of us. Maddox moves me in front of him for the last couple of snaps. I feel his cock against my ass.

"Thank you," I say, taking my phone back.

Maddox turns and dives into the water. All I can do is giggle. But before I dive in after him, I take a quick selfie—getting a good shot of my cleavage—then put my phone away.

"Come on," Maddox shouts from the water.

I smile at Captain Jimmy and then stand on the edge of the boat. Pigs frolic around the water, splashing happily around Maddox.

A lump grows in my throat as I think about how unlikely all of this is. I'm in the Bahamas, but not with the man I booked the trip for. I'm here with Maddox, the guy I never thought I'd date. We're swimming with pigs, something I wrote off weeks ago as being impossible for the time being. And I'm happy. At this moment, right now, *I'm so fucking happy*.

I dive into the water before I can think about it.

Maddox is in front of me when I come up. His face is one big smile.

"Okay," he says, laughing. "I thought this was going to be stupid as fuck, but it's pretty cool."

Two small pigs, babies, I think, swim up to us. We paddle around them, diving under the water and looking up at their little hooves treading water.

"Look at that one," I say, pointing at a black pig with long white spots. "It's almost like a zebra."

"That one is my favorite." He motions toward a baby pink one with a black circle around his eye. "He looks like he got in a fight and won."

I laugh.

We float to shallower waters and sit at the water's edge. The water laps against us as the pigs swim and play, putting on a show for the two of us. I swear the little creatures are smiling.

"Isn't it so unexpected?" I ask, watching Maddox practically cuddle his fighter pig. "There's this scenery—some of the most beautiful, pristine beaches in the world. And then there are pigs. It's wild to me."

"What does it make you feel like?"

"What do you mean?"

He shrugs. "When you see the pigs swimming around you like this —the juxtaposition of it all—what does it make you feel like?"

I don't know.

"Think about it. I'll be back."

Maddox goes into the water and swims to the boat. He speaks to Captain Jimmy, who then retrieves something from our things and hands it to Maddox before he swims back to me.

He doesn't get settled on the sand before his pig is back. Whether Maddox admits it or not, he loves it.

I take his phone with a waterproof cover from him and stand. While he scratches his new friend, I snap some pictures of it with his phone.

"So?" he asks.

I sit beside him again, turning my face toward the sky. "This makes me believe in magic, I guess. Not wizard magic but magic in the universe."

"I see that."

"You do?"

He doesn't answer me, so I glance over my shoulder. He's watching me while he pets his pig.

"Can I take a picture with you two lovers?" I ask.

He laughs. "I guess."

I lift the phone and snap a couple of shots of the two of us and Fighter. Then Maddox pulls me between his legs so he's behind me, and I take a couple more.

He kisses my cheek. *Snap!*

He kisses my neck. *Snap!*

He cups my breast. *Snap!*

He licks the side of my face. *Snap!*

The last picture is of Fighter trying to push the two of us over—or me out of Maddox's lap, rather.

We play on the beach before swimming back to the boat, then use the apple sticks to feed some of the pigs still loitering. But as the dark skies start to roll in, Captain Jimmy tells us it's time to go.

I climb out of the water first. Maddox follows me. We get covered in towels and cuddle up again on our seats.

As we pull away from the place I'll never forget, Maddox brings his lips to my ear.

"The pigs represent determination and courage," he says softly. "Beauty, even where it's not expected. Wonder. Possibility."

My insides turn to mush.

"You look at them and see those things," he whispers.

I nod.

"That's what I see when I look at you."

I can't look at him, or else he'll see my tears. So I hold his arms around me and repeat his words in my head so I never forget them.

"Determination and courage. Beauty, even where it's not expected. Wonder. Possibility."

"That's what I see when I look at you."

How does this end with someone who thinks that about me?

CHAPTER 20

Ashley

"I'M GLAD THE SUN DECIDED TO COME BACK OUT," I SAY, STRETCHING MY toes behind me. "It's nice to have our farewell evening out here by the pool."

Maddox looks over from his lounge chair and makes a show out of checking me out. I pop my ass in the air a little, arching my back as I lie on my belly, to give him a taste of his own medicine.

He's wearing his board shorts from the boat today and no shirt. He couldn't be more edible if he tried.

"What are ya reading over there?" he asks, his eyes still glued to my bottom.

"It's called *Sway*."

He hums. "Who is your favorite character?"

"That's a hard question. It's about this politician named Barrett but his brother, Lincoln, is sort of stealing the show."

"Little brothers are fuckers."

I laugh. "Are you getting Banks flashbacks?"

He rolls his eyes. "What chapter are you on?"

I shrug. "I don't know." I flip to the start of the chapter. "Seventeen."

His eyes darken. "Keep going. Eighteen is a good one."

I press up on my elbows and look at him curiously. He smirks and goes back to his phone.

"What's that mean? How do you know?" I ask.

"Sleeping Beauty slept in yesterday, and I had to get out of bed so I didn't disturb her. I might've seen the book on the coffee table, and I might've picked it up."

What? Okay ... "Did you enjoy it?"

"It wasn't awful. I respected Barrett's game, you know, chasing the girl. I feel a little kindred spirit to the man." He winks. "Your boy Lincoln needs to stay in his lane."

I burst out laughing.

"Just get to eighteen and let's revisit this conversation," he says.

What is he talking about?

"*Fuck it.*" He gets up and walks to me. "Stay there."

I lay flat on my stomach again, dropping my book to the ground. Maddox sets his phone beside it.

"I just put that on when I came out here," I say, noticing the sunscreen in his hand.

"Not on your back."

"No, you put it on my back."

He undoes my bikini top and then squirts sunscreen in his hand. He straddles the back of the chair.

"And then you started talking about chapter eighteen—or I did, whatever—and now I just need to touch you."

"*Oh,*" I say, sighing as his hands slide down my back. "I think I like you reading romance novels. I might get you a subscription to a book box."

His phone rings, but he ignores it. "What's in a book box?"

"Books."

"No shit?"

I giggle. "Paperbacks, free eBooks, swaggy items like pens or stickers or magnets. Cup koozies. That kind of thing. Or you can get some that send shirts or mugs. There's even one that donates their proceeds to charity."

"Buy me that one." He cups my shoulders and brings his thumbs to the back of my neck. "I'll bring the books to your house, and you can read them to me."

I moan as he massages the spot just under the base of my skull that perpetually aches. "Can't you read? And why can't we go to your house? I don't have a house, remember?"

"Yes, I can read, but I anticipate I'll be busy doing other things while you read. And we can't go to my house because Banks will be there."

I giggle. "Can't you make him go home?"

"Yeah. Sure, I can. But I don't trust him not to peek in the windows if he knows you're there and naked. Then I'd have to kill him."

He rubs down my back, around my side so he can palm my breasts, then down to my ass. A fire I've grown very familiar with over the past few days burns hot in my stomach.

"I didn't say I'd be naked at your house," I say. "I'd be there to read to you."

"Oh, like you're going to be at my house and make it longer than ten minutes with clothes on. Right."

Does this mean he thinks he might see me when we get home? Hope blossoms in my chest.

"I might just choose erotica then," I say, lifting my hips as he removes my bottoms. "Who needs a plot?"

His phone rings again. And again, he ignores it.

He squeezes my ass cheeks, taking his sweet time. Each flex of his palms, every press of his fingers increases the ache between my legs.

"What kind of erotica do you read?" he asks, his voice lower. "Are there types of it?"

"If I'm going for erotica, it better be taboo and right to the point. Give me a little choking or breeding—"

"What?"

I laugh. "It's what it sounds like. The point is for her to get pregnant."

"*Oh.*" He clears his throat. "Not sure that's my thing."

"Maybe harem is good for you? One guy and a lot of girls?"

"I'm a one-woman man, thank you very much."

I grin into the chair.

His phone rings again, and he sighs. "Who is that? Can you see?"

"You want me to look?"

"Yeah, if you can see."

If I can see.

Eton kept so much of himself hidden, shrouded in a veil of business of private family matters that made me feel like a jerk for inquiring about. But Maddox is so transparent.

Determination and courage. Beauty. And honesty.

It's no wonder I love this man.

I peek over the side of the chair and see his screen. "It's your mom."

"How many times has she called?"

"Three?"

"Fuck it. Answer it."

I look at him over my shoulder like he's crazy. "Hard no."

"Just answer it. She'll keep calling because now she thinks I'm dead. Doesn't matter that I'm almost thirty. I understand that's completely out of pocket, but I'm not arguing with her."

I just stare at him as it starts to ring again.

He holds his hands up. "I have grease all over me. Please fucking answer it."

I whine as I reach for his phone. *What the hell do I say to her? It's not like we're in Publix. Clearly, I'm here fucking her son. And even more clearly, I'm butt-naked with said son's hands all over my body.*

Oh, dear God …

"Hello?" I say, wincing.

Maddox moves his hands over my hips.

"Ashley?" she chirps. "Well, *hello.* How are you, sweetie?"

She's happy to hear it's me? And she knows it's me? How does she—
Banks. Funny how his name answers so many of life's questions.

"I'm good, Damaris. How are you?"

"I am so sorry to bother you. For some reason, I thought Maddox was home today, and I wanted him to swing by the office and pick up a package for me before he came home. I'm in Daytona Beach today and don't want to have to drive all the way back to the office to get it."

"He'll be home tomorrow. Our flight is at two."

My heart sinks. I've been working so hard to avoid that.

Maddox's massage slows at the reminder too.

"Are you having a good time?" she asks.

"Yeah." I struggle to keep a steady voice as Maddox's hands slip into my inner thighs. "We swam with pigs today."

"You know, I've always wanted to do that. Kix and I keep saying we're going to go to the Bahamas for an anniversary trip, but we never do."

Great. Let me hang up now.

"I'm trying to talk him into a couch right now, but I might just book a trip. See how he likes that." She laughs. "I think I've almost worn him down on the couch. Little does he know that I've already ordered one, and it was on backorder. So by the time he agrees, I'll send him to pick it up at Swayze's in Sunnyvale."

I laugh. "Smart. I like your style."

Maddox stands and pulls me to my feet too. I think we're going to go inside because I'm naked, but instead, he adjusts the back angle and then lies on the lounge.

"What are you doing?" I mouth.

"Marriage is a funny thing," she says. "I learned a little trick from Kix's mom, actually. Want me to tell you?"

"Sure."

Maddox takes my hand and brings me to him. My body tenses as his plan begins to lay out in front of me.

"No," I mouth, my eyes wide. But while my mind may say no, my body screams yes.

He grabs me by the waist, his fingers dipping into my hips to the point it nearly burns, and positions me over his face. I straddle the chair with his mouth just beneath my opening.

My body tingles without him touching it. What the hell am I supposed to do with Damaris? His mother! How do I end this damn call without sounding rude? I sure as hell can't give the phone to her son and stop what he's about to do.

"Have selective hearing," she says, laughing as her son blows on my wet folds. "Because lord knows that he will."

Maddox tugs on my hips until I squat down. I grip the back of the chair with my free hand and hold myself steady. His tongue drags through my flesh before he sucks gently on my swollen bud.

I hiss, moving the phone away from my face. I try to pull away, to get some control over the stimulation, but he freezes me in place by my waist.

"Ashley? Are you still there, sweetie?"

A shiver shoots through me, and I shake from head to toe.

"I'm here," I say, fighting to stay calm. "I think we have a bad connection. There … was a storm …"

Maddox fucks me with his tongue, careful not to touch my pussy with his hands. Each stroke sends a wave of euphoria through my body.

"Okay. Please tell my son that I called. Did you say he was in the shower?"

I did not. "Yup!" There's definitely something wet involved. *Currently, me.*

Oh, fuck … He tortures my clit with his tongue, rubbing slow, hard circles over it. I move my hand to his hair and tug at his roots. He chuckles against me. That only makes it worse.

"Okay, well, let him know I called, but it wasn't important. It was so nice talking to you, Ashley. I hope to see you soon."

"You too, Damaris," I say, her name hiccupped. "Goodbye."

"Goodbye."

I pant, grinding against his mouth. I fiddle with the phone and double-check the call is disconnected. "I'm going to come in about two seconds."

He grabs my ass and shoves me *hard* against him.

"Fuck, Mad!" I moan into the air, my head falling back.

I ride his face until every drip of pleasure is gone. Completely sated, I sag against him for a long moment, cradling his head against me.

Why can't it always be like this?

I pull back and drop to his lap. His face is wet, coated with my orgasm. He licks his lips.

"You ever do that again with your mom on the phone, and I'll—"

"Come?"

I laugh, reaching under me and taking his cock out of his shorts. Before he can say a word, I sit all the way down.

He growls as he hits the back of my pussy. I capture his mouth with mine.

I rock against him, needing him to feel as good as he made me feel. He grins against my lips.

"Do you taste yourself?" he asks, his voice low. "That's pretty fucking sexy."

I blush. "You don't have a condom on."

He slows the tempo of our movement and searches my eyes. "I haven't fucked anyone in a long time. I'm clean. You don't have to believe me. I won't be mad."

I kiss him again, my heart pounding out of control. "I was tested as soon as I suspected Eton cheated on me—which was a couple of weeks before I knew for sure. I didn't have sex with him after. I'm good. On birth control."

He holds my gaze. "You sure? Don't make bad decisions in the moment."

I think I love this man. "Same goes for you." I press a kiss to his forehead as he flexes inside me.

I know Maddox well enough to know that he'll stop unless I tell him that I'm absolutely okay with this. It's the kind of guy he is. He's a good one.

"Mad?" I swirl my hips against him. "Will you do something for me?"

"Always." He pauses. "Well, maybe not always, but I'm probably inclined to right now."

I laugh. "Will you come in me?"

His brow furrows as his eyes widen.

"I just want to feel you explode deep inside me one time. Before we leave tomorrow."

"Good grief, woman."

"I won't ask you again," I promise.

He peers up at me and grins. "Please do."

We kiss as he moves again. I lose myself to this man willingly, knowing that by the time I go to bed tomorrow, this will all probably be over.

But for tonight, he's mine. *And I'm going to enjoy every single minute that I have.*

CHAPTER 21

Maddox

I PLAYED WITH FIRE, AND NOW I'M ABOUT TO GET BURNED.

My juice is untouched, sitting in the glass in front of me. James brought our breakfast by an hour ago, but I haven't touched it either.

I should go wake Ashley so she can get packed. *Give her more time than half an hour.* I smile sadly at the memories.

We stayed up well into the morning. I don't think either of us wanted to go to sleep and waste our last night together. We fucked hard by the pool—her sweet, naked body in the sun was like a glorious gift from heaven. *She's a gift from heaven.* Then back in our bed later, with the moon streaming in our room, we took it slow—appreciating each other's bodies and voices to the soundtrack of the ocean outside our suite.

Our conversations varied, but we strayed far away from the topic on our minds. *Going home.*

I stand and walk through the suite onto the back patio.

I've known my whole life that I wouldn't survive Ashley. When she blinked her little eyes at me behind the coatrack after I cut the wad of gum out of her hair in first grade, I was smitten. But she was too pretty for me—too smart and funny. And as we got older, I could laugh with her, have fun with her, but I couldn't approach her like that. I wasn't worthy of Ashley Thompson.

Then we graduated high school, and I got smarter and realized that I was worthy of her. But I'd had enough experience with women to know how shit worked. And I knew that breaking up with them before it all went bad was the only way to go—the only way to save feelings and friendships.

I also knew I could never do that with Ashley.

"Basically, I'm an idiot right now," I say aloud.

So much is at stake here. If we go back to Florida and treat this as an uncomplicated vacation fling, I don't know if I can see her again and not think she's mine. How do I see her at the bar with some other dude? I can't just be her rebound. Fuck. That. But what other option do I really have?

If we extend this and get into a relationship, I'm never going to be able to break it off. What happens if it goes south? Do I just stick it out, and we're both miserable? Or do we end it there and never speak again and I lose her completely? I can't look in her eyes and know that I caused her misery. That I failed her. That I did anything but treat her like I have the past few days.

So what do I do?

I never should've come here.

But someone else would've. And these last few days would've included another man with her like this.

I growl into the air.

We're going to pay for this somehow, at some point. The question is how and when.

My phone buzzes in my pocket. I pull it out.

Banks: Please tell Moss that I'm right.

Moss: See, Banksy? He knows you're on
bullshit already.

I've missed these guys.

Me: What's going on?

Banks: What is the make and model of the
Scooby-Doo van?

I burst out laughing.

Me: What are you talking about? Why?

Moss: Just answer the question.

Me: It's a van. I don't recall seeing any badges
on it as a child, but it's been a while.

Banks: THE ANSWER IS OBVIOUS.

Moss: Yeah. It's a 1960s Chevy G-body
panel van.

Banks: You are so freaking dumb, Moss.

Moss: Says the guy who had me glue his finger
shut.

Thank God I wasn't there for that.

Me: Why are we having this discussion?

Banks: Long story. Tell him what it is because
he's wrong, and I know you're not an idiot.

Banks: Please don't be an idiot.

Moss: He gave you his answer. "A van."

Me: What do you think it is, Banks?

Banks: I KNOW it's a Dodge A100. Two words —round headlights.

Me: He has a point.

Moss: Mom and Dad stopped having kids because they got to the two of you and realized they'd hit rock bottom.

Me: Funny.

Banks: When do you come home?

Me: In a few hours.

Banks: Shit.

Moss: See you tonight then.

Me: Why shit?

Banks: No reason. See you tonight.

Me: Banks …

I wait, but no one texts me back.

"Dumb fuckers," I say, shoving my phone back in my pocket.

I take a deep breath. *It's time.* Time to wake her up and get ready to go.

With more dread than I've ever felt, I climb the stairs to our room. I feel the breeze from the open doors as soon as I step onto the landing.

She's lying on her side, facing me, her lashes splayed against her cheeks. Her bare shoulders are relaxed, and she looks more peaceful than I've ever seen her.

I sit on the edge of the bed. "Hey."

She stirs but doesn't open her eyes. *I don't blame you.*

"Hey, Birdie," I say a little louder.

Her eyes flutter open. A slow grin splits her cheeks. "Hi."

"I hate to be the bearer of bad news, but you should probably wake up so we can get out of here."

She pulls a pillow over her head.

I know.

I slide into the bed beside her and pull her into me. Her cheek goes against my chest. Her arm drapes over me.

"You know, we could probably just stay on this island as castaways," I say, making her smile. "I'm not much of a hunter, but we could probably get a boat and fish. And charge tourists to go see the pigs."

"I could be a pig excursionist."

I chuckle. "I don't think that's a thing."

"Not until I make it one."

My fingers dance along her arm. "If anyone could do it, it's you. People would give you money just to spend time with you."

"I wouldn't charge you much."

"*Hey*," I say as if I'm offended. "I'm your partner in this scenario. You can't charge me. We're in this together."

She giggles.

"I got breakfast for you. No strawberries this time. James recommended French toast and blueberries, and James is my bud. I trust him."

"I'm glad you got so close to the butler."

"*The butler*," I say with a terrible British accent. "I could never be a person with a butler. I couldn't take myself seriously."

She laughs. I pull her closer to me.

"Is it bad to admit that I don't want this to end?" I ask.

She stills. "I don't want it to end either, Mad."

I stare at the ceiling, my chest burning. *Why is this so hard?*

She sighs. "I know you think you're just fling material. But why does our fling have to end here? Why can't we just ... fling it out for a bit longer?"

That sounds fucking amazing. "Is that responsible?" *I hate myself right now.*

"Why wouldn't it be?"

I shrug. "I just don't want us to wind up hating each other. I love you too much for that."

My throat tightens. I freeze.

She takes a deep, shaky breath. "We're friends. We've always loved each other. I'm not sure how we could ever hate one another."

I close my eyes. *Thank you for that save, Ash.*

"Promise me," I say.

"Promise you what?"

"Promise me that you'll always be honest. That you'll walk away before you hold on to this just because it's what we're doing." I suck in a breath. "That it won't be like fizzle-fuck and you where things weren't working, but you stayed anyway."

"Fine. But *you* promise *me* that you won't drift away from me like you do everyone else because you don't want to put the work in to building something real."

I flinch. "I don't do that."

"No, you do. You've had so many women who would've loved to try something with you, and you just keep it so loose so they don't get too close."

I swallow. *That's not what I do. I keep them loose because they aren't you.*

The realization is so plain and simple it makes me want to puke.

As soon as the thought rolls through my brain, it's like a fog clears in my head. A fog that has been trying to clear for a long time, but I've clung to it.

It's true. It's always been true. She's always been the one that I want. From the moment her little lips trembled in first grade because she was going to get in trouble, I loved her. I fell for her that day, if I'm being honest.

She's why I've never settled down. She's why I've never felt anything with anyone else. She's why I could never see myself married or with kids because it was never with her.

It's never been a childish crush like my brothers have thought. It's always just been … her. The girl who I knew would fit. Whose joy I want to swim in. Whose hugs I want to enjoy daily and whose heart simply won't quit.

I want that forever.

But the thought of committing to her like that, putting that responsibility on my shoulders, is terrifying. What if she looks at me someday and I can't give her what she needs? What if I can't protect her? What if I fail her?

I'd never live with myself.

"Promise me?" she whispers.

"Promise."

She smiles against my chest.

"Want one more round of vacation sex before we leave?" I ask.

"Hell, yeah." She springs up, throwing the blankets off her. But before she straddles me, her phone buzzes. "Who could that be?"

"How do I know?"

She crawls across the bed, her bare ass up in the air as she reaches for her phone. She sits up and scrolls the screen. Her forehead is wrinkled.

"Who is it?" I ask.

"It's my credit card company."

"Is everything okay?"

She sets her phone in her lap and looks at me. "I need to make some calls."

"Okay. What can I do? What's happening?"

"My credit card was just refunded for this trip," she says, her brow furrowed. "It was the only card on file, so I don't get it. I paid in full weeks ago, and obviously, we took the trip. We're here."

Oh shit.

I thought I'd have more time. Mostly, I thought she'd be somewhere else when this happened.

She sighs and starts to get off the bed. "Let me go look up some numbers."

I put my hand on her thigh. "Wait."

"What?"

"So …" I swallow nervously. "I might've had my buddy James help me out and figure out how to refund your payment and place it on my card."

Her eyes almost fall from her head.

"I just … I couldn't …" I shrug.

She spins around to face me. I'm not sure if it's anger or surprise or happiness or disbelief in her eyes, but it's something.

I grimace.

"Maddox ..."

"Look, maybe some men," I say, refusing to use her ex's name, "would let you pay for a vacation, but I'm not that man. And I'm sure as hell not the man who's going to let my wife pay for our honeymoon."

A slow smile tickles her lips. "You know we're not married, right?"

"We are until we board that plane home." Might as well tell her everything. "In first class."

She gasps. "You did that too?"

"I was late. Thanks to Sara. And I was worried you were gonna be pissed if I showed up, so I wanted to sweeten you up just in case."

She smacks my chest, but I pull her on top of me.

"This was my trip," she says. "I didn't ask you to come to pay for it."

"You're right. You didn't ask me at all, and if you would've had your way, I would've been booking a ticket home from the airport." I lean up and kiss her. "This was *our trip*. I got just as much enjoyment out of it—actually, probably more—than you did."

"I got to swim with pigs."

I drop my jaw. "That's the takeaway here? After all I've done for you?"

She giggles, her eyes twinkling.

"I've fucked you and fed you and taken you shopping—I bought you a beautiful forty-dollar wedding ring," I say, holding up her hand with the ring on it. "And you say you got to swim with pigs."

She cups my cheeks and smiles. "I got to swim with pigs with you. Better?"

"Slightly."

She laughs. "I'll give you one more chance to be more memorable than the pigs. But you better hurry because we have a flight—*ah!*"

I flip her onto her back and take advantage of the offer. Even though I might just get lucky and have more opportunities in the future than I thought.

I hope so, anyway.

CHAPTER 22

Ashley

"HI, HONEY! I'M HOME!"

I pull a Sara and close the door with my foot. But, unlike Sara, I'm clad in flip-flops and not fancy stilettos.

Rebecca and Sara spring to their feet—a plate of Doritos spilling to the floor—and nearly tackle me in the entryway. As much as I dreaded coming home, I'm so glad to see them.

My bags hit the tile with a thud. "I was only gone a few days." I laugh as they pull me into a wiggly group hug.

"We want all the details," Rebecca says, pulling away.

"Start with the bedroom stuff." Sara leads the way into the living room. "I'm glad the water was pretty, and the beaches were great, but I want to hear about the sex."

I dig in my bag and pull out two small boxes. Then I head into the living room.

"I can start with the bedroom stuff," I say, dropping one of the boxes in Sara's lap and the other in Rebecca's. "But the good stuff was the pool stuff. Bathroom floor stuff. Against the windows, kitchen counters, on the steps—which was mildly awkward, but I highly, *highly* recommend."

"Start with that," Becca says, her eyes wide.

Sara laughs and opens her box. "I take it that it went well."

It went well? Ha.

I take my seat on the end of the couch and let my mind do what I know it's going to do for probably the rest of time—float right back to Maddox.

I don't think he stopped touching me in some way from the moment we left the suite until he escorted me to my car in long-term parking. He held my hand, touched my leg, had his shoulder touching mine—something at all times. I'm not sure if he realized he was doing it, but I didn't complain.

My cheeks flush. "This is the moment when I humbly come to you and express my sincere gratitude."

"He was that good?" Sara looks at me through her lashes before going back to the box. "Oh, what's this?"

I grin as she pulls out the beaded coin purse with a snap clasp. "Mad took me inside this little shop to buy a metal bird—don't ask. And I saw those and thought of you and the random coins that are always all over your car."

"What a good idea and *how beautiful*." She clutches it to her chest. "Thank you."

Becca gasps. "Ash …"

Sara and I turn to her. Becca's eyes are wide and full of unshed tears as she takes the earrings and bracelet out of the box.

"I saw them and had to get them for you," I say, her reaction making me emotional. "The earrings are pretty, but the bracelets felt like you—with the cord and all. I know you love things like that."

She sniffles and sets them gently back in the box. I steal a glimpse at Sara and notice her lowering her guard, smiling softly at our friend too.

"I do. I love them," she says. "You'll never know what they mean to me."

"Okay, enough," Sara says, shivering. "Thank you for the gifts. We love them. They were unnecessary, but we do love presents, so there's that. But if you guys want to get all gooshy about this, do it once I'm gone. I don't want it tainting me."

I giggle.

"What's on your finger?" Sara points at my left hand. "That's a little suspicious."

"Oh, this little thing?" I wiggle it in the air. "That would be my wedding ring."

"What?" Becca laughs.

"Mad bought it for me as a joke. I forgot I had it on."

Sara's eyes widen, and she nods knowingly. "I see."

"What do you see?" I ask.

"I see it too." Becca grins. "We were right, Sara. I wonder if we get to be bridesmaids?"

"What are you talking about?"

Sara scoots to the end of her chair. "Look, we can be double maids of honor, but I get to plan the bachelorette party. And I'm not wearing blue. Cool tones on this skin are a no-go."

I burst out laughing. "Slow down, fairy godmother. We're not even in a relationship, so don't get too far ahead of yourselves."

I keep my smile on my face, but inside, I squirm.

"Promise me that you'll always be honest. That you'll walk away before you hold on to this just because it's what we're doing."

I've intentionally not focused on *what* that means. Are we not going to be together now that we're home? No. He made me text him when I got back to Becca's, and he's already sent me a selfie with a kissy face. But are we *together* together? I don't think so. I think he's labeling us as a fling.

What do labels matter anyway? I know what it feels like when he touches me, and I can read the look in his eyes. *"I just don't want us to wind up hating each other. I love you too much for that."*

It's fine. This is as real as it can be.

My heart swells.

"You're obviously in a relationship," Sara deadpans.

"Eh ..."

Rebecca smiles. "You should've seen him when we met him at The Shade House and talked to him about the honeymoon. He was freaking *adorable*."

"He was sexy as hell. Adorable? Sure. Dimples are cute, and he was so sweet about you. But there's not enough adorableness to hide the orgasms he gives by walking into a room."

I grin. It's wicked and dirty, an effect of the orgasms he gave me.

Over and over and over …

"That." Sara points a perfectly manicured finger at me. "That's what I mean. Spill."

"Spill what?" I ask. "You know the guy can fuck."

"Well, technically, I don't. But I can imagine."

I fill with unadulterated heat. *If Maddox was here, I'd be figuring out quickly how I could get Sara and Becca to leave so I could have him naked and inside me.*

"Stamina. Like he's *never* not hard." I swoon. "He kisses, gives the best oral ever, and cuddles. It's hard and fast, long and sweet. Outside, inside. He had me naked by the pool, *riding his face*, while I was on the phone with his mom."

Rebecca's jaw about hits the floor.

Sara claps her hands, impressed. "Damn. I'm so proud of you."

"Why? For being an exhibitionist? For probably never being able to see Damaris again because I'm afraid she heard me moan while she talked about couches?"

"For all of that." Sara nods, grinning from ear to ear. "That's my girl."

I snort.

"So what now?" Becca asks. "Obviously, you and Maddox are a thing. Where does that leave you? Are you moving in with him or—"

"No."

My pulse soars. I don't want my friends thinking this is more than it is … even though I think it's probably more than it is. But it's soon, probably too soon, to be talking about comingling our lives like that. I need time to adjust to this situation. In the few hours I've been away from him, I'm overwhelmed with how *happy* I am. And the longer I sit in that space, the bigger the anxious bubble grows in my stomach.

It's going to be fine. Have faith.

I clear my throat. "I'm still going to buy a house. I'm moving forward with my life, and whatever happens with Mad happens. We'll work it out."

Becca and Sara exchange a look.

"What?" I ask.

Becca squirms. "I hadn't planned to focus on this yet. Because, you know, Maddox and the Bahamas and your orgasm-y face ... But once my lease ends, I'm going to move back to Texas."

"*What*? Why? Are you sure, Bec?"

I want to be sad and beg her to stay, but there's something incomplete in Rebecca—a wound that has festered since she got here that she's never been able to heal. I only wish I knew what it was. Maybe going home is an extension of that, her attempt at moving forward. *I'm going to miss her so much.*

"I need to go back there," she says. "It's time."

"Do you want to talk about it?" I ask.

She shakes her head.

"I'm here if you ever want to talk," I say. "Sara and I both are. We don't pressure you because it makes you uncomfortable but just know that we love you, okay? We love you, and we're here for you always."

Becca blinks back tears.

"That's it for me," Sara says, getting to her feet. "I will always listen if you want to talk. I'll help you bury a body—but I'll need a heads-up so I can bring proper footwear. I'll even, and I hate this, curl up on the couch and watch those sappy movies you love when you're sad. Just let me know."

I laugh. "That's big of you, Sara."

"I have a meeting shortly, so I have to go. I just wanted to be here when you got back."

"Hey," I say, stopping her in her tracks. A sense of freedom washes over me—a glorious, powerful, easiness about my life settles in my bones. "Want to have that divorce party?"

Sara's eyes twinkle. "Hell yes, I do. Mega Pint tomorrow night? Is that good for you guys?"

"I'm free," I say.

"I actually have tomorrow night off at Smokey's," Rebecca says.

"Great. Let's meet there at nine. Wear your dancing shoes, ladies." Sara waves. "See you then."

"Bye," we call after her as the door clicks shut.

Rebecca and I sigh, then laugh.

"She's a whirlwind," Rebecca says. "I need to get to work too. I picked up an evening shift, and it starts in twenty minutes. I won't be home until late."

"Go. I'll see you tonight."

She stands and straightens her Smokey's work shirt. "I'm glad you went and had fun. It gives me hope."

My brow furrows, but the look in her eyes stops me from asking her what she means.

"See you tonight," she says, heading for the door.

"Bye, Bec."

And for the first time all week, I'm alone.

I sit still for a few minutes and relish in the quiet. I use the time to replay the past few days and enjoy the peace in my soul.

Then I miss him.

I sort through our pictures from the trip. The pictures with my wedding ring. The shots from the boat with the pigs behind us. Selfies that we snapped randomly at the pool, on the balcony, and during our walks on the beach.

I've never seen myself that happy. I've never seen joy on my face like that. I'm radiating it—even I can see it—and I think I can see it on his face too.

I grin and pull up his name.

Me: I miss James.

His response is immediate.

Him: I'm glad he was so memorable.

Me: I also miss you.

Him: I stopped at the office to make sure nothing fell apart while I was gone. It didn't. Know what that means?

Me: Nope.

Him: That means if you know a travel agent, we should totally take another trip.

My cheeks ache from smiling.

Me: I happen to know one, actually. Any time you want to get away, just let me know, and I'll make it happen.

Him: How about a week at the end of next month? Tati's kids will be in school, so it'll be easier on her to manage this place.

I fall back on the cushions and laugh out loud. *Is this real?*

Me: Anywhere in particular?

Him: Somewhere warm so I can have you naked outside. Fuck, that was one of the best afternoons of my life.

Same.

Him: I'm leaving now and heading home. Want
to have phone sex later?

I laugh.

Me: Sure. Audio or video?

Him: VIDEO. Wear that purple-y lingerie that
you wore for me on our trip.

Me: Okay. 😊

Him: I'd have you come over, but I'm sure you
have a million things to take care of, and I can't
swear my family won't come by. And I think I'll
be dealing with Banks and these fucking
stickers.

Me: 😊

Him: 😊

Me: I have a lot to do tonight anyway. So
sexting it is. What time are you calling?

Him: I'll text you first. Around ten?

Me: Perfect. I'll be ready and waiting.

Him: 😊

Me: 😊

I start to put my phone away but have another idea. I swipe through
my photo album until I find the one I'm looking for.

With a few swipes, the selfie I took on the boat—the one of a clear shot of my cleavage and body in my bikini—is sent to Maddox's phone.

Immediately, my phone buzzes.

> Maddox: And to think that I've touched and licked every single inch of that tight little body. 🔥 Lucky guy.

I look at the ceiling and swoon. Lucky me.

I begin to text him back when another message pops up. This time, every muscle in my body tightens.

> Eton: Are you finished being ridiculous? You've proven your point.

Instead of getting angry or sad or confused—instead of needing time to even think about his message—I laugh.

I find a picture of the pigs and me and fire it his way.

> Me: Fuck off.

I turn off my phone and go unpack.

CHAPTER 23

Maddox

HOME, SWEET—*HOLY SHIT*.

I drop my bags by the door and then close it behind me. *What the hell happened here?*

The lights are on. *All of them.* Even the one in the coat closet that I don't use. Banks's boots and socks are all over the entryway—the socks not in the boots and the boots not together.

Did he move in while I was gone?

I tiptoe into the kitchen, fully expecting a marked disaster. It's a good thing I prepped myself.

A cereal box is on the island with the top unsealed. Fruity Pebbles are scattered around it. A jug of milk—empty, I assume—is next to the refrigerator, and the microwave is wide open. Yellow dust that I can only assume is cheese powder from microwavable mac-and-cheese cups faintly covers the countertop.

I'm gonna kill him.

I head toward the living room, fearing what I might find there, when the front door slams. Banks comes into the kitchen and swallows me in a hug before I have the chance to say a word.

"You're home," he says, patting my back before releasing me. "It's been so quiet without you."

"Well—"

"You're out of milk, and your Easy Mac things are trickier than I anticipated. Got them figured out, though." He moves around the island. "I went to the store and restocked everything but the milk. It's so hard to remember everything. I even made a list—Paige's idea—and I still forgot the milk. Can you believe that?"

"Yeah, well—"

"I fixed your garage door. It was squeaking like a motherfucker. How do you even live like that? Moss came over and helped me hold it in place but do *not* let him steal my glory."

I don't even try to say anything this time. Besides, where would I start?

Banks hops on a stool, smug. "I saw a palmetto bug by the toaster, and Mom called the exterminator who will come next week. I was going to do it, but she said she'd handle it because something about seeing a mouse at Laguna Homes or something, I don't know. *Oh*—I tried to take the fall for the chicken noodle soup being left out, but I don't think she believed me. Which is weird. She always thinks I'm at fault for everything."

Does he breathe?

"Brooke might be pregnant, but you didn't hear it from me. I was thinking we could take Moss out and congratulate him or something. Isn't that what you do when you have a baby on purpose?" He furrows his brow. "To be honest, he might be setting me up to see if I tell you. So maybe forget that I said that."

I can't help it. I chuckle. *He's such a mess, but he means well.* "All of that happened while I was gone?"

"Yup. And I took care of it all. I wanted you to come home and know I held down the fort while you held down the girl." He smirks. "Wanna talk about *that*?"

I ignore the cereal driving me crazy and sit beside my brother.

"Banksy, I think I'm in trouble."

He grins.

"What did I do?" I ask.

"Hopefully, you did it all, and you did it well."

My chest shakes as I laugh.

"Okay, seriously," he says. "I know you had a great time because she's awesome and you're acceptable. I mean, you're not me, but you're not Jess either. You're a good middle ground."

I look at him and laugh again. *He's a nut.*

"If you didn't get on that plane and know you'd come back fucked up, you intentionally had your head in the sand," he says, holding his hands up in a shrug.

I hate to admit it, but he's not wrong. I knew what I was getting into, and I dove in headfirst. *Did I tell myself it was manageable? Did I use Jess's stupid rebound comment as my excuse?* Yup. I did. *Did I also know in my gut that this was my chance to have her to myself?* Also, yes.

But I don't want to admit that, and thankfully, this is Banks I'm talking to. I don't have to admit anything. He already knows.

Banks takes a quarter out of my pink bowl and taps it against the counter. "Ashley has had you by the balls since we were kids."

"Not true."

He rolls his eyes.

"We were perfect in the Bahamas. We were cocooned in this suite away from the world. It was this sweet spot between real love and real life."

"Real love, huh?"

"It's a figure of speech."

"*Okay.*" He tries not to laugh at me. "And that sweet spot that's not real love, just a figure of speech, has to end, why?"

I shrug. "I don't know. I hope it doesn't."

"So I've never been in your position. But I did watch Moss lose his shit over Brooke, and I took notes. Figured I'd learn from his pain. No need for all of us to be tortured, and here's what I got—once you're in the headspace where you don't want things to end, and you have *that look in your eye*"—he points at me—"you're done. It's a harbinger of things to come."

"Learn that word from your delivery guy too?"

"From a lady at the grocery store, actually. But thank you for noticing." He lifts his chin. "The point is that excuses are like opinions—everybody's got one."

I snort. "You sound like that Salt-N-Pepa song. Remember it? We had to listen to it that whole summer in high school. The words are burned in my brain."

"That's opinions and assholes. Anyway, don't change the subject." He fires me a look. "Ashley Thompson is your girl. You can do something about that or not. But if not, prepare to eternally torture yourself and watch her wind up with some other guy who won't treat her nearly as nice as you but does have the balls to say she's his."

I stare at him.

He shrugs. "I don't make the rules. I don't even play this game. I'm a benchwarmer over here. I just know how it works."

"Banks, how can you manage not to clean up your spilled Fruity Pebbles like a four-year-old and then give me advice like that?"

"Easy. I don't waste my time on the little stuff." He grins. "Speaking of which—*Jess is in Tampa tonight.*"

"*Oh, no.*"

"Dad sent him there for something—I tuned that out, doesn't involve me. But that means Jess's house is sitting empty."

Every muscle in my body hurts. I need to unpack, sort through emails, and clean this place up. "No. Don't do this tonight."

"I've already started."

"*Banks.*"

"I underestimated how long this was going to take. I think I have four sheets left. I made an executive decision and put one on every condom wrapper in his drawer. That was time-consuming and used up a big chunk of my stash because apparently, Jess buys in bulk. But I do love the idea of him getting ready to bang some chick and seeing my face."

"He'll murder you."

"Eh ..."

Take me back to paradise. "He has cameras, you know. He'll know you're in there before you get out."

"I happen to know that his cameras don't pick up the side of his house facing Mom's. So we use that door, and we're home free."

I stare at him, pleading silently for this to go away—or for him to do it alone. But the longer I sit, the more certain I am that I'm only delaying the inevitable.

"You're sure he's not coming home?" I ask.

"Yup. Dad made an offhand comment that Jess would be home tomorrow evening."

I sigh, resigned to my fate. "Fine. But we're going to make quick work of it. And if we get caught—if Jess finds out—you're taking the blame. Not me. Got it?"

Banks grins mischievously. "It's not gonna happen. I got this. Relax."

Right.

———

"You're a dead man. I hope you know that."

I stand in the middle of Jess's bedroom and take in the sight. Banks's face is everywhere.

On his pillows. Mirror. On the ends of his free weights on the floor.

In the closet, the stickers are in the soles of his shoes, on shirt buttons, and inside the pockets of some of his jeans.

I scratch my head, a throb beginning in my temple, and walk down the hallway again. Banks's face smiles at me from the pictures hanging on the walls. Every person shown is now him.

"I covered his tools, every file in his file cabinet, lamp shades—on the ends of his tweezers," he says, somehow proud of himself. "I basically have the kitchen left."

"This is not something I want to be doing," I say. "I really, really implore you to reconsider."

"Fuck that. He stole Betsy. He expects me to retaliate."

I scrub my hands down my face.

"I'm thinking one in the center of every tile," he says. "Backsplash and floor. We can hit the bottom of his glasses, some of his forks, random pantry items. What do you think?"

I sigh. "I think you're entirely too excited about this."

He thrusts a couple of sheets of stickers in my hands. "Let's get to work. If we're going to do this, let's do this."

Banks starts on the backsplash. I lean against the island and look at the sticker up close. It showcases him shirtless, flexing in front of a car with a shit-eating grin. *I hope these peel off easy.*

"Don't forget that he almost had you arrested," Banks says, lifting a brow. "I mean, I was involved in that, but Jess put everything in motion."

That's true.

I start sticking Banks's face to the bottom of Jess's mugs. "What will it take for you to settle down with a woman?"

"Me?" he asks. "I don't know."

"It feels like such a trade-off. My life is great. But it could be greater, maybe." *Probably. Definitely.* "But …"

Banks stops and looks at me over his shoulder. The levity usually inked on his face is gone. "What are you scared of, Mad?"

The question, so point-blank, coupled with his expectation of an honest answer, hits me hard.

We watch each other, Banks not backing down, for a few moments. I'm acutely aware of my rapid breathing and my heart thumping blood noisily in my ears. Of the bead of sweat coating my palms.

I've confused myself, intentionally, perhaps, about the answer to this question. Over the years, I've explained my behavior in a myriad of ways. But there's one truth, one singular reason that holds me back.

"I'm scared she'll need me, and I won't be there," I say.

My confession hangs in the air between us. Banks looks around the room before dropping his gaze on me.

"The thought of having that responsibility on my shoulders …". I suck in a breath. "It strangles me. I can't breathe just thinking about it."

"Well, you know people can take care of themselves—especially Ashley, right?"

I sigh. "Yeah. I know. I get that. But it doesn't work that way."

"Then how does it work?"

Annoyed, I move around the room, slapping the stickers on random surfaces. "If I admit to her, to myself, that she's mine—*then she's mine.* I know me, Banks, and I know what I'm going to feel like. I'm barely on the other side of that line now. It'll consume me. *She'll consume me.* I'll drive myself nuts trying to make her happy." I stop and look at him. "And what if that doesn't work?"

"And what if it does?"

I throw my hands up. "Where's your brilliant advice now?"

"That's brilliance. Simplicity is brilliance." He goes back to his stickering. "You're focusing on the negatives. Have you ever thought about the positives? What if you make her happy? What if you make her life better? What if you give her a reason to get up and make her feel safe? Because that's what I think would make her happy."

That's what I want to happen.

Banks moves his production to the floor. I go to the other side of the room and start adding them to the tiles to hurry things along. I'm too antsy for this. Too wired.

I need to see her face.

"And what if it does?"

That's a big what-if, Banks. A huge what-if.

We make quicker work of the floor than I anticipate. The stickers run out before we get under the table.

Banks grins. "If nothing else, this is a lot better looking than it was before."

I smack the back of his head. "You're a dipshit. This is the last thing I do with you. Do not pull me into anything else."

"No promises."

We sneak out the side door, checking to make sure no one sees us, and then bolt to my house. Banks parts ways with me at my back door to go to his house for a shower. *Thank God.*

As soon as I'm inside, my phone buzzes. A picture of a certain set of lingerie on a bed is on my screen.

I glance around the kitchen and do quick work of how long it will take to get the place respectable.

I can hurry.

Me: Busy?

Ashley: I send you that, and you ask if I'm busy? Buzzkill.

. . .

I grin.

> Me: Want to come over? Lingerie is optional because I'll just rip it off you anyway.

> Ashley: Oh, what happened to sexting?

> Me: It's been a night. I want to hold you after.

> Ashley: You really want me to come?

> Me: More than once, if I have any say in it.

> Ashley: Be there in fifteen.

> Me: Fuck the lingerie.

> Ashley:

I laugh.

Yeah. I love her.

I love Ashley. Banks is right—she's my woman.

"What if you make her happy? What if you make her life better? What if you give her a reason to get up and make her feel safe?"

Can I do those things? Or have I been right all along—I'm better fling material?

CHAPTER 24

Maddox

"Need a vacation from your vacation?" Tati laughs, leaning against my office doorframe. "You look … handsome. And tanned. But freaking tired, boss."

Tati, that's not from vacation. That's from last night.

I lean back in my chair, so easily distracted, and remember the feeling of waking up next to Ashley. In my bed.

It was a completely different experience from waking up next to her in the Bahamas. There was no ocean breeze or the promise of a decadent breakfast courtesy of the butler. There was no indulgent view of the sea as far as you could see or a pool to slip into to cool down.

She was in my shirt, under my sheets—her toothbrush was on my bathroom counter.

It was simple. It felt like a version of normal. Of what life could be like.

The weirdest part? *I liked it. A lot.*

"Did you know that pigs swim in the Bahamas?" I ask. "There's a whole island of them. They swim right out to your boat, and you can get in with them. It's wild as hell."

She makes a face. "Pigs swim?"

"Right? Here. I have pictures."

She walks to my desk as I flip through the album that I created for our vacation photos. I find the shots with the animals and show her.

"This one was my guy," I say, showing her the pink one with black around his eye.

"He's cute in a pig kind of way." She sits across from me. "The setting looks beautiful, but I'm not sure that the pig part is for me."

"I wasn't sold on it either, but Ashley wanted to do it. It was definitely an experience. Reminds you not to take the world too seriously. I mean, there are pigs living in paradise getting hand-fed fruit by humans like they're royalty. It's ridiculous."

Tati crosses one leg over the other and watches me curiously.

"What?" I ask.

"Just wondering if you left my boss on the islands."

"What's that supposed to mean?"

"I think you're beaming, Mr. Carmichael. I think you're positively smitten, and I'm here for it."

I roll my eyes. "Mind your own business, Tati."

She laughs.

"Speaking of business," I say, turning to my computer and hitting the print button on an email. "I just got an offer on the Ugly Door House that you showed while I was gone."

"I knew it. *I knew it.*" She fist-pumps. "Was it decent, at least?"

"It's not bad. The seller will counter, obviously, but I bet this goes through." I rock back in my seat. "Good work."

"Thanks."

"And thanks for taking over for me on such short notice. Not sure what I would do without you."

"Definitely not what you were doing while you were gone, that's for sure." She winks as she stands. "I'm glad you had fun. I'm just as happy that you're back. Now stay focused, and don't be sitting in here daydreaming about your new girlfriend."

I start to argue with her and tell her she's not my girlfriend. But I stop.

"That's what I thought," she says. "Door open or closed?"

"Closed."

It shuts behind her.

I manage to focus on my work for a solid hour, pushing all thoughts of Ashley out of my mind. It's easier than it was earlier today or yesterday. It's easier because I accepted reality.

I'm in love with her. Plain and simple. That's what this feeling is all about. As soon as I acknowledged that, the panic in my stomach settled.

"Go with the flow," I say aloud, hoping that hearing it as well as thinking it helps stamp it in my head. "There's no need to rush to do anything. We're so good together. We'll figure it out."

I nod, turning back to my computer when my phone buzzes.

Paige: Make it home, lover boy?

Me: Had a great time, thanks for asking.

Paige: I didn't.

Me: I was willing to ignore your lack of manners. Don't draw attention to it.

Paige: Should I put Ashley on the Christmas present list or not yet?

I stare at the question. *Christmas is months away.*

Me: Yeah. She likes romance novels and birds.

Paige: 😏

Me: What's so funny?

Paige: Didn't expect you to fall THIS HARD.

Me: Strangely enough, your brother Banks helped me work some shit out last night.

. . .

My phone rings, and I look down. *Huh?* "Why are you calling me? I have shit to do, Paige."

"I have to tell you something, and I don't want to text it."

Why? "Tell me then so I can get on with my day."

"So when you were gone, Banks called me. And he's like—*Mad is gonna come home, and I don't know what to say to him.*"

My brows pull together. "About what? About the cereal on my counter? Or the cheese powder? Or why the tube thing that you put the toilet paper on is gone from my guest bathroom?"

"Hey, you gave him a key."

"Nope. That's false. I did not." I think. "I'm not even sure how he has a key, now that you mention it."

"Reason six million that I'm glad I live far away."

"Such a liar, little sister," I say, laughing. "Anyway, back to Banks. What was he wanting to talk to me about?"

"Honestly, I think he was trying to help himself as much as you because he didn't want you all moody and ruining his sticker fun."

I groan. "Fuck those stickers."

"I heard that went well," she says, laughing.

"For whom? Because let me tell you something—this isn't ending well for anyone involved. He put his face on every tile in his kitchen, Paige. On his condoms. He covered a toilet seat with them."

Her laughter gets louder. "He sent me pictures before you got home. I was nervous even opening the images because that could implicate me later, right?"

"I'm glad someone else has blood on their hands."

She sighs. "Anyway, Banksy and I had a few chats about being a good listener. I told him to let you bring up Ash and then to just ask you questions and let you work it out."

My brain scrambles. *That's exactly what he did.*

Is this the toddler phase with Banks? Is he trying to grow up? This is unexpected but pleasantly received.

"Seems like you worked it out," she says.

"I guess I did." And for once in his life, Banks did too. To say I'm shocked is an understatement.

"When you're ready to propose, *call me*. Do *not* listen to any of our brothers. Don't ask Mom, or it'll be a huge production, and she'll probably be peeking through the bushes to watch. Don't make it weird."

I sigh, enjoying this odd but totally normal-feeling conversation with my sister.

"I'm not proposing anytime soon," I say.

"We'll see."

"Yeah, we will."

She yawns. "Okay, go do your … whatever it is you do all day. Nate is working with Troy today, so Ryder and I are going to the zoo, I think."

"Fun."

"Probably not." She laughs. "Call me later. You never call me."

"You never call me either."

"I just did."

I roll my eyes, but I'm smiling. "Gotta go, Paige. Love you."

"Love you, Mad."

I eye my computer and the many emails I need to return. Instead of doing that, I open my photo album. I didn't see Ashley take her cleavage shot, but I truly love that she did, and she sent it to me. Not just because she's sexy, but because it's a sign that she's mine.

A knot begins to twist in my stomach. It cinches tighter and tighter until I find it hard to breathe.

My fingers fly across the text screen.

> Me: Hi.

> Ashley: Hi.

> Me: Want to go to dinner tonight?

> Ashley: Would love to but I'm going to see Mom for dinner and then meeting Sara and Becca at Mega Pint at nine.

. . .

Oh.

She sends me a picture of her in the tub. Her toes are sticking out of a bunch of bubbles.

Me: Remember you're a married woman.

Ashley: LOL

Me: No laughing about it.

Ashley: I thought our marriage ended at the airport? And we're just a fling now?

I did say that—kind of. And when I said it, I meant it—mostly. But now, sitting here, imagining her getting hit on and not knowing that the two of us are definitely a thing, it burns through me.

Me: Nope. Still married. You didn't return the ring.

Ashley: Why don't you come tonight too? Make sure I'm wearing it?

Me: Isn't it a girls' thing?

Ashley: Yeah, but it'll be fine.

Me: Go and have fun. Call me if you need me.

Ashley: 😘

Me: 😘

Kissing emoji, my ass.

She wouldn't do anything with anyone else. I trust her implicitly. And honestly, she doesn't owe me any kind of loyalty.

I tap my chin.

Is this the way it's going to be? She'll be out with her friends as a free woman?

Of course, it is. Why wouldn't it be?

It wouldn't be if I'd just tell her I love her.

> **Me:** Wanna go to Mega Pint tonight?

> **Banks:** Sure. I'll meet you in the kitchen around nine?

I sigh and get back to work.

CHAPTER 25

Ashley

"You look hot," I say to Sara.

"Thank you. You are glowing in matrimony yourself."

I roll my eyes as we stop for Becca to catch up.

Mega Pint, a little bar tucked between a bank and a barber shop away from the tourist traps, is our favorite local watering hole. Sometimes Gordie, the owner, has live music or a deejay. Most nights, it's just the usual hits through a new touch-screen system that Gordie is quite proud of.

Once Becca has locked her car and joined us, we step across a giant crack that's been in the sidewalk since we were in junior high and enter the darkened building.

The crowd isn't too bad, consisting mostly of locals. We weave through the small mass of bodies by the door and make our way to the bar.

"Three amaretto sours, please," Sara says.

"I really love that ring," Rebecca says, touching my left hand.

I grin. "I reminded Maddox that we are just a fling, and he told me I better be wearing my wedding ring." I take my drink as Sara pays. "Curious if he'll show up tonight."

"This place is pretty quiet tonight," Sara says. "I didn't open a tab just in case we decide to go back to Becca's or something. Or we could go to mine if you guys want to go to Sunnyvale."

Rebecca points at a booth in the back corner. "Let's claim that now while it's available."

We walk to the booth, losing Sara temporarily in the process. A guy she sees every now and then—Bama Boy, I think she calls him—catches her attention as we pass.

Rebecca watches her longingly. "I wish I had her confidence."

I look over my shoulder. "Yeah. Same."

"Who are you kidding? You have confidence. I think you've had a boyfriend or fiancé the whole time I've known you."

I sip my drink and think about that. "Have I?"

"Yeah. One after the other."

Huh.

I've never thought about that before, oddly. But I can't think of a time that I've been single for long. *I wonder what that says about me?*

"Who was your last boyfriend, Bec?"

"It was a long time ago."

"You had dinner with Benny Marjero a few months ago," I offer.

"Yeah, but it was dinner a few times. Nothing serious."

Joan Jett comes on overhead, and I don't have to look at the dance floor to know Sara's on it.

"So who was your last real relationship?" I ask, taking another drink.

She plays with her bracelet, the one I got her in the Bahamas. "He was the sweetest guy. So kind and thoughtful and softly spoken. Everyone loved him."

"Why did you guys break up?"

"He died."

I set my drink on the table and try to keep my composure.

He died? Becca's boyfriend died?

She gives me a tight smile and directs her attention to her phone. Pain is painted on her face.

"Bec, I'm sorry," I say. "I didn't know."

"Of course, you didn't know. How could you? I just don't really like to talk about him, you know?

"Yeah. Okay." *Shit.*

Sara dances up to the table. "Gotta pee. Anyone else?"

"I'll go." Becca scoots out of the booth. "Be right back."

I nod, my heart twisting.

I hope I didn't upset her. Why did I push? I wouldn't have questioned her if I had known.

My poor, sweet friend.

My eyes close, and I take a long, deep breath. *And I think my problems are bad.*

I'm alerted to motion across from me by the sound of the booth squeaking. I pop my eyes open, expecting to see Maddox.

But it's not.

Eton is staring at me like he wants to rip my head off. *What the hell? Why is he here? How the hell did he find me?*

Panic bubbles in my stomach as I reach for my phone. Eton won't hurt me, but that doesn't mean I want to be here alone with him either.

I glance toward the bathrooms, but I don't see either of my friends.

"You aren't an easy woman to track down," Eton says, his voice bone-chillingly cool.

"Apparently, I'm easy enough. You found me. Find my friends? I'll be blocking you. Now, if you'll excuse me ..."

I start to scoot out of the booth when Eton's oversized friend, Jason, blocks me in.

My gaze whips to my ex-fiancé. "What the hell is this?"

"We need to talk."

"No, Eton, we don't." My blood boils. "Who do you think you are?"

He laughs. The sound is like nails on a chalkboard.

How did I ever find him attractive? How did I ever consider spending my life with him? Was he always this rude? Arrogant? Despicable?

"Get your goon out of my way," I say, leveling my gaze on his.

"Please don't speak about my friends with that kind of language. What's gotten into you, anyway? Just because you came back to the gutter doesn't mean you have to act like gutter trash."

My eyes nearly fall out of my head. "Do you want to know what boggles my mind?"

He hums.

"That I ever, *ever*, gave you the time of day," I say.

He laughs as if I'm kidding. "If you'd be nice and show me you remember how to behave, I might consider letting you come back to civilization with me."

"I wouldn't go with you if the world was on fire and you had the only boat to safety."

He rolls his eyes. "Speaking of boats, I saw you went on your embarrassing, paltry little trip. How pathetic to have to go on your own. Did you learn something from this, Little Miss Thinks She's Independent?"

"*Yes.*" I smirk. "I did go on my *little trip*, and it was the best trip I've ever had. Must've been the company. Quite ... *orgasmic* if you will."

His face darkens. This man is such a coward. *Total fizzle-fuck.*

I grin.

"It was unforgettable in so many ways," I say, taunting him. "I made so many memories, did so many things for the first time. Want to hear about them?"

"Don't."

"Then leave," I say, narrowing my eyes.

"Not until we have a discussion."

Fuck this guy. "Guess how many times I got off, Eton. *Guess.*"

"*Ashley—*"

"In four days, it was probably ... ten? Fifteen?" I tap my chin. "Oh, I forgot when I rode his face at the pool."

His fist pounds on the table. "Enough!"

"*Fuck you.*"

"Don't talk to me like that, you little tramp."

I laugh. It's louder than I expect, but damn, it feels good. "Oh, it irritates you that *I'm* screwing someone else now? But it was okay for you to screw around on me when we were engaged?" I lift a brow. "Is that what you're getting at? What did you expect, Eton? Did you think I would come back to Kismet Beach and miss you? *I've not thought about you once.*"

The rage spilling out of my mouth is cathartic. Even when we broke things off, we were on his turf. I stayed in my lane. But now? The lanes are gone.

"How do you expect me to want you back when you're talking such filth?" His breathing becomes ragged, his nostrils flaring. "You're better than this."

"I am. *I'm better than you*. Get out of my world, Eton, and never come back. Got it? We are so done—*ah!*"

My eyes water as soon as his palm connects to my cheek. My skin stings, burns, flames in a way I've never felt before.

I touch the side of my face gingerly as shock mutes my anger. *Did he do that? Did he hit me?*

"Don't ever touch me again," I yelp.

Our eyes lock, hatred pouring from one to the other as I steel myself against him.

I grip the table and start to get up, to stand on the booth's table if I must and get someone's attention, when my gaze connects with someone else's.

Maddox.

"What the fuck is happening here?" he says, eyes darting from mine to Eton to Jason, then back to me. "Are you okay?"

I nod, tears streaming in relief.

"Step back," Jason says. He towers over Maddox, broader than him too. "Move it."

"I want to get out, Jason," I say.

"Sit down," Eton says to me, seething. "I'm not done with you yet."

Maddox extends a hand to me. "Come on."

I reach for him when Jason's fist swings at Maddox.

"*Ah!*" I yell. *This is not happening.*

Maddox rolls easily under the shot. Jason doesn't see Banks's punch coming at him from the other side. Banks connects to Jason's cheek. The sound of fist to bone cracking pops through the bar.

The music goes off. I see Sara and Rebecca off to the side, Sara with her arm around our friend. Tears stream down my cheeks as Jason stands back up.

"Look what you've caused," Eton growls. "Are you happy? Did you get the attention you wanted?"

I don't answer him because I'm watching Maddox.

Jason swings at him again. This time, Maddox steps outside the punch and drills him in the face. Jason's head snaps back.

So much for being big.

The bar is silent, the patrons making a wide circle around the booth. The smell of adrenaline is unmistakable as Jason tries to rush Maddox.

They end up on the ground, and I lose track of what's happening. Punches are thrown in the skirmish until Maddox manages to mount him. I've seen him do this a thousand times in wrestling, but I've never seen him *like this.*

Banks grabs my hand and pulls me out of the booth. He inspects me quickly.

"Are you okay?" he asks.

I nod.

He turns to go back to Maddox but spots the side of my face. His eyes run cold.

"What's this?" he asks, his voice rising.

"Nothing. Don't worry about it. Help Mad."

"What is this, Ash?" He rips his gaze from mine. It lands on Eton. "You hit her?"

Eton chooses violence. "What's it to you?"

I move toward Sara. My heart breaks for this situation—for the blood on Maddox's lip as he stands. For the fury on Banks's face. For the sound of sirens outside.

But I'm also angry. So fucking angry. *At Eton. How did it come to this?*

Tears pour down my cheeks.

"You motherfucker." Banks has his fists in Eton's shirt and is dragging him out of the booth before I realize what's happening. "You like to hit people? Hit me. Come on, motherfucker. *Hit me.*"

Banks's eyes are wild—dark, brooding. Angry. "Throw, prick."

Maddox stands behind his brother while Jason is on the floor behind him.

"What?" Maddox asks, glancing at me quickly. "What's happening?"

"Should've hit me." Banks grins at Eton before nodding at him. "He hit Ash."

Eton doesn't even see the first punch coming. He doesn't have time to react to it. Not that it would've done him any good.

Maddox is on top of Eton, rocking him in the face with punch after punch. "You fucking piece of shit," Maddox seethes. "How does this feel? You like this?"

"Mad! Enough! Hey!" Banks grabs his shoulders and pulls his brother away.

Banks stands between Maddox and Eton, who is lying half on the booth, half on the floor. Maddox glares at Eton as he struggles to catch his breath.

"You ever talk to her again, I will rip your throat out with my bare hands," Maddox says, pointing at Eton. "I swear it. I—"

"Enough, man," Banks says, blocking Maddox's line of sight. "Let's not verbalize all of our plans in case we have to use them."

Banks grins, but Maddox doesn't flinch.

"Where's Ash?" Maddox turns, springing to life, and finds me by the wall. Before he can move, an officer barrels in and grabs him, leading him away. *No!*

It's a chaotic mess as the police come through the door and attempt to sort out what happened.

"I need to tell them my side," I say. "That Eton hit me."

"He did what?" Sara shrieks. "I'm gonna get mine in—"

"Stop," I say, tugging the back of her shirt and pulling her into me. "He got enough."

Maddox and Banks are taken to the end of the bar with Skylar Schultz, an officer we went to school with. Eton and Jason, once he wakes up, are taken to the opposite side of the room.

Maddox's eyes find mine through the crowd, just like they always do. He lifts a brow, a silent question asking if I'm okay. I nod. His eyes close briefly, and then he looks at me again. He presses his lips together and dips his head subtly. Then returns his attention to Skylar.

I want to go to him. I want to thank him for being there for me, *for defending me.*

"Ma'am," an officer I don't recognize says. "We're going to need a statement from you."

I nod, watching Eton and Jason get taken out in handcuffs.

"Want me to come with you?" Becca asks.

"I'm okay." *I think.*

The next half hour or so is a blur of conversations, paperwork, and medics.

Do I want to press charges? Yes.

Did I see who hit whom first? Yes.

Did I know the man who Maddox attacked? Yes.

I'm drying my eyes with a piece of paper towel that the bartender, Brittni, gave me when Skylar comes over.

"Hey," he says.

"What's going on? Can we leave?" I ask, leaning on Rebecca's shoulder.

He winces. "I have to take them in."

"*What?*" I stand straight, my heart dropping. "*No.*"

"I have to, Ashley. It's protocol. They'll have a bond, and they can call someone when that gets set." He pats my shoulder. "Go home. Get some rest. They'll be out soon."

I watch over his shoulder as Maddox and Banks are led out in handcuffs.

It's a sight I never want to see again.

Tears flood my face, burning my swollen cheek, and I cry into Sara's arms.

CHAPTER 26

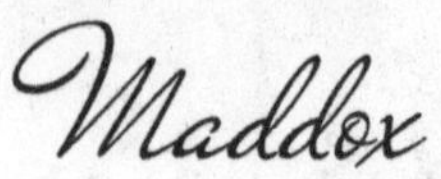

BANKS'S WHISTLE ECHOES THROUGH THE CELL.

"Can you stop it?" I ask, scratching my scalp with my fingernails just to feel something outside of my body.

"What song was it?"

"Banks."

"Come on. Do you know?"

"Can we not do this right now? We're sitting in jail, for fuck's sake."

"It was the *Andy Griffith Show*." He sighs. "I'm disappointed you didn't know that."

I get up and pace the length of the holding cell. It smells like piss.

"Ash was okay, wasn't she?" I ask with my heart in my throat.

The events from the moment I stepped into Mega Pint to the moment I was shoved into the back of Skylar's car are hazy. My adrenaline is starting to wear off. I'm going stir-crazy—needing to get the hell out of here. *How did I literally go from heaven yesterday to hell tonight? What the fuck happened?*

"She's okay," Banks says. "Swollen cheek. She'll be all right."

Just when I thought my anger was starting to subside.

I would've killed Eton tonight. If Banks hadn't pulled me off him, I don't know when I would've stopped.

I never cross a certain line. I'll always defend the weak, but I always check myself. That's why I sent Banks to talk to the dad at wrestling practice. But tonight, there was no line. *And that scares the shit out of me.*

Fuck. I run my hands down my face.

All I can think about is Ashley's face when I walked into the bar. I've seen many expressions on her face over the years, but I've never seen abject fear. Sure, there was anger mixed in, but she was spooked.

It turned my blood cold.

The closer I got, the angrier I became. Not that two men were in a booth with my girl, but that she didn't want them there. She didn't feel safe. She was vulnerable. And she was alone.

I saw red.

My throat constricts. *But Banks felt it too. For Ashley and for me.*

"Thanks," I say, blowing out a breath. "You probably saved me from prison."

Banks hops off the bench. "That's what I'm here for. I'll always have your back, Mad."

I face him, my little pain-in-the-ass brother. The guy who annoys me daily. Who eats my food. Moves into my house when I'm gone.

Who would do anything to defend me … or my girl. He stepped up. He stepped in. He got to that fucker before I did because he touched Ashley.

Banks might be a fool, but fuck, he's fierce. Loyal. The best friend I could ever have.

I pull Banks into a hug. He pats my back before letting me go.

"I don't know what I'm going to say to Ashley," I say, a ball of nerves bouncing around my stomach. "What does she think about all of this?"

Banks shrugs.

"It's like our life went from friends to …" I look around.

"Felons?"

"Asshole," I say, shaking my head.

Footsteps come down the corridor. Banks and I face the bars and wait to see who it is. Finally, Skylar comes into view.

"All right, you're in luck," he says. "Made some calls. We're going to get you in front of a judge tonight so you can get out of here. Bail will be eight hundred dollars each if you guys want to call someone and have them be ready."

"Thanks, Skylar," I say. "We appreciate it."

"Hey, no problem. Hate this happened. Ashley is pressing charges against Eldridge, so that'll make his life fun for a while."

I tense.

"Any way you could stick us in their holding cell for five minutes?" Banks asks. "We forgot to tell them something."

Skylar just laughs. "Haven't you caused enough mayhem for one night?"

"What are we getting charged with?" I ask.

"I'm waiting for the final paperwork. I doubt Gordie presses charges, but Ashley is on Eldridge. The witnesses all said that Eldridge's sidekick threw the first punch, so it's really a wash. I doubt much will come of it, but I can't make promises."

I nod.

Skylar sighs. "I'm going to check on a few things, then I'll be back for you to make your call."

"Thanks," Banks says as Skylar walks away.

My brother and I sit on the bench. Slowly, we look at one another.

"So," I say, biting my lip.

Banks shakes his head.

"What are our choices?" I ask. "Moss and Brooke are out of town. I'm not calling Mom or Dad."

"That leaves Jess and Foxx, and to be honest, I'm really not feeling either one of them."

"See how stupid the sticker thing is now? I'd call Jess a hundred times before Foxx, but if we call him now after he's seen your face *a thousand times*, he's gonna take us in the parking lot and try to fight us, and we'll all end up in here again."

Banks rolls his eyes. "He's not found them all yet."

I rub my forehead.

"We gotta call Foxx," Banks says. "*You* gotta call him. I was an innocent bystander in this?"

"How do ya figure?"

"It was your girlfriend we were defending. I really feel like I should get a break somewhere, considering I'll also be catching charges if you do. The very least you could do for me is to call Foxx for bail and a ride."

"How about rock, paper, scissors?" I offer.

"Nope."

I take a deep breath. "Is it bad that I'm questioning if he'll really come?"

"Ah, he'll come. He won't pass up an opportunity to hold this over our heads for the next ten years."

We sit quietly as we wait on Skylar to come back. I try to keep my mind busy, occupied, and not on Ashley.

It won't do any good right now.

But how am I not supposed to think about her? How can I not see her swollen cheek? The tears falling down her beautiful face. The pain. *The disappointment.*

Is she disappointed in me? *Fuck.*

Will she want anything to do with me?

"We're friends. We've always loved each other. I'm not sure how we could ever hate one another."

I guess the answer is yes, but she probably shouldn't.

"Hey, Mad," Banks says.

I look at him.

"Your mount was a little weak. Need to sharpen up a little. And turn your hips when you throw. You gotta ..."

Banks keeps talking, and I hold my head.

It's gonna be a long night.

CHAPTER 27

Maddox

"I DON'T KNOW WHY YOU GUYS DIDN'T JUST CALL ME," JESS SAYS AS WE climb into Foxx's truck. "You could've saved us all the pleasure of dealing with him tonight."

Banks leans behind Jess's seat so Jess can't see him. *"What the fuck?"* he mouths to me.

I shrug.

Foxx, clearly unhappy about having to get out of bed at two in the morning to bail his youngest brothers out of jail, glares at us in the rearview mirror.

"Grace is free, Foxx," Banks says. "Kindness doesn't cost a thing."

I fire him a look to shut up.

"You're so wise. Is that what you thought when you put your fist halfway through a man's orbital socket this evening, Banks?" Foxx asks.

"In Banks's defense, that motherfucker had it coming," I say.

Foxx backs out of the parking space and then pulls onto the road.

The dark and drizzly night is as sullen as I feel. Jess hands me my phone, and I turn it on to see if Ashley has messaged me.

Ashley: Let me know when you are out and that you are okay. I'm going crazy worrying about you.

I type out a quick text.

Me: Sorry if this wakes you. Just got out of jail. Foxx and Jess picked us up, so you can imagine … I'll call you tomorrow?

Her response comes immediately.

Ashley: Thank God. I've been dying over here. Is everything okay?

Me: Yeah. It will be. They told me you were pressing charges.

Ashley: Yes. Fuck him.

That's my girl.

Ashley: Are YOU okay? Not everything else? YOU.

Me: I'm fine.

Ashley: Thank you for that tonight. For protecting me. I don't really have words to express all the things right now but thank you.

Me: Do you want to come over? I can come and pick you up.

Ashley: I'm in bed and seriously exhausted. I'm sure you guys are running on adrenaline anyway. Maybe I'll just come by tomorrow? Will you be home, or do you have to go to the office?

Me: I'll be home.

Ashley: I'll see you then. Get some rest.

Me: You too.

Ashley: And Mad …

Me: Yeah?

Ashley: Thank you again. 🩶

Me: Always. 🩶

Jess looks at me over his shoulder. "You guys hungry? Want Foxx to stop and get you a sandwich?"

Foxx says, "*No.*"

At the same time, Banks says, "*Yes.*"

"You're not eating in my truck," Foxx says.

"I'm starving," Banks tells him. "I've been in jail. Where is your empathy?"

"It's like you just met me. Do you honestly think I'm going to feel sorry for you tonight?" Foxx asks.

"It wouldn't kill you." I shrug. "We're not asking for affection or nice words."

Foxx ignores us.

"I tried, guys," Jess says.

I shift in my seat. "Jess, why are you being so nice tonight?"

"Why wouldn't I be?"

I glance at Banks. He looks terrified.

"No reason," I say. "It's just the middle of the night, and Foxx isn't thrilled." I pause. "How did you even know that Foxx was coming?"

Did Foxx smirk? Surely not. What would that mean?

"I just got home," Jess says. "Traffic was awful, so I ended up stopping and ... long story. But I was in the driveway when Foxx went by, and I flagged him down to see if something was wrong or if he was going on some late-night surveillance mission."

Makes sense. But I don't know if it helps or hurts Banks's state of mind.

Foxx pulls up in front of my house and stops.

"Thanks for coming," I say. "We'll pay you back in the morning."

"Cash, preferably," Foxx says.

"Thanks, Foxx. See ya, Jess." Banks hops out of the truck and is halfway up my driveway before I get both feet on the ground. "I'm going to my house."

I laugh. "Why? To hide? Think he won't look for you there?"

"He's gonna look for me at your house first. Gives me more time."

I wipe the rain off my forehead. "I told you not to do this."

He walks backward across the yard. "I didn't expect to be going to jail the same night. It's a lot to manage in one day."

I laugh as I watch him jog to his back door. *What a fool.*

I step inside my kitchen. It feels like forever since I've been home. I make a quick drink.

My energy dumps, and I slump against the counter.

What the hell happened tonight?

My eyes squeeze shut.

I acted out of instinct tonight. I saw Ashley in trouble, and I reacted. I didn't think about it, and *I always think about it*. I never act without thought. I know better; I've trained it out of me.

Or so I thought. Clearly, there was a crack in that mindset.

My whole life could've been over in the blink of an eye. It might've if Banks hadn't been with me.

"Holy fuck," I grumble, still processing everything.

How did everything move this quickly? Paige said she didn't expect me to fall this hard—how right was she?

How is this affecting Ashley? Her ex hit her. *Holy fuck.*

Who is with her? *Becca. Becca and maybe Sara. Maybe she called her mom.*

But I wish it was me. *It should be me.*

I wander around my kitchen, wishing she was here. Wishing I was holding her. Wishing she was holding me.

"This has all gotten away from me," I say, setting my glass on the counter. "I've lost control of this whole situation."

What will this look like in another week? A month? A year? The thought scares me. I already feel so strongly about her that I'm not sure that I'm even thinking clearly anymore.

I start heading to my bedroom when a knock raps on the door. *The fuck?* I go to the foyer and peer out the peephole.

Banks?

I yank open the door and burst out laughing.

"This is not funny," he says through his closed mouth.

I wipe tears out of the corners of my eyes. "What in the hell happened to you?"

He stands on the porch covered head to toe in pink glitter. The rain is burrowing the sparkles in his hair and gluing them to his eyelashes, and his shirt, which I know was black earlier in the evening, looks like a unicorn shit on him.

Pink sparkles *everywhere.*

I pick an especially shiny piece off his forehead. "Is this a heart?"

"Fuck off," he mumbles.

"What happened? Did you find a unicorn and try to fuck it?"

He starts to step inside, but I block him.

"No way," I say. "You aren't tracking that into my house. Sorry."

"Mad ..." His eyes go wide. "I'm afraid to go back home."

I smirk. "Why?"

"Every time I turn on a light switch or open a door, another bucket of this shit dumps on my head. My house is covered in fucking glitter."

I can't control my laughter. I dig my phone out of my pocket and look at the screen.

Jess: 😊

"That's why he was so nice to you," I say, blowing out a breath. "He was setting you up."

"How'd he know about the stickers? He had to know to plan this."

I shrug. "Paige wouldn't have told him. She's solid."

Banks exhales, and glitter flutters in the air. "Stop laughing at me."

"I can't." I chuckle and snap a couple of pictures before he can stop me. I send one to Jess. *Maybe it'll keep me on his good side.* "This is the best. You're going to find glitter for years."

"Can you just let me come shower?"

"No. It's raining. Go stand under a gutter or something."

He sighs. "I just stood up for your honor, or whatever, and you're turning me away?"

"Glitter is a hard limit."

His shoulders slump, and his head falls forward. "Tell your brother Jess that this is war."

I laugh as he walks back across the lawn. "I think he already declared war, Banksy."

He flips me off and keeps walking.

Me: You win.

Jess: I know.

Me: How did you know?

Jess: Moss. He knew something was up and opened that package. We figured it out pretty easily. So we got Dad to lie for me and say I was out of town so Banks would feel ballsy. And as soon as I knew I was right, I got him. Little shit.

Me: I HAD NOTHING TO DO WITH IT.

Jess:

Me: Jessssssssssssssssss

Jess: Going to bed. Glad you're okay.

Me: Night.

I need a vacation.

I go into my room and straight to the bathroom. I need to wash the jail off me. The smell of the bar, the filth of the jail cell, the rain mixing it all together.

As soon as I'm in the shower, I'm taken back to Ashley's "honeymoon." The warmth, the passion, the peace.

Her cheeky comments. Her shy smiles. Her soft touches.

I shower quickly, wishing I was still in the Bahamas. It just pisses me off that it's over.

It's all over, I fear.

Once I've toweled off and brushed my teeth, I flop on the bed. Rummaging around, I find the pillow that Ashley used and pull it to me.

My chest physically aches without her. My body screams without her nearby. My heart breaks knowing what she went through tonight.

What if I'd arrived later? What if I had been too late?

Is this what love is? Is this what deep, soul-deep love feels like?

"I don't know if I can survive this," I say, breathing in the faint traces of her perfume as I drift off to sleep.

CHAPTER 28

Ashley

"Hey," I say, falling into Maddox's arms.

He holds me tight to him as he moves our bodies as one unit and closes the door behind me. His face buries in my hair, and he kisses the top of my head. I nuzzle against his chest and breathe him in. *Spiced cherries.*

"I feel terrible," I say.

"For what?"

He untangles us and gently turns my face. He inspects my cheek from every angle. I hold still and let him see that I'm okay.

"Does that hurt?" he asks, his voice gravelly.

"Not really. It burns. My jaw is sore."

His teeth clench.

After a kiss is placed in the center of the spot that still burns, he takes my hand and leads me to the living room.

"What do you feel terrible about?" he asks again.

"Oh, I don't know. For you getting arrested last night."

"*That's not your fault.* You know that, right? That's wholly on that dumb piece of shit you were engaged to."

"Yeah. I know. I still feel sad that it happened." I sit next to him on his sofa. "I didn't sleep at all."

"Should've come over. I was up too."

His fingers toy with mine in the space between us. It feels good to have him close. But it also feels … askew.

Maybe I'm still in shock. I've blocked Eton's number from my phone and disconnected him from any apps he might be able to access. Has he been tracking me?

The thought came to me last night. It kept me awake. But so did replaying the fight.

Maddox's face as he used his skills to overpower a man at least two inches taller than him. His ferocity, something I've never seen from him, as he pummeled Eton.

He focuses on the little pink ring he got me in the Bahamas. I haven't taken it off since he put it on my finger. It's so silly and fun, and when I see it, I smile. He usually does too … but not now.

"Are you okay?" I ask.

"Just thinking about this ring. That was a fun day."

"Yeah. It was."

"It was a hell of a lot easier than it's been here."

I swallow. "Yeah. I wonder if it's because we just jumped into the deep end. You know, we didn't have time where we felt each other out."

"Oh, I felt you out."

I laugh. "You know what I mean."

He nods. "I do."

My chest constricts as I watch him fiddle with my ring. He looks no worse for the wear despite his brawl last night. He's utterly handsome, and I want to climb into his lap.

But I don't.

I sit where I am and watch him.

"I was coming to Mega Pint to tell you I love you." He looks up at me, his eyes clear. "I do love you, Ash."

I smile and bite my lip. *This man.*

"I love you too."

My voice is shaky, not confident or elated like it should be.

Maybe I'm not shocked by his declaration because I already knew he loved me. It also could be that we're both too exhausted this morning to put a lot of energy into it. I don't know. But this isn't the way we should be saying *I love you* for the first time. That I'm sure of.

"I love you so much, so completely, that it … it worries me," he says, working his neck around his shoulders. "I could've killed Eton last night. I don't even remember the moment. I just remember Banks telling me he hit you."

I pull my finger out of his grip.

"Do you think … do you think we did this the right way?" he asks. "Did we go all-in too fast? I mean, we didn't even say we were doing it, but obviously, that's what happened—for me, anyway."

A lump settles in my throat, refusing to let anything go around it. I don't know if I'm still in shock or if I expected this or if the thoughts that have been swirling around my head since last night are the same as what he's saying.

I don't want to admit that I understand. No part of me wants to tell him that I lay in bed last night and, on top of replaying the fight, thought about what Rebecca said to me, about how she's never seen me single.

I've jumped from one relationship to the next my whole life. There's probably something there to be explored in therapy. But none of my relationships work out—they all fail. Is that because I don't know myself well enough to succeed in a partnership? Is it because I jump in too fast—*into the deep end*—and don't give it a chance to build naturally?

The thought terrifies me. It makes me nauseous.

What does that mean? What does it mean for Maddox and me? Is it a sign that this won't work, that we'll meet the same sad fate as the rest of my relationships? Is this the turning point for us like Maddox said?

"I guess … I guess you entertain it as long as it's good and enjoy it until it stops working. Then you walk away before you hate each other."

Is this all we get? *Surely, it can't be. Maybe you knew all along. Maybe you knew that you'd never get to keep him. To have this level of happiness forever.*

I understand what he was saying now. I'd rather walk away from that now than hurt him down the road.

I look at his face—his beautiful, soulful eyes and the lips that can make me feel treasured by a simple kiss—and I can't risk giving us a chance. I love Maddox Carmichael. I love him with all of my heart. And I truly believe, from the bottom of my soul, that he's the one for me.

But maybe you can't force those things. Maybe it's like a pot of soup, and you have to let it simmer to develop the flavors. Maybe it'll get better if it's put in the fridge for a while. *Put on ice.*

My stomach tightens so hard that I think I might vomit.

"Ash?"

"I don't know," I say. My words are a whisper as if I can barely find the courage to utter them. "I went all-in too. From the plane. I was all-in with you."

"Honesty?"

"Always."

"I'm terrified that this is my one shot … No. I *know* you are my one shot. And I feel like I've shown up to take the most important test of my life—the test to see if I can take care of you and love you like you need it—and I didn't prepare well enough. That I wasn't … ready."

He nibbles his bottom lip as he watches me for my reaction.

I fight the tears that well in my eyes. I try my hardest not to let him see them.

He groans and stands up, running his hands through his hair. "I'm fighting my instinct to break this off." He looks at me. "That's what I always do. I wait for this part, where it gets hard, and I walk. You were right. There are a million excuses why I do it, but it all boils down to this—before you, *they weren't you*. They weren't worth fighting for."

The dam breaks, and the tears stream down my cheeks.

"And here I am, actually fighting for you." He chuckles at the irony. "If I was presented with that situation a thousand times, I would do it the same way every time. I want you to know that."

I watch him drift away, just like he promised me he wouldn't. But I promised him I wouldn't hold on to this just because it's what we're doing.

"What do we do, Ashley? Help me understand."

I watch him look at me and see the reverence in his eyes. I feel the love radiating off him in a way I've never felt before. He's a good man,

Maddox Carmichael, and that's why we must do the hard stuff. So someday, maybe we can get to the good stuff.

I get to my feet and swallow my pain. My agony. This isn't how this was supposed to go. We were meant to fall into each other's arms and find comfort.

However, like the confident person I don't feel like I am, I wipe my face and lift my chin.

"Well, I have a terrible track record when it comes to this stuff. Hence, the reason you came on my trip and the reason we're here," I say.

He grins sadly. He knows what's coming.

"It's best if we take some time to think," I say, begging my voice not to crack. *Don't betray me.* "We might just be amped up from the vacation, and when the dust settles, we might feel differently."

"Or we might feel the same way." *Or that.*

"I just think we've both had a lot of big events that we probably need to reflect on. And come back *to this conversation* ..." I cover my mouth to try to catch the hiccup of a sob before it comes out, and I don't cry.

He wraps his arms around me and holds me so tight that I can't breathe. But I don't care because I'm not going to be able to breathe without him either.

"I love you," he says. "This isn't about that. I didn't bring this up because I don't."

I shake my head. "I love you too."

"A step back for a minute?"

"Yeah. A step back for a minute." *I hope.*

I extract myself from his arms. I feel him resist, not wanting to let me go. He should know that I don't want it either.

"I'm going to go," I say.

Panic flashes through his eyes as reality sets in.

"Um ... yeah. I'll see you around, I guess," I say.

I offer him the best smile I can manage and bolt for the door.

"Ash!"

I don't stop until I've pulled the door open. Then I turn around.

He's standing in the kitchen next to his pink bowl, his eyes betraying the same fear I feel. I see his hesitation. I know what he's going to do. He's going to recant. He's going to tell me to come back because this part is too hard.

But we both know we'll end up in this spot eventually. It might as well be now.

Tears build in the corners of my eyes again as a wave of overwhelming heartbreak threatens to drown me.

I hold his gaze. *I love you.*

"Turquoise," I whisper.

I don't wait to see his reaction or give him the opportunity to tell me no.

I do what's best for us and end things. For how long? I don't know. But I do it while I can.

CHAPTER 29

Ashley

I KNOCK GENTLY AND THEN TUG THE DOOR OPEN. "MOM? ARE YOU home?"

"In the kitchen!"

I enter her house and breathe in the smell of apple pie. *I've never had apple pie make me want to cry before.*

"I didn't know you were coming—*oh, sweetheart.*"

She sets her knife down and comes to me. I lean against her shoulder, losing all control of my emotions.

My tears fall free and fast. They race down my face and onto her shirt, making the yellow fabric nearly brown.

"*Shh,*" she says, rubbing the back of my head. "It's okay, baby girl. It's okay."

I pull away and make a futile attempt to dry my swollen eyes.

"Ashley, what's wrong?" She grabs a tissue and hands it to me. "You're scaring me."

I find her table through the haze and sit.

The thought of having to go through everything with her right now, when my whole life feels like it's in chunks on the floor, is almost insurmountable. But that's why I came here. If I've ever needed my mother's advice, it's now.

"I don't know where to start," I say.

"People say to start at the beginning, but sometimes that doesn't make the most sense. So pick the spot you're most comfortable talking about, and we'll engineer the story around it."

I smile sadly in relief.

"Why is your face red?" She touches my chin gently and moves my head side to side. "Is it swollen?"

"Probably."

Anger paints her face, and she stands. "Why?"

I watch her move to the kitchen and fill a bag with ice. She grabs a dish towel and covers it before handing it to me.

"Ashley, you better start explaining."

"Eton showed up at Mega Pint last night."

She stills. "And?"

"He hit me."

She storms to the kitchen and swipes her phone off the counter.

"Who are you calling?" I ask.

"Sara."

"Why?"

"We have business to take care of."

I laugh. "What are you going to do? Honestly, Mom. What's your plan?"

"I'll have quite a drive to figure it out. Sara's pretty creative. We'll make it work."

"Sit down," I say, tapping the table. "Put the phone down and sit. Eton has already been taken care of."

She stops swiping. "How?"

I blow out a tired breath. The sound makes her pause.

"He was arrested, and I'm pressing charges, for one."

Mom lowers herself slowly across from me. "And two?"

"Maddox and Banks showed up."

It's all I can say without crying again. But it's all I *have* to say.

Mom sets her phone down and looks relieved.

"They were arrested too," I say. "I called the police station this morning, and of course, they won't tell me shit. But I tried to make sure they knew that Mad and Banks were defending me—and themselves."

"Were they bailed out?"

"Last night. Perks of a small town, I guess."

She nods, furrowing her brow. "Did you get checked out? Are you okay? Is anything broken?"

"The medics looked at it, and I'm fine."

She narrows her eyes. "Maddox didn't blame you, did he?"

"*No*," I say emphatically. "Not even a little. I'm the one who felt bad."

"It's not your fault."

"I know. I had a moment when I felt like it was kind of my fault, you know? Maddox was there for me and so was Eton—I was the link. But then, on the way over here, I realized the truth. None of this is my fault. I don't know why my automatic response is to blame myself."

She covers my hand with hers. "It's partly because you just feel sad that this exists, and you feel in the middle of it—like you're the connecting piece of the wheel so it should all funnel to you."

"Yeah," I whisper. "But I know, logically, that's ridiculous."

"It is. Blaming yourself makes you feel in control of a situation. It makes you feel safe. If it's Eton's fault for this, then your brain tells you that *he* has the power. That's scary. If *he* has the power, *he* could do it again, and it's out of your control. So your brain twists things so you don't feel so vulnerable. If *you* did this, then *you* could've stopped it. *You* can control whether it happens again. But you know that's not true."

I think about what she's saying and she's exactly right. *How fucked up is that?* And how wise is my mom? And the therapists who helped put her back together after what Dad did to her.

Did she ever wonder if that was her fault too?

I bury my face in my hands and just sit. *Maybe that's a discussion for another day.*

This whole situation is so fucked up. I woke up this morning and thought I had a bad dream. *How can this be real?*

"I think I'm kind of in shock," I say, dropping my hands. "I'm numb one minute, and then my brain is going a million miles an hour the next. I can't get myself steady enough for long enough to make sense of anything."

She pats my leg. "Give yourself some time if you need it. Or if you need to march on with life today, let me grab my shoes, and I'll march with you. No one can tell you how traumatic things like this are going to feel or how long it'll take for you to process it."

I sit back in my chair and look at my mother. She's had her fair share of trauma. I'd venture to say I'm right—she's been in my shoes.

Mom sits stoically in front of me, proof that situations don't break people. People break people. She didn't allow my father to break her.

No one will break me either.

I sit a little taller. "Maddox and I …" I struggle to find the words. "We're on pause, I guess."

"Over this?"

I shrug. "Maybe. Probably not. I don't know. In a way, I feel like this was probably going to happen eventually, and Eton's bullshit just expedited it."

"Why do you feel that way?"

"Because things were too good. I was so happy." *She knows. She saw me the last night when I was high on love.* Yet only a day later, I'm here with a very different outlook.

My eyes fill with tears. *"We were so happy.* I've seen it a thousand times. When things are too good to be true, they're not true."

"That's a terrible way to look at life, sweetheart."

"But that's how it goes. Have you ever been happy and just … were happy?"

She presses her lips together. "Life is full of bumps and ditches and … and volcanoes."

I laugh quietly.

"But you keep going, and eventually, the landscape changes. It's the way of the world, honey. Don't get in a ditch and turn facedown. You might miss the sun coming up."

I get to my feet, twitchy from the conversation. I know she means well. What she's saying makes sense too. But my love life is a series of ditches. I just keep falling.

"How does Maddox feel about this?" she asks.

"Oh, he's all too happy to take a break. It's his modus operandi.

Once things start looking hard, he stops. He's been this way his entire life."

Mom gets up too and heads back into the kitchen. "So this is it for the two of you?"

"I don't know. A part of me doesn't think so. But a part of me also thinks that ..." I sigh, irritated. "Here's the thing—we jumped into this so fast, Mom. And when I looked at him this morning, I knew what he was thinking. He was drifting away even though he said he wouldn't. He was already questioning us." I swallow, blinking back tears. "And maybe I was questioning us too."

I bare my soul to my mother, and she continues slicing apples like we're discussing the weather.

"I'm having a crisis here," I say. "Can you pay attention to me?"

She grins but doesn't look my way. "What do you need me to say, Ashley? What can I help you with?"

"*Mother*, my heart is broken, and I need some advice. Or a hug. Or for you to tell me what to do. Okay? Pick one. *Pick the spot you're most comfortable talking about, and we'll engineer the story around it.*"

She snickers.

"*Mom.*"

She sets her knife by the pile of apple slices and sighs. Her eyes are alight with humor. "Do you listen to yourself?"

I glare at her.

"Ashley ..." She sighs. "You've been through the wringer in the past twenty-four hours. No, the past few years. Between your father and Eton and moving away from me, which had to be hard on you, even if you refuse to admit it, you've had to handle a lot of balls thrown your way."

And?

"The sun came up, sweetheart. Sometimes its rays can be so strong it blinds you for a moment. Even when you can't see it, on the cloudiest of days, it's still there, causing burns."

My soul stills.

Mom's eyes search mine. "I've been scared twice in my life—when I married your father and when I had you. I mean, I've been scared at other times but not like that. I was scared to drop out of college, to leave your father, and also to job hunt after being a stay-at-home mom. But I knew I'd figure out those things eventually." She leans against the counter. "But when I got married and when I had you, I was *scared*. Soul-shaking, knees-wobbling, cry-in-the-shower scared."

"Should've been a red flag with Dad."

She shakes her head. "No, because I loved him. And that was real and true and good, even if he didn't reciprocate it after some time. The point is that the two moments that have wrecked me like no other were the two moments that changed my life dramatically. That attached my soul to someone else's. I acknowledged I was giving a piece of my heart away to both of you. That suddenly, I was going to have to feel things times two, and then three."

"What are you saying, Mom?"

"I'm saying that you're questioning things right now because it's the right thing. You're doing what's healthy. What's smart. And of course, you're scared—you're scared because you're in love. If you weren't scared, I'd tell you to move on. That he's not the one."

My chest burns as tears fill my eyes yet again. "I don't know what to do."

"You'll figure it out."

I throw up my arms. "What kind of answer is that?"

"The honest one." She goes back to her apples. "I've known you would end up with that kid since the day he showed up at your birthday party in third grade. He bought you a Barbie umbrella. Do you remember that?"

I grin. "I do. I'd forgotten that."

"He was smitten with you then."

"But what if he doesn't come back to me? What if he decides that he doesn't want this responsibility?"

"*That's exactly how it works. You move on to the next thing. Every happening can't be a cataclysmic event with six kids in the family or else you'd be in panic mode all the time. You stand, brush yourself off, and keep going.*"

My fingers tremble as I rub my finger over my gaudy wedding ring.

"Then you, my child, don't believe in love," she says.

She takes another apple out of the bag and peels it. Methodically, she runs the knife just below the skin in one long, smooth ribbon.

My head is stuffed, overflowing, and I can't make sense of all of this.

"I'm going to go," I say. "Thanks for talking to me."

She looks up and smiles. "It pains me to have to watch you hurt."

"Then why are you smiling?"

"Because the sun isn't aimed at me. I know as soon as you acclimate to it, you'll feel its warmth too."

Whatever. "Bye, Aristotle."

She laughs as I walk out the door.

CHAPTER 30

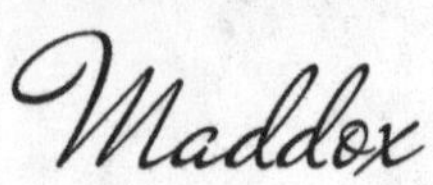

"WHY ARE YOU HERE SO EARLY?" TATI STOPS OUTSIDE MY OFFICE DOOR. "You're never here before me."

I look up from my desk, head in my hands, shoulders slumped.

"*Oh.* May I come in?" she asks.

"You're going to start asking now?"

"Good point."

She comes in and sits across from me looking all breezy and put together. I haven't had another shower since the one I took after I got home from jail two days ago.

I got to the office three hours ago—well before most of the staff was even awake in their beds. But I couldn't sleep, Banks was passed out on the couch, and I couldn't pace anymore.

At least, not in the same space. I paced here. Different view.

"Okay," she says. "Talk."

"I'm the boss, remember?"

She fakes a smile. "I know you got arrested. I also know why. I'm sure you're not loving that things got out of control like that, but they did because you were protecting your woman. It's instinct."

"Yeah."

"I didn't call you at home yesterday to talk about it. But now you're here, so talk."

"I don't want to."

"Did I pose that as a question? Weird. I don't remember doing that."

My hand falls to my desk and I lift my head. *Why does it feel like it weighs ten pounds?* "Sounds like you know what happened. What's there to talk about?"

"This … *mess*." She draws a circle in the air around my face. "That's not about you getting in a fight. Why do you look like you slept in that shirt last night?"

I glance down. The green polo is wrinkled as hell. It does look like I slept in it last night.

"Banks tried to do some of my laundry while I was gone. I didn't have the energy to iron it."

She snorts.

"This is about Ashley. We're on a break," I say.

"That's very *Friends* of you, Ross."

What?

"Never mind," she says. "So you're on a break. Does that make you feel better about things?"

"Obviously not."

"So it's safe to say this isn't working for you?"

"I'm fucking miserable. I can't eat without her. I can't sleep without her. I worry about her twenty-four seven. I texted her last night, and she didn't text me back."

Tati furrows her brow. "Is she pissed at you?"

I shrug. "I don't think so. I mean, probably, but she didn't leave pissed. We weren't in a huge fight or anything. We didn't break it off because of that. It was a mutual agreement."

"A step back for a minute?"

"Yeah. A step back for a minute."

"Well, this is one of your easier problems," she says. "If it isn't working for you, why are you still doing it?"

Didn't I have Ashley promise me she wouldn't do that—she wouldn't stay with me if it wasn't working? But now this pause isn't working for me. So what do I do?

"I hate when you make things sound so trivial," I say.

"Then make it make sense."

I stand, rolling my chair backward and into the bookshelf. "I can't make it make sense, Tat, because the only thing that makes any sense is for her and me to be together. I'm not stupid or blind."

"Huh."

I glare at her. "How can things be this intense already? Like, where do I go from here? I'm scared out of my mind."

"And now we're getting somewhere."

"Are you being a smart-ass?"

"Smart, yes. An ass? Maybe also yes." She stands and moves behind her chair. "It's scary to get exactly what you want sometimes."

I stare at her.

She's right about one thing—Ashley is exactly what I want. She's the *only* thing I want.

"So what happens when you get what you want in life?" she asks. "The only thing that can possibly happen is that you lose it, right? How could you possibly sustain something for a lifetime—especially something that took you decades to get?"

Shut up, Tati.

"This isn't about you wondering if you're doing the right thing or whether it can be this intense already. You're not thinking it might not work out because you already know the answer. The real answer. You love her."

I nod. *Where is she going with this?*

"Maddox, this is about you realizing that you got what you wanted, and the risks now seem so damn high that you're panicking. You're worrying about losing something that, right now—you don't even have."

I sit back down. *I might fire her.*

"You're conjuring up all of these scenarios in your head, all of these excuses because you're scared. You're trying to make yourself feel better, and I get it. I'm a hell of an excuse-maker myself. But what's gonna kill you more, boss? The fear of having her or the certainty of not?"

Friday. I'm firing her Friday.

"Now, I'm going to work. Someone"—she points at me—"has been slacking lately, and I'm trying to keep the place going. There's an offer from Armitage in your email if you haven't checked it. That might brighten your day a little."

She turns to go.

"Tati?"

"Yeah?" She looks over her shoulder.

I sigh. "Thanks. For everything."

"You've very welcome. Now, don't be a fool."

She laughs down the hallway.

CHAPTER 31

Ashley

The waves break beneath the gloomy clouds.

"I can't breathe," I say, holding my hand to my chest. My other one lays on top, feeling my wedding ring beneath it. "I miss him so much."

Becca rests her head against mine. "Then go to him. Call him. Text him."

Maddox texted me last night, and I didn't have the courage to text him back. I didn't know what to say or how to respond to anything he might bring up. I didn't trust myself not to just blurt out that I love him and beg him to take me back—to get back together before we're ready.

"But before I do that, I need to know that you didn't agree to this on the plane because you felt pressured. You were my friend before this, and you will be my friend after."

Back at ya, Mad.

I've thought a lot about what Becca said about me never being single. I kept thinking that the next relationship would somehow make me happy. That it would heal my heart. That it would prove that I was okay because someone wanted me.

Probably because my dad didn't. He walked away.

That caused me some issues, I know. I believed, because he manipulated me into thinking it, that I was the reason for our failed relationship. I was too much like my mother, too headstrong. I demanded too much of him. I wanted too much attention. *"You're an attention whore, Ashley. Leave me the fuck alone."*

But no relationship is going to heal my heart. No man is going to walk in and make anything better, and moreover, trusting someone else with that kind of power is asinine.

It's not up to anyone to make me happy. It's up to me. And, by the grace of God, I'm getting there. With baby steps and clarity—acceptance that shitty men like my dad and Eton do shitty things—has freed me from some of the burdens on my soul.

Those aren't mine to carry.

What *is* mine to carry is the source of my life's joy. What feeds my soul? What makes me the happiest? What makes me feel whole and beautiful and strong? I need to answer that and find someone who can share in it.

I don't need to be single. I need to love myself and find love—true love, not just another guy willing to give me a crumb.

True love like Maddox.

"Can I tell you a story?" Becca asks.

"Sure."

Her gaze settles off in the distance. "I grew up in Texas, and my home life was epically shitty. I needed to get away and start fresh where no one knew my name. In a series of events, fortunately or unfortunately, depending on how you want to look at things, I ended up in this little town of Jackson, Indiana."

"Do you think it's fortunate or unfortunate that you ended up there?"

"Depends on the day."

I pick up a handful of sand and let it filter through my fingers as I wait for her to continue.

"I fell in love with that little town," she says. "I fell in love with the beauty of it. They have a town square that's always filled with flowers and flags for each holiday or school event. There's a soda stand, a total throwback, called The Fountain. It has the best Cokes ever."

A ghost of a smile is on her lips as she remembers.

"The people there are salt of the earth. Good people. They took me in, loved me, fed me, protected me. They included me, which might've been the most important thing of all." She sighs. "Just having people around to care about you and check on you matters. Like you and Sara do for me now."

"And you do for us." I bump her shoulder with mine.

She picks up a shell and tosses it toward the water. "I fell in love *in* that town. Completely and desperately. He was unlike anyone I'd ever met. He was an angel, really." Tears fill her eyes. "He had the sweetest smile you've ever seen on someone. The gentlest, easiest way that just put you at ease. The biggest heart."

Her voice breaks, and her tears fall.

I've never seen Rebecca cry. I've never heard this much about her life either. Now I know why.

I wrap my arm around her. She lays her head on my shoulder and sniffles.

"Cord dated me old-school style. He took me to dinner. On picnics by the river that separates Indiana and Illinois. We'd sit on the bluff and look over the water and talk and laugh and share our lives. He held doors and had manners. He was truly one of a kind."

"He sounds amazing, Bec."

She takes a long breath. "We hadn't dated long, but we started whispering about the future. Hinting at it, really. We were both so cautious, so burned by our pasts that we were afraid that a relationship would prove us to be the worst part of where we came from."

My heart pulls for her. *What has this sweet girl been through?*

"He tried so hard, every day, to be the best person he could be—as if he could possibly get any better."

She lifts her head, and I watch the rivers of tears flow down her face. When she turns to me, her eyes are filled with an agony, a pain that makes me tear up too.

"Every bit of hesitation that I had … if I could go back, Ash, I'd go all-in. I'd feel everything. Give me all of it. The joy, the happiness, the pleasure. The pain, the heartbreak. The warmth of his hugs and the sweetness of his kisses. The sound of his voice with that little twang when he would sing me George Jones songs by the bonfire." She hiccups a sob. "I'd take a string of all the worst moments between us if I could just have him back again."

She bursts into tears, her body shaking with the force of her pain. I hold her, crying softly and wishing I could help her.

Thunder cracks overhead, and rain starts to mist from the sky. It's like the world is brokenhearted too.

"All I have of him are memories," she says, struggling through her sobs. "Everything else was stolen from me. I'll never have a chance to do any of it again, and I wonder every freaking day why I didn't just love him like he deserved to be loved. It kills me, Ashley. It kills me."

I hold her tighter, gently rocking her back and forth. "I'm sure he knew. I'm sure he knew how much you loved him."

She pulls back, wiping her eyes with the end of her shirt. "I got a letter from him just after ..." She fights not to sob again. "And he told me that he loved me and that he wants me to always remember that I deserve to be happy. To never settle for anything less than that."

I want to ask what happened, but that seems too ... cruel. *She lost him. That tears my heart in two for her.*

How would I cope with losing Maddox forever? Never getting to see his smile again or feel his body against mine?

A shiver races through me.

"He sounds amazing, Bec. I'm so glad you had him, and I'm so sorry he's not still here."

She takes my hands in hers. Her eyes clear. "But you have Maddox. He loves you like Cord loved me."

I think of his cheeky smile on the plane. His face lit by the candles on the beach. The strawberry in the kitchen and bringing snacks to bed. His laughter with the pigs and the warmth of his body in bed the night before we came back.

"Make the memories, Ashley. Make them while you can. I'm not promising you that it will work out, but I am saying that you don't know if you'll get tomorrow. If you want him today, that's enough."

We sit quietly for a long time, the mist billowing around us. I think I know what I want to do, but will Maddox? Will he try too?

"Make the memories, Ashley. Make them while you can. If you want him today, that's enough."

After a long while, I pull out my phone.

Me: 🖤

Maddox: 🖤

CHAPTER 32

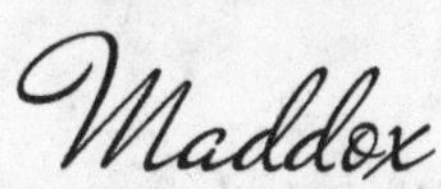

"Hey, hey," I say, coming into my parents' kitchen.

Mom looks up at me from the table. She sets a notebook down. "What are you carrying? You better not have anything alive in there."

I roll my eyes. "I'm not a child anymore."

"Debatable." She grins. "Really—what's going on?"

"How do you feel about making soup?" I set her kettle down on the counter. "I found this in my kitchen this morning, so I thought I'd bring it back. But then I wanted soup. So I went to the store and got chicken, onion, celery, carrots, and egg noodles. You're on your own when it comes to spices. Oh! This lady in the egg noodle aisle told me you'd need chicken stock. Got that too."

She stares at me.

"What?" I ask.

"Nothing," she mumbles, getting to her feet. She joins me in the kitchen and peers in the pot. "I think you got it all."

"Why do you sound surprised?"

"No reason." She takes everything out of the kettle and sets it on the counter. "So how was work today?"

Long. Terrible. No good. Very bad.

Tati kept looking at me like she was disappointed in me. *What does she want?* I ironed my shirt and took a shower last night. That's progress.

Kind of. I really just figured it was better to be productive while I commiserated over Ashley instead of lying prostrate thinking of her.

"Banks said that you and Ashley are on the fritz," Mom says.

I sit at the table. "Banks did not say fritz."

"Oh, he did. Believe it or not." She shakes her head and shrugs as if Banks perplexes her too. "Anyway, what's going on there?"

How do I put it? "I'm an idiot."

"Noted. Anything else?"

"That was the wrong response," I say. "Come on. Where's the mom spiel? The—*my baby boy isn't an idiot. What did she do to you, buttercup?*"

She lifts a brow. "Buttercup?"

"You know what I mean."

"Well, you said you were the idiot. I would venture to guess that you could be an idiot in relationships under the right circumstances. I'm not going to argue with you."

"Wow, Mom. You're the best. And we wonder where Foxx gets it."

"Do you want this soup? If so, you better shush." She washes the kettle like she doesn't trust me. "She answered your phone, you know. When you were in the Bahamas."

Do I know? How could I forget that?

I close my eyes and try not to go there—not again and not in front of my mother.

"I know," I say. "I was … otherwise occupied."

"Figured as much."

My eyes fly open. "I don't even want to know what you mean by that."

"Good, because I'm not telling you."

"Tell me." Jess walks in and plants a kiss on Mom's cheek. "Making soup? In this heat?"

Mom doesn't look up. She just points at me.

"Oh." Jess sits across from me. "How are you?"

"On a scale of one to ten, I'm a three. You?"

"Ten. Have you seen Sparkles today?"

I snort.

"Hey, what happened to Banks?" Mom holds a knife in her hand. "I saw him this morning, and I swear he … shimmered."

Jess tries desperately not to laugh. "I think he had an accident while mixing paint at work. That's my guess, anyway."

"Terrible excuse," I whisper.

He makes a face at me like he was thinking quick and had to say something.

"Oh," Mom says, either believing it or choosing to let it go. "Anyway, back to Ashley. What's going on, Maddox?"

Ugh. "We're … slowing our roll."

Mom's gaze flips to mine.

"I think we've probably slowed enough," I say with a sigh. "But now I don't know what to do. Nothing is fixed. I want her back, but I don't have the solutions to the reasons we slowed in the first place. Follow me?"

"Sort of," Jess says.

"We're on a break," I tell him simply.

"Oh, *Friends*," Mom says.

"Why does everyone keep saying that?" Irritated, I rock back in my chair. "Did I miss something?"

"It's fine," Jess says, grinning. "Let's just *pivot* back to Ashley."

"Well done," Mom says, laughing.

Jess bows from his chest.

"You guys are so weird," I say.

Mom pours the stock into the kettle. "Sometimes in life you don't get all the answers, Maddox. Sometimes you live with questions your whole life."

"Well, my question was more like—did we dive into this too fast?"

"Probably," Jess says immediately.

"I'm sure you both had heightened emotions after the bar brawl." Mom looks at me sternly. *That conversation didn't go over well.* "Maybe it just feels too fast."

Jess leans against the table. "Let's think without emotions, okay?" he suggests as if he's talking to a teenager. "The pace isn't going to create additional problems. The problems are the problems. They'll all come out eventually. If you move faster, you'll just find them sooner. On the other hand, you can fix them sooner too. It's science, really."

Mom smiles at my brother.

"I read this the other day too," Jess says. "If you have a why, you'll discover the how. Something like that."

"Jess, I love that," Mom gushes. "Think about that, Maddox."

I roll my eyes and get up. *Jess is Dad's favorite. He can't be Mom's too. Damn.* "How long until the soup is ready?"

"Give me an hour."

"I'll be back." I head for the door.

"We'll text you if we come up with anything else you can use," Jess hollers.

"Don't."

The door slams behind me. I imagine Mom is in the kitchen telling Jess that she should make me come back and close it softly, but I keep walking.

The air is thick, hot, and so humid that it makes your clothes stick to your body.

Today's knot in my stomach is different than yesterday's. It changes every day. Just as I'm starting to live with it, it mixes it up. Keeps me uncomfortable.

There's a hole in my life today. A large, gaping void that I can't escape. It makes me feel untethered as if I'm drifting through my day with no anchor.

No why.

My pace slows.

Tati was right. The certainty of not having Ash is killing me slowly. Having to call Sara every night to check on her is ridiculous—almost as ridiculous as not having her in my bed. And although I'd never admit it, Jess is right too.

It kills me to think that.

Maybe this *is* just life, and we sort it out and go on. Move forward.

Aren't I having to sort shit anyway? Just a different kind of shit?

You stupid fool.

I rip my phone out of my pocket and find Paige's name. She answers immediately.

"Hey," she says. "You called."

"I need your help …"

CHAPTER 33

Ashley

"I don't want to, Sara." I pull the blanket over my head. "Let's go tomorrow."

She jerks the blankets down. "No."

"Sara …"

She takes my hand, ignoring my puppy-dog eyes, and tugs. "Up."

I allow her to pull me to a sitting position, but I don't get off the bed.

"You were supposed to be up and ready," she says, digging through my suitcase. "We're going to be late."

"Can't be late if you don't go."

She glares at me over her shoulder. "Go brush your teeth and comb your hair."

"I don't want to go to La Pachanga. I don't want to meet your friends from work. I don't need new friends." I smirk. "I don't even like the two I have all the time."

She tosses a sundress at me. "Right now, I really dislike you. And unless you want me to sit you down and comb your hair, you'll go do it yourself."

"Fine."

I march into the bathroom, cursing Sara's name the whole time, and make quick work of changing into the dress and brushing my hair and teeth. I add a little mascara to make myself a tiny bit more presentable since I'm apparently going out in public.

I don't want to go. I have no appetite. No energy. No hope for the future—which Sara says is dramatic. *When she's calling something dramatic, it must be.*

"Why do I have to go?" I ask, tossing my dirty clothes into my luggage.

"You just mixed those with the clean ones."

"So?"

She shivers. "You must go because they're bringing their friends and I don't have any. Rebecca is at work, so you're the last option."

"Gee, thanks."

"Here. Twirl."

She spritzes perfume in the air. I twirl just to make her happy and don't think about Maddox twirling me in the Bahamas.

Everything reminds me of him.

"All right." She peers over me like I'm the subject of a study. "Do something with your hair."

"I don't want to."

"You need to put it up."

"If I'm going to embarrass you, leave me here."

We glare at each other. I think she's going to bite my head off, but she doesn't.

"Fine."

She glances at her phone. "We better get ready. I'm going to grab a drink—I'm so dehydrated today—then we'll go."

Okay ...

I take another peek in the mirror. *Damn, I look terrible.* My face is pale. Bags have taken up shop under my eyes. My hair looks like a rat's nest despite the brush.

It only takes a few seconds to get it into a bun. *Better.*

The doorbell rings as I grab my purse off the chair.

"Can you get that? I'm peeing!" Sara yells.

I thought she was getting a drink? "Yeah." She probably doesn't even know what dehydrated means. Dehydrated people don't pee much—*oh shit.*

Maddox stands in the doorway wearing my favorite black button-up. His hands are shoved in his front pockets, and he watches me carefully.

Sara squeezes by. "Fairy godmother is going to head out."

"You set me up," I tell her.

"He was coming regardless. I just made sure you were presentable. I take thank-yous in the form of gift cards to the salon."

She blows me a kiss, winks at Maddox, and practically jogs away—in heels.

Maddox and I face each other. The air between us swirls as if it's pressing us closer.

"Do you want to come in?" I ask softly.

He steps inside, and I close the door behind him.

I feel alive for the first time in days. It's awash in a nervousness that threatens to make me vomit, but it's *feeling*, nonetheless.

His chartreuse eyes, the ones that I love so much, search mine so deeply that I wonder if he can see my soul.

"I wasn't sure if you'd let me in," he says sheepishly.

"You know I wouldn't turn you away." *How could I?* "How have you been?"

"Shitty. You?"

"Shittier."

We exchange a grin. Relief begins to loosen my muscles.

"I'm sorry," he says. "I'm sorry for drifting away from you like I promised you I wouldn't. I'm sorry I made you feel like you were optional in my life. I'm sorry I ever thought that taking a pause was the right answer."

Gingerly, I take his hand. As soon as we touch, he clamps his palm around my fingers.

I dip my chin and lead him into the living room. We sit on the sofa, closer than the last time we sat together.

He strokes the ring on my finger—the beautiful conch shell piece that I haven't been able to take off. It gives me so much hope—reminds me of so much goodness—when I look at it that I can't part with it.

"I'm sorry too," I say. "I should have been wise enough to see through my own bullshit. Instead of leaning into you, I pulled away. I pulled away like it wasn't working when it's the only thing that has ever worked."

"Loving you scares the shit out of me," he says. "I would do anything for you. Anything. You're … an extension of me somehow. I can't explain it. If you aren't with me, I don't feel like I'm all there."

Tears tickle the corners of my eyes. "I understand. I feel that too."

"Here's the thing—I guess it might not always be good. It's going to get hard like it is now. But going through the hard with you is so much better than going through it alone."

"I thought about being single for a while."

He narrows his eyes.

"I thought that maybe I needed it. Maybe it would help me learn who I am. Maybe I needed to be alone to figure out what makes me happy. But I don't." I grin at him. "You make me happy. When I'm with you, it's like the sun is up. And even when I'm in a ditch, no matter how deep, as long as you're in it too, we can hold each other until the sun rises again."

His brows pull together. "Have you been hanging out with Banks behind my back?"

I burst out laughing. "No. Why?"

"No reason." He grins, his posture releasing some of the stress he walked in carrying. "So what are you saying? We're going deep ditching together?"

The smile on my face feels like a miracle. I laugh freely, happily. I'd almost forgotten what this felt like.

"Deep ditching?" he repeats. "No offense, but what the fuck is that, Ash?"

"My mom was all philosophical, and she was talking about the sun and ditches and volcanoes." I shrug. "She lost me a little, but I think the ditches are the problems in life. And you can't lie in them and wallow. You have to wait for the sun to rise and then climb out."

He nods like I've lost my mind. I shrug because maybe I have. I don't even care. He's here. That's all that matters.

"So …" He clears his throat and stands. "I have something else."

"What?" *Please don't ruin this. Don't break my heart.*

Maddox gives me his shy smile, my favorite, and drops to one knee.

My heart bursts and my hand covers my mouth as I watch him pull a box out of his pocket.

"I asked your mother before I came here if I could do this, and she said to tell you one thing," he says. "She said to remind you that on rainy days, you only need an umbrella."

I grin although he can't see it because of my hand.

"Ashley," he says, grinning. "You make me believe in magic. Not wizard magic, but magic in the universe. Wonder. Possibility."

Tears fill my eyes. *How does he do this? How is he so perfect?*

"I've been yours since I cut the gum out of your hair. Will you be mine forever?" He opens a small box. "Please be my legal wife?"

I laugh through the tears. "Are you just wanting another honeymoon?"

"Every day will be a honeymoon with you, Birdie."

I smack him, only to be hauled into his chest.

He presses kiss after kiss against my lips, cheeks, neck, and forehead. Through each kiss, he promises me all kinds of things—some sweet, some absolutely filthy.

I want all of them. I want all of him.

He pulls away, grinning like he's won a jackpot, and slides a ring on my finger—in front of the one already there. "I don't know what we do about that."

"Good problems to have."

I take in the piece of jewelry. It's so unique, yet so familiar.

"This is not the ring I wanted to propose to you with," he says. "But Paige instructed me to use it because I had it, and I shouldn't wait. She said you'd understand."

"It's not about the ring, Mad ..." I inspect the one he just gave me. It appears to be handmade with a stone on top that doesn't quite look like a stone. It's white and gold and brown, flecked, I think, with a glaze or resin on top. "What is this? It's beautiful."

He grins. "I got that in the Bahamas, actually. Well, I got it today, but I ordered it when we were there. Do you remember the shop where we got Becca's gifts?"

I laugh. "Yes."

"Well, they had rings made by a local artisan. She took sand from the beaches and crafted rings. So when we were with the pigs, I grabbed some sand and had James get one made for you."

I drop my hand. "You're kidding me? Are you serious, Maddox?"

He smiles. "I thought it would be a fun souvenir for you, something to remember your pig day. But it was in the mail when I got home today. I was talking to Paige about how to propose to you, and she said I should use it. We can pick out a ring for you together."

I wrap my arms around his neck and bury my face in his shoulder. I don't know how I got so lucky to be his, but I am, and I'll never take it for granted as long as I live.

I kiss him slow and tenderly before pulling back.

"This is my engagement ring," I say. "Period. I don't want another one because you couldn't find anything more perfect than this."

He dips his head and smiles. "I don't know how long it will hold up, though. There's no warranty or anything."

"Then we'll have to go back to the Bahamas. Shucks."

"I hope it dissolves monthly." He smiles. "So that's a *yes*, right?"

I laugh, tracing his jawline with my finger. "That's the biggest *yes* in the history of yeses."

He visibly relaxes. "One more thing?"

"Are you about to ruin this?" I make a face. "If so, no more one thing."

He laughs. "I found a house for you today."

He did? "Really?"

My heart skips a beat as I stare into his eyes. *What does that mean?*

"It has a lot of perks," he says, swaying me back and forth. "Immediate occupancy. The owner is willing to accept any concessions you want. There's a neighbor who thinks he can just walk in, though, so you'll have to figure that out …"

I light up. "What are you saying, Mad?"

"Move in with me. I don't want to spend another night without you."

"I might have some requests."

"Name them."

"The first one is I really like it when you—*ah!*" I giggle as Maddox lifts me in a bridal hold and carries me to the door. "What are you doing?"

He stops and stares at me. His smile is as big as his heart.

"I'm taking you home."

I've never heard four more beautiful words in my life.

Maddox Carmichael is my fling-to-forever. Who knew?

CHAPTER 34

Maddox

THIS IS THE WAY IT SHOULD ALWAYS BE.

Ashley is curled up next to me, her arm draped over my chest. Her cheek is pressed against my shoulder as we plan for the future. *Our future.*

"When do you want to get married?" I ask her.

I feel her grin against me. "Friday sound good?"

"You can't have the wedding of your dreams planned by Friday, Wondergirl."

"I don't need it."

I move until she's looking up at me. "I want you to have it."

"It's not necessary, Mad."

She sits up, my sheets pooling around her waist. Her bra covers her breasts only because I was too eager to get inside her once we got through the door.

There'll be time for those later.

Like immediately after this conversation.

I stroke my finger up and down her arm. "You've wanted a big wedding forever. You should have one."

"I should have what I've always wanted—you." She winks at me. "Honestly, Maddox. I just want to be your wife. I don't need pageantry or a fancy venue. I just want to marry you."

Huh. "Okay. Friday it is. And you're sure you want to live here? You're okay with it?"

"Absolutely."

"Just repeating, you know Banks lives next door."

She laughs. "Yes. I expect to see a lot of your brother."

"They all live on this road."

"Okay, plural." She practically glows. "If something doesn't work out, we can deal with it then."

"We can go deep ditching."

She giggles and leans down to kiss me. "I do have one thing, though."

"What's that?"

She climbs on top of me. With one knee on either side of my body, she sits up.

I hold her waist and look up at her like a dork. She's a poster girl, a centerfold—a fucking dream. And she's pinned me to my bed and looking at me like she wants to devour me.

Yes. Fucking. Please.

She moves her hips in a slow circle, grinding against my cock. "It might be more than one."

"Fine."

Her heat covers my cock as she slides back and forth.

"Maybe three," she says.

"Fine."

"Actually, odd numbers are bad. Four."

"Fine." I've always known that Ashley wanted a big family. Knowing that I get to help her create that? Fuck, that turns me on more than I *ever* thought possible.

I want everything with her. She is my everything.

My fingertips bite into her hips, gripping her flesh like it's my lifeline.

"Remember when we were talking about books?" she says.

"Yup."

"And I mentioned erotica?"

My cock throbs. "Do you want to be choked?"

She grins. "Maybe. But I was thinking of something else."

"Spit it out because all I can think about right now is coming in your pussy."

Her eyes flare. "Perfect. I was thinking maybe you could do that. *Come deep inside me.* Put a—"

I capture her kiss and the rest of her words.

I told her that I would give her anything she wants. *Who am I to deny this?*

She grips my cock and slides down on it with a hiss. Then she stills and watches me.

"I love you, Maddox. Thanks for being my fling."

"I love you, Ash. Thanks for being my forever."

Epilogue

ASHLEY

A few days later

The Carmichaels buzz around me. It's all chaos and noise and energy. I wonder if it's always like this.

Damaris and Kix are in the kitchen. Damaris organizes the pizza boxes on the counter, batting away her sons' hands every six seconds. Kix, who is supposed to be helping her, has gotten sidetracked by Foxx at the sink.

Banks, who looks especially shimmery, sits beside me, arguing with Moss about privacy. Moss's girlfriend, Brooke, just left to pick up her grandmother. Damaris made it clear that my mom is invited to every Sunday dinner, too, and I told her that she would be here next week. She had a date. Her third this week. *Thanks, Sara.*

Apparently, family meals mean anyone who is loosely considered family can come. I love that about these people.

Jess stands beside his mother, giving her hell about having pizza on a Sunday. She spars back with him, standing her ground. He looks up at me and winks.

"You okay?" Maddox whispers from behind me. "This can be a lot."

I turn my head to see him. "It's great."

"And now I can't just go to Maddox's," Banks says, playfully glaring at me. "He kicked me out for her."

"I think he kicked you out before that," Moss says. "You just didn't listen."

"Yeah, Sparkly," Jess says. "You didn't listen."

Banks glares at him, making everyone laugh. Everyone except for Foxx. He just looks at them like they're children.

"Hey," Maddox says, trying to get everyone's attention. "Hey!"

Everyone turns to look at him.

"Yes, Maddox. You can have the floor," Jess says.

"I would like to make an announcement," Maddox says, standing behind me. He laces his fingers through mine and puts his other hand on my shoulder. "What are you guys doing on Friday?"

Damaris looks suspicious ... and cautiously hopeful. "Why?"

I think I might burst. Each of the Carmichaels looks at me with smug grins—like they know. Like they expected it. Like they wanted it.

"Well," Maddox says. "Ashley and I are going to be at Cornerstone Church on Friday evening at six. There will be a pastor there and—"

"Are you getting married?" Damaris shouts. She covers her mouth and races to the table. "Oh, Maddox. Come here, Ashley."

I barely get to my feet before her arms are wrapped around me.

"Welcome to the family, sweet girl," Damaris says, pulling back. Her lashes are wet. "I am ... I'm thrilled, honey. Thrilled. Does your mother know?"

"Yes," I say, laughing.

"Okay. What can I do? I'm a do-er. Point me in the right direction—"

"Don't do that," a voice says from behind us.

"Hey, Paige is home," Moss says, getting up to hug her.

Banks bumps knuckles with her as she walks by.

She gives Maddox, Jess, and Foxx quick hugs. Then shares a long one with her dad.

"Ashley," she says, smiling as she comes to me. "Don't let my mom have any leeway. Trust me. Nothing is simple with her."

Damaris swats at her before they embrace.

My heart overflows with the love of this family—for each other … and maybe for me too.

Maddox holds me from behind, locking his hands around my waist. He's so sturdy and strong, so protective and good.

And mine.

"Mad called and said he was getting married, so I booked a ticket home," Paige says.

"Glad you get to know before the rest of us," Banks says.

"We were trying to figure out how to break it to you easy, Sparkles," Maddox says.

I smile at Banks as his family laughs at him.

"Fuck," Moss says, tossing his phone on the table.

"What?" Jess asks.

"I keep getting these fucking penguin texts."

"Someone, well different numbers, keeps texting me about flamingos," Maddox says.

Paige makes a face. "Where have you been hanging out, guys?"

"Nowhere," Maddox says.

"It's been happening to me for weeks," Moss says. "It's driving me nuts."

"Yeah, I've been getting flamingos for a couple of weeks. I got them in the Bahamas. I'm so confused."

Jess sighs. "Sucks to be you guys. I'm eating."

"You are not," Damaris says, going back into the kitchen. "We have to say grace."

Everyone quiets. Banks and Jess take their hats off. Heads are bowed and Kix begins the prayer.

Maddox squeezes my hand. I peek at him and he winks.

"Amen," Kix says.

"Come on," Maddox whispers, leading me through the house and out the front door.

"Where are we going?" I ask.

"You'll see."

"But your dad just said grace, Mad. We can't just leave."

"We'll be back in time to see if there's any pizza left after my family attacks the boxes. Brooke will be back soon with Honey, her grandma, so there'll be more chaos. They won't even miss us."

"Okay."

We walk, hand in hand down the road toward his house. *Oh my gosh.*

"My bird," I say, laughing. "You put that thing in front of your house?"

"*Our house,* but yes. Your bird sculpture has a new home right beside our mailbox. Moss hates it, so I made sure it was nice and visible."

We keep walking, and I'm not sure what for—I see the sculpture. *Really, how can you miss it?* I'm about to ask him what's happening when I stop.

Now I get it.

"Maddox …"

A giant truck comes down the road and then backs into Maddox's driveway. The name on the side of the truck is the same name as the storage unit where my things are stored in Orlando.

"All of your stuff is here," he says. "Sara and Banks went and loaded it into the moving truck yesterday and then we paid the storage place to drive it down. They're going to unload it into the garage so you can go through it when you want to." He cringes. "Sara and Banks —that's a story for another day."

I laugh. I can only imagine.

"But I wanted your life to be settled. Here. In our home. I know you've missed your stuff …"

I wrap my arms around him and look into his eyes. I am that. Settled.

And it's not because of my stuff, although that was a sweet thing to do. It's because I've found myself again. I took the risk and exited things that weren't right for me … and look what I have for it. I *entered* into the most beautiful life possible. I never knew it could be like this.

"How do you think of everything?" I ask.

"I've been reading romance novels in my downtime and picking up tips."

I laugh against his lips as he kisses me.

"Did you ever read that chapter I told you about?" he asks. "I have ideas ..."

He wiggles his brows as he walks toward the truck to instruct the delivery men on what to do.

I stand in the middle of the road and can't help but feel like with the delivery of my things comes a closing of a door. The end of a chapter of my life.

Maddox and I are going to write the next chapter together. We're making *our* entrance. Together. Side by side. Hand in hand. Because this is love.

I know what it looks like because of Maddox Carmichael.

Want more of Maddox and Ashley? Grab a bonus scene here.

Don't miss Jess's book, FLUKE. Chapter One is next. Keep reading...

Fluke

Chapter One
   Pippa

"Seeking a fake ex-husband."

My words fall into the air, sounding just as ridiculous as I imagined they would. I sigh and lift a brow at Kerissa, my best friend and troublemaker extraordinaire, sitting across the table from me. The mischief in her eyes complements the smug grin on her face, and I know, beyond the shadow of a doubt, that I need to rethink this attempt at crisis management.

"I can't do this," I say, slamming my notebook closed.

"And why not?"

I level my gaze with hers. "You've come up with a lot of bizarre things in your life, but this one takes the cake."

"Takes the … *wedding cake*?"

She laughs at her joke—one that I don't find especially funny under the circumstances.

How do I get myself into these situations?

I grab a couple of Cajun fries—the whole reason we came to Shade House for happy hour—and pop them in my mouth. Tables around us begin to fill with patrons ordering drinks and appetizers. I side-eye my root beer float and consider breaking down and ordering an amaretto sour. The only problem is that my problem-solving abilities go down with each drink. At this point, I need all the help I can get.

"We could use this as an excuse to throw a divorce party," Kerissa says.

"Kerissa—"

"Will you just think about it? Hear me out." Her eyes twinkle. "We'll go to Savannah and get a room at Picante."

I sigh happily. "I do love that hotel."

"*Right*? We can hit up a Georgia Hornets game, get a massage, and shop. Maybe find a couple of unassuming bachelors to ravage for the weekend."

"Well, I did see that Lincoln Landry is the general manager of the Hornets now." I wiggle my eyebrows. "I'm thinking about buying a Hornets shirt with Landry on the back."

She laughs. "They don't have shirts with the GM's name on them."

"Oh, no. *They do*." I point at her. "You can get them online. I've already looked."

"How did you know all this, Miss I Hate Sports?"

"Because Lincoln Landry transcends baseball. He went viral last season for nothing other than a smirk and the way he licked his lips." I shrug. "Who am I not to follow a fan account dedicated to giving me delicious videos every morning? LandryLover0808 works hard at her craft, and I support content creators, *thank you very much*."

Her laughter grows louder. "Sometimes I wonder if I even know you."

I laugh too.

"There's this little place called Judy's down the street from Picante," Kerissa says. "We can grab breakfast there."

"Yes, and maybe we can …" I stop as reality knocks me sideways. "Wait a minute. *I'm not actually getting a divorce*, remember?"

Kerissa frowns.

I flop back in my chair, the legs rattling against the tile floor, and huff.

Ten minutes ago, I was frustrated that I was a fake divorcée. Now I'm irritated that I'm not a real one.

Why am I the way I am?

Kerissa leans forward, folding her hands on the tabletop. "Is it wrong if I say I'm sad you don't have a marriage in trouble?"

I can't help it. I giggle.

"I'm kidding," she says, although I'm not sure she is. That's okay because I'm not sure I am either.

A trip to Savannah sounds like the perfect antidote to the mess at work. But taking trips to avoid my problems is almost as unhealthy as working with Chuck "the Schmuck" Collins.

My jaw clenches at his name rolling around in my head.

I shouldn't let him get to me. I'm a grown-ass woman who should be able to bite her tongue and let douchebags be douchey. But I was born lacking a filter to prohibit myself from snapping back at assholes.

It's not one of my finer qualities and certainly doesn't do me any favors. If I wanted to play the blame game, I could credit it to having two uber successful, brilliant parents who embodied the definition of hubris. The only way to survive surgeons as parents when you grow up wanting nothing to do with the medical field is to learn to stand up for yourself. It took me a long time to learn that.

Ten years later, I'd say I've mastered it—maybe a little too well.

"Now that you're calm-er," Kerissa says, "tell me what happened today."

Ugh. I take a deep breath. "My boss, Bridgit, wants to expand Bloom Match again. Originally, it was a small online matchmaking service. Then they got the idea to make it a regional thing where we blind-match people from this area, set up the dates, host mixers—all that stuff."

"Right."

"Business has been going well—exploding, even. Bridgit asked everyone a couple of months ago to brainstorm ways to take the company further. We all proposed our ideas, and it's come down to me and Chuck the Fuck."

"We hate him."

"We do." I nod, my blood pressure rising. "I dislike him on a good day. Even if I got up on time, had the perfect latte, and a great hair day, I'd still hate Chuck. If I had to nominate someone for the Hunger Games, it would be him. I wouldn't even have to think about it."

She snorts.

"I hit the alarm three times this morning, Muggers screwed up my latte, and my hair looks like this." I point at my head. "I woke up emotional, which makes me ragey itself because emotions are inconvenient and make me feel weak."

Kerissa rubs a hand against her forehead. "This does not bode well for Chuck."

My teeth clench as I remember the smarmy look the jerk gave me.

"So we're going back and forth about our ideas, right? The whole office is in the conference room listening to us weigh the pros and cons of our proposals. I wrap up my little impromptu presentation—*which I nailed, by the way*. He must've felt threatened or something because he leaned back in his chair, his arms behind his head like he's proudly displaying his sweat stains in his armpits, and says"—I pause to channel my inner Chuck voice— *"'I'd like to point out that we're taking relationship advice from a woman who has no verifiable experience with them.'"*

The top of my head might blow up.

"He did not," Kerissa says, eyes wide.

"Everyone was staring at me. I had flashbacks from high school when everyone found out about my mom's chandelier debacle. I just opened my mouth and spewed ... I don't even know what I said, Kerissa. *I was so pissed off.* Something about being touched he pays so much attention to my private life but that I had been married before." I stop to drag in a hasty breath. "Then, because I'm petty and I know from office gossip that he and his wife are having problems, I said that at least I knew when to walk away, unlike others who live a loveless life in misery."

Her jaw drops.

"Not my proudest moment," I say, shifting in my seat.

"Well, silver lining—at least you put it in past tense. You could've said you *are* married. That would've been way more awkward."

I stare at her.

"What? I'm trying to help here," she says.

"What would've helped is if you'd gone to work with me and clamped a hand over my mouth. Because everyone started jabbering about how they didn't know that about me. I stood there with red freaking cheeks, constructing a fake marriage that we ended after a couple of years when we realized it wasn't right for us. *Oh*—he's still smitten with me, too, because why not? If you're creating an ex-husband, you might as well make him worth the fake marriage, right?"

Kerissa chuckles as I groan.

It's fine. Everything is going to be fine.

Hannah, our server, slides up to the table. A wad of pink gum snaps between her teeth.

I rest back against my chair and take a long, deep breath. I had big plans for today after work, including a walk on the beach and making a cold tomato soup with tarragon crème fraîche for my new neighbor. It's been a long time since I made something for anyone besides Kerissa, and she has the palate of a child. I was excited to take my sweet new friend a bowl of soup and listen to her stories about years gone by.

"You ladies look like you're in the middle of a serious conversation, but I wanted to make sure you don't need anything else," Hannah says.

Kerissa cups her chin in her hand and smiles at Hannah. "I'm fine. Pippa told her coworkers that she was married. For the record, she's never sniffed a wedding veil."

"I'm sitting right here."

"I know," Kerissa says. "I saved you the trouble of explaining. You're welcome."

Hannah grins. "That sounds like a prickly situation."

"How do you mean?" I ask, fiddling with my straw.

"Well, don't you work at a matchmaking company in Lakely?"

I nod.

"What if someone asks who you were married to?" she asks. "What do you say then? He's just someone from out of town? Because Lakely is a good forty-five minutes from here, and while there's not tons of crossover, someone might ask just to see if they know them."

I know. Dammit.

Kerissa sits up and laughs. "No, because that would've been too easy. She told them that she has dinner with him once a month."

I glare at her. "I said *sometimes,* not once a month." I shrug. "He still loves me. I can't help it. I'm lovable."

Kerissa rolls her eyes.

"I'm sure you are," Hannah says, cackling. "But I think you should plot out the rest of your story before you return to work tomorrow. You don't want to be caught with your pants down … unless your ex-husband is coming around. Maybe he was good in bed."

"He was. I might've mentioned that too."

Kerissa and Hannah laugh at the heat in my cheeks.

"You both suck," I say, joining in the laughter.

"I'm with you on this," Kerissa tells Hannah. "I told her she needs to find a fake ex-husband to have on hand just in case. I know people who have done this kind of thing, and it worked out very, *very* well."

"Well, good for them," I say, holding my head in my hands. "I'm glad they found their knight in shining armor. But I have no interest in finding a man to deal with for the rest of my life, nor am I super excited about having a fake one either."

Hannah taps on the table. "Let me know if you need anything. I have a couple of new tables to check on."

Kerissa takes my notepad and slides it across the table as Hannah leaves.

I love my job, and Bridgit, more than any job I've had before. And while a part of me knows she would understand my predicament—especially since I think she dislikes Chuck too—I don't want to give her a reason to think poorly of me.

I don't want to disappoint her.

"Okay, I think this was a solid start," Kerissa says. "Just look at it. You'll feel better if you have an option in your back pocket."

She's right. Options are good.

She turns the notepad around, and together, we read.

Seeking a Fake Ex-Husband

I need a fake ex-husband.

Let me explain ...

I may have let it slip to my new coworkers that I have an ex-husband. Now they're fascinated with the details, specifically with him.

Why wouldn't they be? He's gorgeous, has exceptional skills in the bedroom, and is determined to win me back.

But there's a problem. He doesn't exist.

The bigger problem? I have to produce him to save my job.

This is where you come in.

I'm seeking someone to play a smitten ex-husband for two weeks. You'll need to remember our love story—details matter when it comes to romance! I need you to be prepared to travel in-state at a moment's notice. We may be in close proximity; sharing a bed may be required.

One more thing—kisses are required for optics as necessary.

If this sounds interesting or, at the very least, entertaining, let me know.

Signed,
Your Future Ex-Wife

"See?" I take the notepad and stuff it into my bag. "That's ... *no*. Funny, but no."

"Suit yourself."

I twist to hang the bag on the back of my chair. "I think I'd rather find an actual husband than post that. I ..."

As I start to turn back, my eyes latch on to a pair of the greenest eyes I've ever seen.

Screw. Me.

Fluke is live now on Amazon, Audible, and free with Kindle Unlimited.

Acknowledgements

First and foremost, thank you to my Creator.

It's almost five in the morning. I'm sitting at my desk, a place that I've been living for the last week. My family will be rising from their beds soon and I will be passing them in the hall in hopes to get a few hours of rest.

Their patience and support when I'm in writing mode—specifically when I'm wrapping a book—is unbelievable. I'm so grateful to have the best five guys in my corner. To my husband, Saul, and my children, Alexander, Aristotle, Achilles, and Ajax—I love you endlessly.

To Rob and Peggy Patterson, thank you for always understanding … everything.

Kari March created an amazing cover. I'm so thankful to have her on my team.

Huge thanks to J. Ashley Converse Photography for the beautiful photo on the cover. Working with you has truly been a dream. And to the cover models, Dane Peterson and Maddi Hansen—this picture caught my attention as soon as I saw it. I'm honored to have you on my book.

My assistant, Tiffany, kept all the things in order while I wrote. Thank you, Tiff.

Susan Rayner, Jen Costa, and Anjelica Grace read for me and gave me invaluable feedback. Crystal Eackers lent me her time and energy in nailing down the first part of this book. Thank you all so much. Yessi Smith joined the fracas and gave me such great insight.

Without Lara Petterson, I would've been stuck researching and never would have gotten to the writing part. Thank you for your calls, solutions, and energy. You made such a difference.

Michele Ficht worked with me again to make this book as error-free as possible. Thank you so much.

Marion Archer stuck it out with me, talking me off a ledge while cleaning up my plot. All the love to you, my friend.

Jenny Simms worked late into the night and I love her so much for it.

Mandi Beck, as usual, was my levity and sounding board. You're the best best-friend ever.

S.L. Scott came in clutch with the one piece I couldn't find. I love you so much.

Jessica Prince and I wrote together every day. Without our Zooms, I wouldn't have finished.

Catherine Cowles, Kaylee Ryan, and Yessi Smith all had a hand in making this story come together, all in different ways. I appreciate you all.

Big thanks to Candi Kane PR for working with me on the promotion of FLING. I adore you.

Huge, huge thanks to The Smuthood (Brittni and Sam) for their energy and creativity in helping me get the word out on Tiktok. My love for you runs deep.

Hugs to Kaitie Reister for always being a friend, managing All Locked Up, and for being the Countdown Queen. Also, squeezes to Stephanie Gibson for everything—just for being you.

And to you, my reader—thank you for taking a chance on me. I hope you loved this story. I hope it made you smile.

USA Today Bestselling author Adriana Locke lives and breathes books. After years of slightly obsessive relationships with the flawed bad boys created by other authors, Adriana created her own.

She resides in the Midwest with her husband, sons, two dogs, two cats, and a bird. She spends a large amount of time playing with her kids, drinking coffee, and cooking. You can find her outside if the weather's nice and there's always a piece of candy in her pocket.

Besides cinnamon gummy bears, boxing, and random quotes, her next favorite thing is chatting with readers. She'd love to hear from you!

Join her reader group and talk all the bookish things by clicking here.

www.adrianalocke.com